Mykonos After Midnight

A Chief Inspector Andreas Kaldis Mystery

Jeffrey Siger

Poisoned Pen Press

First Edition 2013

10 9 8 7 6 5 4 3 2 1

Library of Congress Catalog Card Number: 2013933483

ISBN: 9781464201813 Hardcover
9781464201837 Trade Paperback

Poisoned Pen Press
6962 E. First Ave., Ste. 103
Scottsdale, AZ 85251
www.poisonedpenpress.com
info@poisonedpenpress.com

Printed in the United States of America

Mykonos After Midnight

Books by Jeffrey Siger

Chief Inspector Andreas Kaldis Mysteries

Mykonos After Midnight

Target: Tinos

Prey on Patmos

Assassins of Athens

Murder in Mykonos

I dedicate this to the People of Mykonos and Barbara Zilly. You make it all possible.

Acknowledgments

Khalid Al-Otaibi; Roz and Mihalis Apostolou; Demetra, Karl Ilias, Alexia, and Dimitri Auersperg; Michael Cohen and Suzanne Lerner; Nikos Christodoulakis and Jody Duncan; Joanne, Aleka, and Michael Daktilidi; Andreas, Aleca, Nikos, Mihalis, and Anna Fiorentinos; George "the Cat"; Nicholas Gryblas; Nikos Ipiotis; Nikos Karahalios; Flora and Yanni Katsaounis; Olga Kefalogianni; Panos Kelaidis; Antonis Kontizas; Nicholas and Sonia Kotopoulos; Katerina Ligoxyngis; George and Maria Makrigiannis; Linda Marshall; Thomas and Renate McKnight; Terrence McLaughlin, Karen Siger-McLaughlin, and Rachel McLaughlin; Nikos and Artemis Nazos; Lambros Panagiotakopoulos; Mihalis Paravalos; Barbara G. Peters and Robert Rosenwald; Theodore, Manos, and Irene Rousounelous; Beth Schnitzer; Raghu Shivaram; Alan and Patricia Siger; Jonathan, Jennifer, Azriel, and Gavriella Siger; Lefteris and Sharon Lock Sikiniotis; George and Efi Sirinakis; Ed Stackler; Pavlos Tiftikidis; Jessica Tribble; Sotiris Varotsis; Christopheros Vasilas; Alejandro Wolff; Barbara Zilly;

And, of course, Aikaterini Lalaouni.

Magick: "It is theoretically possible to cause in any object any change of which that object is capable by nature."

—Aleister Crowley (1875-1947)
The Wickedest Man On Earth

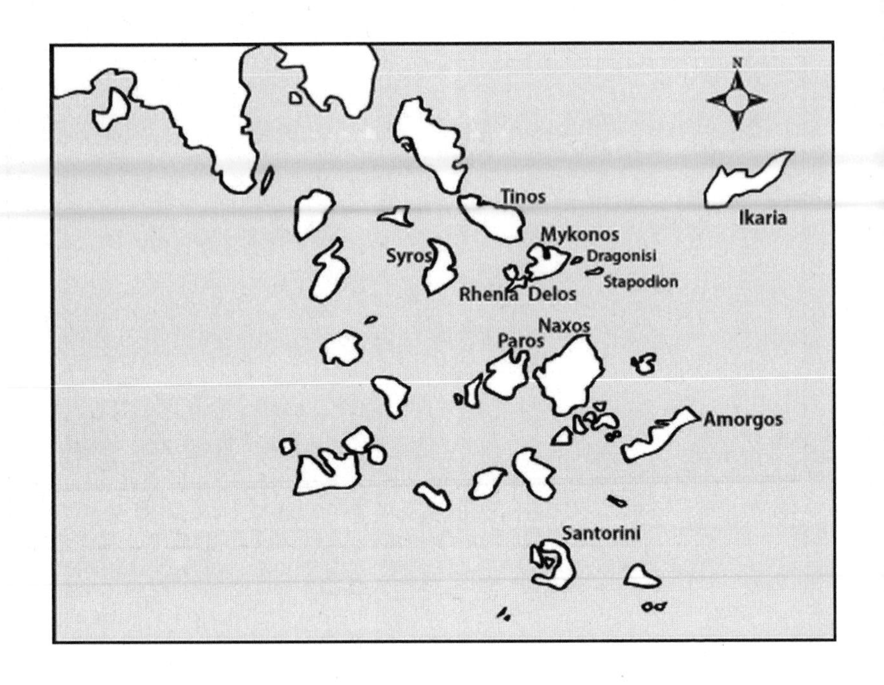

The Cyclades Islands and Ikaria

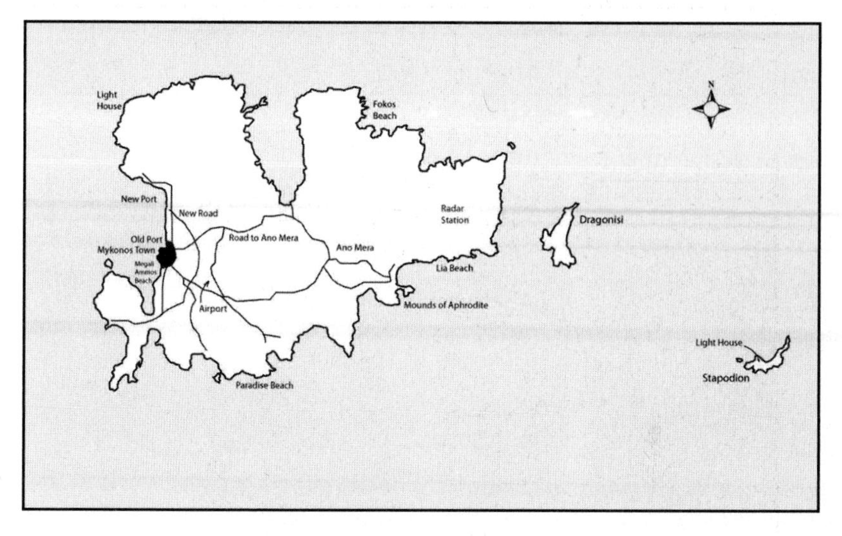

Mykonos Island

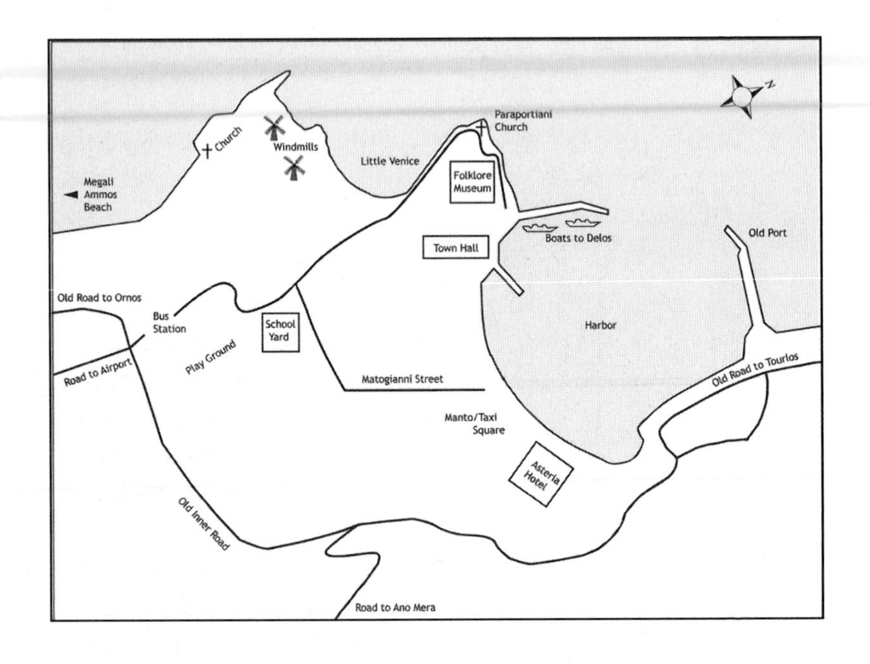

Mykonos Town

Chapter One

The man kept pressing on the doorbell. He'd come this far and was not about to leave without speaking to his friend. Maybe he'd been wrong to call Christos an "old fool," but that was no reason for ending a fifty-year friendship. For two days in a row Christos had been missing from morning coffee in the harbor. That wasn't like him.

They'd been friends since practically the day Christos got off the boat to open his nightclub here. And what a club it was. They all came: Brigitte Bardot, Grace Kelly, Sophia Loren, Jackie Onassis, Yul Brynner, Paul Newman, Gregory Peck. Christos' place had changed Mykonos forever. The times and crowds were different now, but the club still prospered from its perch above the old port following Christos' indefatigable philosophy: "I try to spend every day doing what others dream of doing just once in their lives."

Trouble was, Christos' approach to life had him falling for a twenty year-old Ukrainian pole dancer.

The man started pounding on the door with his fist. "Come on, Christos, it's Ted. Open up."

Ted had never actually called Christos an "old fool." His exact words were, "The trouble with Viagra is it fucks up an old man's mind a hell of a lot more than it ever gets up his prick."

No answer.

Ted turned right and followed a narrow, blue-gray flagstone path toward a white gate just beyond the edge of the house. The gate was of solid steel, a foot taller than Ted, and the only interruption in an eight-foot high natural stone wall surrounding Christos' property.

He tried the gate handle, but it was locked. He looked down a row of weather-beaten, terra-cotta pots neatly spaced along the base of the wall, walked over to an amphora filled with bright red geraniums, stooped down, dug his fingers into the soil, and came out with a key.

"At least you're not so pissed off at me that you changed the hiding place."

On the other side of the gate the flagstone path tripled in size, its left border lined the side of the house and its right sat perpendicular to a dozen parallel rows of grapevine plantings running up to the stone wall on the property line sixty feet away.

As Ted reached the back of the house, he yelled, "Christos, it's Ted. Ready or not here I come."

No answer.

He carefully peered around the corner. Behind the house, flagstone covered all open ground except for a ten-foot soil perimeter abutting the rear wall and bursting with pink and white oleander, pomegranate, lemon, olive, and fig trees. It was Mykonos' blue and white version of the Playboy Mansion, complete with outdoor kitchen, bamboo-covered beach bar, marble dining table for thirty, sixty-foot-long heated pool, hot tub for ten, and linen-draped outdoor beds.

"Hello, anybody home?"

Still no answer.

He wondered whether he should leave and come back later. Christos had a quick temper, and showing up unexpectedly could set him off big time. And when Christos took offense, his stubborn side kept the anger boiling well beyond his recollection of what had set it off in the first place.

Ted stared west at the sea beyond the treetops. He had to give his friend credit: Christos knew how to pick locations. This place was unlike any other on the island. It sat a little more than a half mile from the old harbor, yet despite all the development pressing upon his property, when you looked west all you saw were rolling hills, the blue Aegean, and magnificent sunsets.

He turned his head and glanced around the backyard. Everything looked normal. "Probably out with the dog," a yellow Labrador Christos had saved from starvation a dozen winters before, one of the many pets tragically abandoned at the end of each summer by self-indulgent, uncaring seasonal residents.

Yes, it's Sunday, they must be out. Otherwise, the mutt would be barking up a storm at me.

He thought to take a peek in the windows but decided it wiser to leave. If Christos was inside and ignoring his shouts, he was in no mood to be disturbed.

The next morning the maid found Christos Vasilakis bludgeoned to death in his living room. Next to him lay his dog, killed the same way. She called the police and when they arrived she was sitting calmly next to the bloodied bodies, her eyes fixed on a sliding glass door opening to the backyard. Flies were everywhere.

One young cop almost lost his lunch at the sight. Another at the smell. A third cop, a sergeant, asked her, "Why are you sitting here? It's a mess. His head is cracked wide open."

She didn't move her eyes. "I am from Kosovo. I have seen many dead bodies. Mister Christos was very good to me. I am honoring him by remaining with him."

The sergeant bit his lip. "Sorry, but you'll have to wait outside with us until the homicide unit gets here from Syros."

Syros, home to the Cycladic islands' central police headquarters, was the capital island of the Cyclades and forty-five minutes away by fast boat in good weather. That's where the homicide cops were based and those were the rules.

The sergeant stared at the body as the maid walked past him toward the door.

What happened from this point on was someone else's problem.

Chapter Two

She wished it had ended differently. It was all her fault. She was certain of that. If only she hadn't worn the fancy clothes and jewelry to surprise Sergey on his release from prison. He never said so, but he had to know she couldn't afford those things on what she made as a dancer. It was obvious she was fucking someone special.

She gazed out the train compartment window at the farmland. It seemed to be passing by so quickly. Just like the weeks since their first visit. She yawned. If she'd stuck to turning tricks during the two years Sergey was away, none of this would have happened. He would have expected that. After all, it's what she was doing when he caught her hustling johns without his permission in that strip club he managed in Bialystok.

She was seventeen then, a runaway from the poverty of the Ukrainian countryside. He was an educated Russian almost twice her age. He didn't hurt her, just made her screw him in his office for free. They kept up that arrangement for about a week until one night her pimp showed up at the club and threatened Sergey to burn it down to the ground if he kept "messing" with his "property." She never found out what happened to her pimp, but within a week she was living with Sergey and working his side of the nightlife business as the go-to person for whatever drugs the customers wanted.

For about a year her life was steady and predictable, more so than she could ever remember. Then a rival club owner arranged for Sergey to get arrested in a major drug bust. With Sergey no longer around to protect her, the only thing she could be certain of was that staying in Poland wouldn't be good for her.

So she took off for Greece and ended up on Mykonos. At five-feet-ten, with busty Grace Kelly looks, getting a job was easy, and the most difficult part of finding someone to take care of her was weeding out the competing offers.

Christos Vasilakis was the obvious choice. He was her boss, he knew everyone, he was rich, he didn't mind if she screwed around as long as she slept at home, and his sexual appetites were far less demanding than a younger man's. That arrangement also made it easier for her to still think of herself as Sergey's girl.

But why did she feel that way? She shut her eyes and tried to think of an answer.

They hadn't written or spoken since she fled to Greece, and his last message to her was that he never expected to see her again. So, why did she return to Bialystok to see him? She'd felt no guilt over leaving him there to face prison alone. If she'd stayed in Poland, the prosecutors would have made her testify against him and his sentence would have been much longer. No, they both knew it was best that she left.

The obvious answer was love. But that would be insanity. Moth-to-the-flame insanity. She opened her eyes and turned her head to look at the two men sitting across from her in the train compartment. Yes, insanity.

And it has cost me dearly.

By the time the homicide unit arrived from Syros it was nearly noon, giving the sun a chance to re-bake the bloody contents of the house to a deep, gag-inducing stench. Even the coroner retched until he could dab some menthol gel above his upper lip.

"It's a nasty one, Tassos," he said.

The man he'd called Tassos held a white handkerchief doused in menthol up to his nose. The two uniformed cops with him did the same. Looking his full sixty years, five foot eight, and unlikely to have missed a meal in many years, Tassos nodded. "Horrible way for Christos to go. Horrible way for anyone."

The coroner pointed at a white marble statuette of the Greek god Adonis that lay toppled on the floor between Christos and the dog. It was covered in dried blood. "If that's the weapon, the first blow to his head probably ended it. The rest was rage. I can't even recognize his face."

"What about the dog?"

"There's a fireplace poker close by the poor thing. Looks like that's what did it in."

"Do you think one blow took it out, too?"

"Does that matter?" Said the coroner.

"Costas, just answer the question."

The coroner knelt next to the dog. "The dog was struck more than once."

"So, either the killer was also pissed off at the dog or had trouble taking it out."

The coroner nodded. "And if he had trouble, the dog might have gotten a piece of him."

"Or her. Make sure the boys are careful, there might be more than one human DNA sample in this…" Tassos waved his hand at the floor but didn't finish his sentence.

"Chief Investigator Stamatos?"

It was a Mykonos police sergeant standing inside the front door.

"Yes?"

"Sorry to interrupt you, sir, but the maid wants to know if she can leave. She has another job to get to and is afraid she'll be fired if she's not there on time."

"Tell her to stay." Tassos looked at the coroner. "Do you need me?"

"How could I possibly do my job without you staring over my shoulder?"

"That's what I thought. If you find anything interesting, just yell. I'll be outside."

Tassos turned to the two uniformed cops. "The same goes for you. And be careful where you step. We've got a hell of a lot of house and outside property to cover, and our glorious ministry's cutbacks leave it all to us, so take your time. Hurrying won't get you back to Syros for whatever you've planned for tonight. It will only piss me off if you miss something."

What he didn't say was how many bad guys were literally getting away with murder because of the country's financial crisis. There simply weren't enough cops, equipment, or time to do a proper investigation. "Not on my watch," Tassos muttered as he walked out of the house.

The maid was sitting out of the sun on a cafe-style, white-wrought iron chair next to the front of the house. The sergeant and two officers leaned against the stone wall about thirty feet away.

Tassos walked over to the woman. The sergeant started toward them but Tassos waved him off.

"*Keria*." Tassos used the respectful form of address for a married woman. "I'm sorry to have kept you waiting, but I'm sure you understand that we have much to do to catch the people responsible for this."

The woman's expression was flat. "With Mister Christos gone, my other job is all that I have."

Tassos nodded. "I understand. Times are very tough. What hours did you work for him?"

"From eight in the morning until two in the afternoon, Monday through Friday."

"He was an early riser?"

"Every day as soon as I got here he'd walk to town for coffee in the harbor with his friends."

"What time do you have to be at your other job?"

"Two thirty."

Tassos looked at his watch. "We have an hour. You'll make it with no problem. What can you tell me that might be helpful?"

"I know nothing. I just found his body and called the police."

"Did you check to see if anything was missing?"

"I called the police from the living room and sat there with Mister Christos until they arrived. I never went anywhere else in the house."

"Did he have a safe?"

"I wouldn't know that."

Tassos walked over to another chair and dragged it into the shade next to the woman. "Looks like I'll need this, *keria*, because if that's the kind of answers you're going to be giving me, we'll be talking for quite a while." He sat down facing her.

"I don't understand. I answered your question."

"How long have you been cleaning Christos' house?"

"Almost three years."

"Like I said, did he have a safe?"

"I don't—"

Tassos raised his hand. "We both know you knew every inch of his house better than he did. So, if you keep playing dumb, you might just convince me you had something to do with his murder. Now, *did he have a safe*?"

She blinked twice. "Yes."

"Where is it?"

"There were two. One in his bedroom closet, in the wall behind an icon, and another in the living room."

"Where in the living room?"

"In a wall covered with large white marble tiles next to the fireplace."

"How did you know about them?"

"Mister Christos never tried to hide the one in the bedroom. Many times he went to it while I was cleaning the bedroom."

"And the one in the living room?"

"A few months after I started working for Mister Christos he asked me to clean out the fireplace in the living room. I noticed some of the marble tiles had separated from the wall. I touched them, and they swung open like a door. The safe was inside."

"Did you say anything to him?"

"No, I left the tiles just as I found them. I didn't want him to know I knew about the second safe."

"Why?"

"He'd never done anything to suggest he wanted me to know about it. I thought he might be testing me to see if I touched things that I shouldn't."

"Did you ever see the marble tiles open again?"

"No."

Tassos nodded. "Did anyone else know about the safes?"

"I don't know."

Tassos looked at his watch. "*Keria*, you're running out of time."

"Many people knew about his safe in the bedroom."

"What about the one in the living room?"

She shook her head. "I don't think so."

"Did his girlfriend know?" Tassos had spent his time on the boat trip over from Syros calling several of Christos' well-known friends. They'd told him about the girlfriend.

The woman's face came alive at the question. "She's a whore."

The "*putana* from Ukraine," was the phrase most often used by Christos' friends. "Why do you say that?"

"I made the beds."

Tassos shrugged. "So?"

"I could tell when it wasn't Mister Christos who'd been with her." She lowered her eyes. "His hair was silver. Not black or brown or…"

Tassos nodded. "I get it. Do you know the names of any of her visitors?"

"No, I never saw any of them. She'd have them over in a guest room after I left and before Mister Christos came home for his nap in the late afternoon."

"Did he know about the other men?"

She shrugged. "If he did, he never said anything to her. At least not when I was around."

"What else can you tell me about her?"

"She had a boyfriend."

"Who is he?"

"I don't know, but he's not from Mykonos."

"How do you know?"

"From the way she talked to him on the telephone."

"She talked to her boyfriend in front of you?"

"Once, in Polish."

"You understand Polish?"

"Enough to know she was talking to a boyfriend."

"Do you have a name for the boyfriend?"

"Sergey. He's in Bialystok. She was talking about visiting him."

"Going to visit him, or having already visited him?"

"Both."

"When did she visit him?"

"She left the island five or six weeks ago, so it was probably then."

"Did she travel a lot?"

"Not without Mister Christos. That was the first time I could remember her traveling without him. They argued about him paying for her trip. Mister Christos said he wouldn't pay for her to go somewhere without him. Even if it was to see her family."

"Is that where she went?"

She shrugged. "That's what she said."

"Any mention of Christos in her conversation with the boyfriend?"

"She said 'the old man suspects nothing.' I guess that was about Mister Christos."

"'Suspects nothing' about what?"

"No idea."

"You never told Christos any of what you'd overheard?"

She looked at Tassos' eyes. "Do you think Mister Christos didn't know what she was? If I told him what I'd heard, it would be nothing different from what he'd already imagined and had accepted as the price of being with her. If I told him, he wouldn't get rid of her, he'd get rid of me, the one who told him what he did not want to hear."

Tassos smiled. "I see you knew your employer well. Any idea where the girlfriend is now?"

"Mister Christos told me she'd left a week ago Sunday for Poland." The maid spit at the ground. "On another visit to her family."

"You think she went to see the boyfriend?"

"That's what she was talking about on the phone."

"Did Christos say when she'd be back on Mykonos?"

"This weekend."

"Any idea of who might have done this to him?"

She gave a quick upward jerk of her head in the Greek gesture for "no."

"No enemies, no arguments, no strangers coming around the house?" said Tassos.

"The *putana* would know about those sorts of things. She's the one who brought strangers into Mister Christos' home."

Tassos said nothing for a moment, smacked his hands on his thighs, stood up, and waved for the sergeant to come over. "Thank you, *keria*."

"Yes, sir?" said the sergeant.

"Please have one of your men give the lady a ride to wherever she has to be."

The maid stood and started to follow the sergeant but Tassos touched her arm to stop her. He handed her his card and whispered, "If you think of anything else that might be helpful, anything at all, please call me. And I'd appreciate it if you'd keep that second safe just between us."

Tassos dropped his hand from her arm and walked back into the house.

We have no signs of forced entry.

We have no signs of the girlfriend.

We have a suspect.

Anna had been away from Bialystok for less than a week but it felt like a lifetime. When they reached the building, she told the two men to wait outside. She wanted to be alone in Sergey's one room apartment.

The fresh flowers she'd left in a vase on the small table next to his bed were gray and shriveled, surrounded by withered petals that had fluttered onto the tabletop.

All it would have taken was a little water.

She looked at the bed. It hadn't been made. Dirty clothes lay scattered on the one upholstered chair in the room. There were dishes piled up haphazardly in the sink and God only knew what sort of a mess was in the bathroom.

Sergey was the same slob he'd been when they'd lived together, always waiting for someone to pick up after him. But now that someone was used to maids.

How can I ever go back to this?

Anna sat on the edge of the bed and stared at the icon on the wall between the room's two dirty windows. She didn't pray, only stared, waiting to hear him at the door.

There were a lot of things she had to tell him.

Chapter Three

Tassos turned back into the house and went straight upstairs to Christos' bedroom. It was messy, but slept-in messy, not ransacked. The safe was where the maid had said, its door wide open and insides empty. He looked around. There wasn't a thing in the closet or bedroom that looked as if it might have been in the safe. The killers must have taken everything in it, he thought.

He went back downstairs and found the coroner working in the living room. "There's a safe upstairs, Costas. It's wide open so let's get the tech boys on it doing their thing. But I doubt they'll find anything more than the victim's prints."

"Why so pessimistic? Even cops get lucky sometimes."

Tassos shook his head. "Not on that safe we won't. My guess is Christos opened it for them. As messy as this killing was, if they'd murdered him first there'd be blood tracked somewhere upstairs or on the steps. Besides, the smart move was to get him to cooperate."

"Unless they already knew the combination."

Tassos nodded. "Yes, but even if they did, I doubt they'd have killed him first. Still, have them check for blood traces up there just in case I'm wrong for the first time in my life."

"What do you think happened?"

"I think Christos opened the upstairs safe but they were looking for more than what was in it. And not just money or jewelry."

"And how do you come to that conclusion?"

"They took everything in the safe. I mean everything. Most people keep at least some personal papers in a safe. Deeds, a will, an old photograph or two, something they think important enough to protect. Sure, there may be some blackmail value in some of those things, but I can't believe every scrap of paper in there would interest a thief. *Unless*, what they wanted wasn't in the safe and they thought the papers might hold a clue to what they were really after."

"But why kill Christos if he gave them what they came for?"

"The point is, I don't think he did. The maid said there was a second safe. Maybe the killers knew about it, maybe they didn't. But I think he died because he didn't give them what they were looking for. Something they knew he had hidden somewhere. Either in a second safe or someplace else."

"What the hell was worth dying for? Certainly not money."

Tassos shrugged. "Who knows what people are willing to die for? You and I know better, because we've seen this before." Tassos waved his hand at the bodies of Christos and his dog. "But most folks, don't think this could ever happen to them. Especially on Mykonos, where violent crime is practically unheard of. When something like this starts to go down, they think it's just a bad dream that'll end when they wake up."

"But if he opened the upstairs safe without a fight, and the killers realized he hadn't given them what they wanted, why didn't they beat him up in the bedroom instead of bringing him down here to do it?"

Tassos shrugged again. "That, my friend, is a question to ask them when we catch them."

Tassos walked over to the fireplace and began tugging at the tiles. When a section of them shifted, he pulled harder, and the tiles swung open just as the maid said they would.

"Bingo." Inside was a closed safe door twice as large as the one upstairs. "Care to bet whether the killers ever found this one?"

Costas gestured no with his head. "But I still don't understand what could be in it worth dying for."

"Me either, but our answer might be inside. Besides, if you're right about the first blow taking him out, Christos may not have had a chance to change his mind and give them what they wanted."

Costas shook his head. "Poor bastard."

"Can any of your boys open a safe?"

"Professionally?"

"No jokes. I need someone who can do it and keep his mouth shut. Too many loose lips among the local police."

"One of my guys has done that sort of thing before, though he might be reluctant without a court order."

"Just get it done."

Costas nodded.

Tassos turned and pointed to a bookcase in the far corner of the room by the door leading to the backyard. "Did you see that?"

"If you mean the camera? Yes. It's pretty well hidden but I saw it. One of your men found where the recorder used to be."

"Used to be?"

"Yes, everything's gone. Whatever was recorded is no more."

"Sounds like whoever did this really knew the house."

"You think so, huh? No wonder you're chief homicide investigator."

Tassos shot him the middle finger as he shouted, "Adonis, where are you?"

Ten seconds later a lanky, dark-haired uniformed cop in his early twenties stuck his head through the doorway out to the backyard. "I'm out here, Chief, looking for footprints."

"Forget about that for now. I want you to check out every house that has a sight line on this place. See if any of them have security cameras aimed in this direction. If you find any, get everything they have going back a week. And I mean everything."

"Yes, sir, right away." He disappeared.

Tassos said, "Good kid."

"Why, because he listens to your every word? And don't bother giving me the finger this time. I'm too busy concentrating on my work to notice."

Tassos gave him the finger anyway.

◇◇◇

Anna lay stretched out on her side across the foot of the bed. The apartment's windows faced front, across a busy commercial street three stories below, and the little light still in the sky came from behind the building. She fell asleep to the din of the traffic.

She awoke in the dark and slid off the bed to make her way to the bathroom next to the front door. She turned on the light, did her business, and stepped back into the room making up the rest of the apartment. That's when she saw the men asleep with their heads resting across their forearms on the kitchen table over by one of the windows.

From the number of empty beer bottles on the table, Anna guessed that she'd had the company of her two traveling companions for quite some time. They must have tired of waiting outside the apartment and come in to pass the time drinking and whispering to each other about what they'd like to do to her as she slept on the bed. But she knew all they'd dare do was fantasize. After all, she was Sergey's girlfriend.

Where is he? She'd spent six miserable days with these degenerates getting to Mykonos and back on schedule, and Sergey couldn't bother to be here waiting for her? *Bastard.* In addition to maids, Anna had become used to better treatment from her men.

The whole trip would have taken two days, three at most, had they flown. But that would involve closely checked identification at security checkpoints. Boats, buses, and trains were a pain in the ass to travel between Bialystok and Mykonos but that was the way Sergey wanted it done. It was his plan and they'd stuck to it faithfully—except for the part about what happened to Christos.

Bang!

Anna jumped up and spun around to face the door.

Bang, bang, bang.

Someone was hammering away at the door with a fist.

"Who is it?" she said.

"Your happiness and joy."

"Sergey!" She hurried to the door, undid the bolt, and swung open the door.

A tall, broad-shouldered man with Romanesque features stepped inside, arms spread wide and smiling as if he were a kid on Christmas morning. Fair-skinned, with pale blue eyes and shoulder-length, bright white hair, he seemed almost albino, except that his eyebrows and lashes were jet black.

She threw her arms around his neck and kissed him hard on the lips.

Sergey brought his arms in toward her body and gave a sort of a hug with his elbows.

She pulled back, her hands still around his neck. "Is this how you show how happy you are to see me?"

He waved with one hand to the two men at the table. They waved back, smiling.

"Where have you been? I've been waiting for hours," she said.

Sergey leaned in and kissed her quickly on the lips. "My darling, I've been buying vodka to celebrate." He pulled back from her grip and brought his hands around to show a plastic grocery bag in each hand.

"Here, put them on the table so we can share with our friends." He handed her the packages and started walking toward the men.

"What's the matter, you couldn't carry them over to the table yourself?"

He paused for an instant, but said nothing and kept going.

The two men stood up and embraced Sergey.

"You did it, my friends. Congratulations. Well done." Sergey slapped both men on the back.

Anna hadn't moved. "'Well done'? These imbeciles beat him to death before we had the chance to find where he'd hidden what we were looking for. They ruined everything. Destroyed our plan."

Sergey turned and walked back to Anna. He took the packages from her hands. "Relax, it was an accident."

"*Accident?* You weren't there. They never gave him a chance to tell us where it was. I did just as you said. I told him the two had kidnapped me and wanted money to let me go. That's when he took us upstairs and opened the safe."

"But what we wanted wasn't in there," said the shorter of the two men.

"There were other ways to get him to tell us," she said.

"We tried," said the tall man.

"Throwing him down the stairs wasn't what I meant."

The tall man shrugged.

Anna nodded toward the short man. "That asshole never gave me a chance to get him to talk. He just started beating Christos with a statuette until his head split open, while *you* did the same thing to the dog." She pointed at the tall man.

"The fucker bit me," said the tall man waving a bandaged hand.

Sergey sighed. "There's nothing we can do about it, my love. Let's just move on." He kissed her on the forehead, took the packages to the table, and gestured for the men to open them.

"How can we move on? I can never go back to Mykonos. I'm no longer a kidnap victim, I'm part of a murder."

"We took all the videos," said the tall man.

She shook her head. "It's still too big a chance for me to take. I'll always be a suspect."

Sergey nodded. "Yes, I'm afraid you're right about that. But look at the bigger picture. Christos is no longer. The king of Mykonos nightlife is gone. Hail the new king." He pointed to his chest.

"Are you crazy? You're not Greek, let alone Mykonian, and you've never even been to Mykonos."

He smiled. "Details, my love, details."

"You *are* crazy! What about all those things he bragged about to me? The things you said we *must* have for the plan to work?"

He shrugged. "I assume the police will find all of that and we'll be able to buy what we need from them. If not, we shall find other ways."

"And what are we going to use for money?"

He shook his head. "Oh ye of little faith. Remember, police aren't as expensive as they used to be."

"Stop bullshitting me, Sergey. What's going on?"

The tall man opened one of the bottles of vodka as the short man put out four mismatched water glasses.

"Like I said, we're celebrating."

"Tell me or I'm out of here!"

"But to where? Where can you go now that is safer than here?" He waved toward the two other men, "With us?"

She blinked.

He walked over to her and put his arm around her shoulder. "Come my love, it's time to celebrate."

And so they did.

◇◇◇

The screen lit up and a buzz vibrated along the tabletop. Tassos put down his coffee and reached for his phone. He looked at the name of the caller, ANDREAS KALDIS, and pressed ACCEPT.

"I was wondering when I'd hear from our country's feared head of its Special Crimes Division." The two cops met when Andreas served as chief of police on Mykonos, and they'd remained fast friends after his promotion back to Athens as chief of the division charged with investigating matters of national concern or potential corruption.

"Tell me about it. If it weren't for a court appearance I had this afternoon, Spiros would have had me on Mykonos busting your balls for answers to feed the press."

"Ahh, Spiros Renatis, our distinguished fearless leader and minister of public order. How nice of him to still take an interest in my work after all these years. He should have dropped by, I'd have been more than happy to see him. At least he could have called. I'm hurt."

"Yeah, I bet. He's more afraid of you than he is of his wife," said Andreas. Tassos had been on the force so long that everyone either owed him a favor or feared what he knew about them—on both sides of the law.

"You mean the one who gives him his social standing?" said Tassos.

"Hey, easy there fella, you're hitting close to home." Andreas' wife was the daughter of one of Greece's oldest and wealthiest families and the socially prominent widow of a shipowner before they married.

Tassos laughed. "How is Lila, Andreas, *mou*?"

"My bride is fine and sends her regards."

"So, what can I do to help you?"

"As if you didn't know. Christos Vasilakis had a lot of friends, he was a media darling, and Spiros sees the chance to become a headline hero again with a quick arrest."

"Well, it won't be quick, but we'll make an arrest."

"You've solved it already? I'm impressed."

"It wasn't that hard. There were three of them. Christos' girlfriend and two other guys. They showed up at Christos' house in a car they'd stolen from the old port, killed him, drove the car back to the old port, left it there, and took the Sea Jet to Athens."

"How the hell do you all know that?"

"Got your attention, huh?"

"Always do."

"I had one of my guys check the neighborhood for security cameras. He found video covering practically the whole route between Christos' house and the old port. Do you have any idea how many cameras are out there? They're everywhere."

"Good thing my secret liaison days at deserted fields and beaches are behind me."

"You better believe it. These days whatever you do outdoors you're likely doing for an audience."

"When do you expect to make an arrest?"

"No telling. That's something we'll have to work through Europol. My guess is the killers are out of Greece by now."

"Anything for Spiros to tell the press?"

"Not yet. If he does, it will tip-off the killers we're on to them, and they'll disappear like smoke."

"I guess that means I tell him nothing."

"I leave that to you. But knowing Spiros as we do, and his penchant for kissing the ass of anyone he thinks might help his career, if you told him the whole story he might think it serves his interests better if they're *never* caught."

"What the hell are you talking about?" said Andreas.

"There's a part to this murder that makes the simple solution I just described far more intricate a puzzle than I dare tell you on a mobile phone. Even a supposedly secure one."

"Jesus, Tassos, you and your dramatics. You're just trying to get me over to Mykonos to buy you dinner."

"Andreas, how many times do I have to tell you? 'We're cops. We don't pay.'"

Andreas laughed. "A perfect description of our different approaches to police work."

"So, are you coming or not?"

"How about tomorrow morning on the first flight? I promised my mother that Lila and I would have dinner with her tonight."

"And Tassaki?"

"If we didn't show up with her grandson, I doubt my mother would feed us."

"Yeah, Maggie said that your mother won't even let you use a babysitter."

"I'm glad to hear that my secretary is keeping you up to speed on my personal life."

"Your secretary is discreet. It's my girlfriend who talks."

"Cute."

Andreas had unknowingly rekindled an old romance between Tassos, a long time widower, and Maggie, Andreas' secretary and mother superior of Athens' police headquarters.

"But seriously, my friend, get over here ASAP."

"Will do. See you tomorrow. Good night."

Tassos put the phone on the table. He picked up his coffee, took a sip, turned his head, and stared at the crescent of tavernas spread out along the harborfront. He watched a few taverna owners trying to lure passing tourists inside with offers of "very fresh fish, special price." The enticers were obviously transplants from other places. Mykonians didn't act that way. They looked down on such pushy practices, considered them contrary to their philosophy that hospitality meant serving, not pressing, your clients. So far, that approach had worked out well for them. Mykonos' tourist draw was the envy of every island in the Cyclades, if not everywhere in Greece.

He took another sip of coffee and thought about how much the times had changed. The island was still paradise, and the old town never failed to enchant tourists wandering its centuries-old maze of whitewashed two-story buildings aligned every which way along narrow, flagstone alleyways. But paths once used to flee invading pirates now served as playgrounds for village children beneath the watchful gaze of black clad grandmothers chatting away across brightly painted wooden balconies.

A pack of scantily clad college-age girls walked by, toying with the taunts of boys calling out to them from the taverna. Tassos smiled. Maybe times hadn't changed that much. Just the places. He'd heard locals say that during the hectic summers of Delos' Third Century BCE heydays as the commercial trading center for the ancient world, Delians would send their wives and children to Mykonos during the hot summers. Not so much to holiday—as many wealthy but busy Athenian husbands and fathers sent them today—but to save them from the advances of thousands of anonymous sailors and traders passing through the island looking for ways to spend their time. Today, the former sanctuary posed the greater threat to virtue than the Delian ruins. A promise that drew even more to the flame.

As with everything in Greece, the history of Mykonos entwined with the gods. Some said the island's name came from Apollo's grandson, Mykons. Others claimed it just meant "a pile of rocks" in keeping with the myth that Heracles fought the Giants in aid of Zeus and after defeating them threw the vanquished into the sea where they turned into the massive boulders found scattered around Mykonos.

The first evidence of human inhabitants on Mykonos dated back to 4000 BCE. For most of the ensuing six thousand years, whether the island prospered or not depended primarily on its proximity to the more commercially developed islands of Delos,

Syros, and Tinos, and to the foreigners then in control—Carians, Egyptians, Phoenicians, Minoans, Ionians, Athenians, Macedonians, Romans, Venetians, Turks, and Russians, were among those who dominated Mykonos at some point.

Two other significant elements played a part in Mykonos' development: piracy and plague. Pirates haunted the island virtually from antiquity, so much so that it became home to many, and legend for its able-bodied seamen willing to sail to wherever there might be commerce or battle.

But sea travel brought with it many perils, including plague. As recently as the mid-nineteenth century, plague so badly ravaged the population that those who survived and did not flee to other islands or the mainland were too few to work the fields or take care of the animals. That's when the Church induced immigrants from islands such as Crete, Naxos, Santorini, and Folegandros to move to Mykonos, offering the promise of a new start for them and the hope of a new beginning for the island.

A flicker of promise appeared after World War I that tourism might take root, but World War II crushed it. The German army's program of taking everything for themselves and leaving nothing for the occupied people brought devastating famine and death to Mykonians on a scale greater than almost anywhere else in Greece.

After World War II, came war on the mainland between the left and the right, and in the fifties and early sixties a mass exodus of the island's youth to Athens and far off lands in search of a better life.

Against that six thousand years of struggle it seemed magic that in little more than a single generation Mykonos transformed into its present-day wonder and the long-impoverished Mykonians became among the wealthiest per capita people in Greece.

Tassos took another sip of coffee. The unusually gentle breeze coming off the sea had a lot of people strolling along the wide, blue-grey-brown flagstone border between the tavernas and ten yards of sand to the water. Some came out to smell the sea, most to people-watch, but all to absorb the in-season energy of Mykonos and a sense that, for the moment at least, all was right with the world.

Tassos put down his cup. Good thing they didn't know what was locked inside the briefcase at his feet.

Chapter Four

When the alarm went off at dawn, Lila mumbled from her pillow, "Is there something you forgot to tell me?"

Andreas hit the snooze button. "Yep, I have to catch the seven-thirty flight to Mykonos."

"Is it about Christos?"

"I won't even try figuring out how you knew that."

"Not hard. It's all over the news. Make that Spiros is all over the news. And when he's all over the news can my husband be far behind? After all, someone has to come up with his answers."

"I knew there was a reason I married you." He kissed her on the cheek.

"That's all I get for such glorious praise first thing in the morning? A peck on the cheek?"

"Put it on my account. I'll settle up later." He pinched her butt.

Lila sat up. "I'll have Marietta make you breakfast." She reached for the phone.

"No time for that. I'll catch a bite at the airport."

Lila smiled but dialed. "Marietta, would you please prepare breakfast for Mr. Kaldis. And pack it to go."

She hung up the phone. "You're still not used to having help." She smiled. "I like that about you."

Andreas nodded. "I'm trying. Yesterday, I let Tassaki pick out my clothes."

"Letting a two-year-old pull all your shirts out of a dresser drawer is not what I meant."

Andreas shrugged. "I'm trying." He leaned over and kissed her. "Now I really have to run."

"Open the drapes, let in the light. It won't bother me."

Andreas picked up the remote control and pressed a button. The drapes parted, revealing narrow, pale-gray horizontal steel slats covering the windows. They were necessary security for virtually every upscale home in Greece, even a penthouse on the most prestigious street in Athens and next door to the presidential palace.

Andreas pressed another button and the shutters rolled up and out of sight as light rushed into the room. An unobstructed view of the Parthenon atop the Acropolis filled the window. This was another thing Andreas had difficulty getting used to: living the life of the super rich. But if he wanted to marry Lila it came with the package. He could not expect her to live a life on what he earned as a cop. Make that an honest cop.

So, this was how he now lived. Not that he resented his good fortune. It was just so very different from his own roots as the son of a working class cop. Another honest cop.

"Do you need a ride to the airport?"

"No thanks, Yianni is picking me up."

Yianni Kouros was Andreas' right hand. They met when Yianni was a brash young rookie on Mykonos and Andreas his chief. They'd been together ever since.

"When will you be back?"

"No telling. Tassos wants to see me. Hopefully on an afternoon flight or, at worst, the last boat."

"Well, at least with Tassos I know you won't be getting into any trouble."

"My love, with Tassos there's generally nothing but trouble."

"I meant of the *other* kind." She smiled. "The Mykonos crazy lifestyle sort of trouble."

Andreas nodded. "Good point. I think I'll bring Yianni along. He specializes in that sort of thing."

Andreas managed to get to the bathroom door before Lila's pillow caught him from behind.

◇◇◇

Kouros sat in a marked blue and white police car in front of the apartment building.

"Morning, Chief. I see you have breakfast."

"As a matter of fact *we* do. Lila had it packed for two." Andreas held up a *spanakopita* as he slid into the passenger's seat. "A bit heavy for breakfast, but easier to eat in the car than yogurt."

Kouros pulled away from the curb and reached for the spinach pie. "Any idea what has Tassos so wound up he won't talk over the phone?"

"Not a clue." Andreas pulled another *spanakopita* out of the bag and took a bite. He struggled to speak around his chewing. "But whatever it is, it must be serious. Tassos is not an alarmist."

"Can't wait to hear what's on his mind. What time's your flight back so I can pick you up?"

"Pick me up? You're coming with me."

Yianni smiled. "I hoped you'd say that." He pointed with the *spanakopita* toward the back seat. "I even packed a bag. Just in case."

"We're not staying overnight."

Yianni smiled. "Better safe that sorry."

Andreas took another bite. "Damn it, I should have packed a bag. But if I had, Lila would have thought I actually intended to stay over."

"We bachelors always plan ahead. You do remember those days, don't you?"

"Detective Kouros, just get us to the airport."

Andreas spent most of the flight reading the report Tassos had faxed to Kouros covering what he'd come up with so far in the investigation. The rest of the time Andreas stared out the window at a deep blue sea, white-edge waves, and beige-brown islands flecked with green and white.

Mykonos lay ninety miles southeast of Athens and less than thirty minutes away by plane, or two hours and fifteen minutes by high-speed catamaran. Approximately one and a half times the size of the island of Manhattan, it had a population of ten thousand year-round citizens that swelled to fifty thousand during tourist season.

The island differed greatly in season from its agrarian and seafaring roots. In summers Mykonos drew a monied crowd relatively immune to the worldwide financial crisis. And, for the most part, Mykonians put aside their way of life during those months as they braced for a tsunami of rich and super rich from around the world, joined by hordes of poseurs, flocking to their island on holiday.

Mykonos also served as a cruise boat mecca, drawing day-trippers to tourist shops and coffee at the port. But it wasn't the rich or the cruise boats that Mykonos relied upon to support its many hotels, shops, bars, restaurants, and clubs. For those, the island looked to sun worshipers drawn by the island's dozens of breathtaking beaches and partiers chasing after its world famous 24/7 action.

Yes, serious cultural reasons also drew visitors to Mykonos, most notably the intensely spiritual holy island of Delos. There one could walk amid restored, millennia-old ruins of the once thriving center of ancient Cycladic life. But one had to get up early to catch a boat to Delos because the last boat back to Mykonos was at three in the afternoon, and that sort of early morning pilgrimage rarely worked for the late night partier, no matter how sincere intentions might have been when falling asleep at dawn.

Tassos stood on the airport tarmac just outside the terminal's arrivals door. He held a briefcase but managed to exchange embraces with his friends.

Andreas pointed at the briefcase. "Never knew you to carry one of those."

"Follow me," was all Tassos said. He led them inside the terminal, through the baggage claim area, and past a doorway to the right leading out of the building.

"Where are we going?" said Kouros.

"I'll tell you when we get there."

At the south end of the terminal building they took a flight of stairs up to the second floor and stopped at a door marked OFFICE OF DIRECTOR OF AIRPORT OPERATIONS.

"In here." Tassos opened the door and waited for Andreas and Kouros to go inside. He pulled the door shut behind him and locked it.

"My friend said we could use his office. He won't be back for an hour. He's having coffee in the harbor with his cronies."

Tassos put the briefcase on top of a desk, walked to a line of windows overlooking the runway, and closed the blinds.

Andreas and Kouros stood in front of the desk watching Tassos.

"What's with all the mystery?" said Andreas. "The police station is only a hundred yards away. We could have met there."

Tassos walked back to the desk. "You'll understand when you see what's in here." He tinkered with a combination, popped the locks, lifted the lid, and spun the case around so the two could see what was inside.

"It's the contents of Christos' second safe. The one I didn't mention in my report."

Anna woke wishing she hadn't. The celebration of the night before had turned nasty. Sergey insisted on getting drunk and that everyone join in. Then he had sex with her. In front of the other two men. She knew where things were headed, and tried to get out of the apartment as soon as Sergey finished. But the two men grabbed her at the door and brought her back to the bed.

She didn't struggle. She remembered what they did to Christos. They hurt her, but other men had done much worse.

Sergey did nothing to stop them. He sat on a chair by the table drinking his vodka, watching it all. By far *that* was the worst thing any man had ever done to her.

She tried rolling off the bed, but the two men were asleep on either side of her. She pushed herself by her elbows toward the foot of the bed. One of the men grabbed her arm. She smacked his hand and cursed him. He let her go and she quickly slid off the bed and onto her feet.

She felt throbbing, burning pain everywhere down there and feared what diseases those sick bastards might have given her. She stared at Sergey sleeping with his head on the table.

And you let them do it to me. She staggered to the bathroom and turned on the water to fill the tub. She prayed for a bit of hot water.

She wondered how she could have been so stupid. How she'd wrecked her chance to get away from scum like this. She stepped into the tub. It was soapy from the residue of past baths never scrubbed clean. But the water was warm. "Thank you, God," she said quietly to herself.

She sat down and lay back in the tub, watching the water spill out onto her toes and creep up along the sides of her thighs to above the places of pain and onto her belly. It had reached her chin when the door opened.

"Good morning, my love." Sergey was naked. "What a glorious party." He aimed his penis at the toilet bowel and began to piss. "And it would have been nothing without you."

"You miserable piece of shit. How could you let them rape me?"

"Rape? But I thought you were enjoying yourself so. I know how much you like making love to other men, so I thought why not let our colleagues enjoy you as well."

What she wanted to say wouldn't come out.

"Besides, those poor men have not been with a woman in a very long time, possibly never with one as beautiful as you. And it was the least we could do for all the generous help they've given us."

"*We!* Those degenerate bastards raped me."

"But, my darling, you are my girlfriend." He bent his head forward, shook it vigorously from side to side, and jerked it back up, causing his hair to fall to the sides of his face. "I also suffered watching those men violate you. I, too, sacrificed—have you no compassion for what I endured?"

She stared at him, the water now up to her lips. She tried to speak but choked on the water. She sat up and turned off the faucets.

Sergey shook his dick, turned, and sat on the edge of the tub. He stroked her hair.

"Perhaps, if you hadn't become so close and special to Christos I would not have let that happen. But you did, and so what was the harm in letting them enjoy you too?"

"What are you talking about? I came back to you."

He nodded. "I know and appreciate that. For without your return I never would have learned of the glorious opportunity awaiting us on Mykonos. A chance for a new beginning."

"And for that you let them fuck me! That's how you show your thanks?"

He shrugged. "But it would have been such a waste not to let them enjoy you."

She started to speak, but he put a finger to her lips. "Shhh, let me explain, my love."

He took his finger away and went back to stroking her hair. "Christos would never give up his club. No matter how much money he was offered. Many had tried. It was his life. And no one could rival him. Not because others didn't know how, but because they would never get permission to do so. Christos owned everyone in government whose approval was necessary to open a place, and not even the largest bribe could shake his grip." He squeezed a fistful of her hair as if to emphasize his words. She winced and he opened his hand.

"There was nothing in the harbor of Mykonos to seriously compete with Christos' place, and as long as he lived, there never would be. Certainly not any by us."

"Why do you say that? You never even met the man. You have no idea how he might have reacted if you'd bothered to ask instead of sending those…those beasts of yours. That was your plan all along, wasn't it? To kill him."

Sergey shook his head. "My love, I know how powerful men behave. How they must behave to remain powerful. I intend to be such a man on Mykonos. One other men fear. There cannot be two such men in the same place. It is against the natural order of things."

"What are you talking about?"

"I had a lot of time to think in prison, having so few visitors. And—"

"I couldn't come and you knew that."

Sergey put his finger to his lips. "Shhh, yes, yes, my darling. As I was saying, and I often wondered about opportunities outside of Poland and our poor Balkan neighbors for one willing and prepared to do what must be done to seize them."

He smiled. "And as if fate were eavesdropping on my thoughts, you showed up on my very first day out of prison bearing a golden goose."

"But Christos is dead. How are you going to get what you needed from him now?"

"His influence died with him, and now it is up to the strongest to step in and take advantage of the vacuum."

"The locals will fill it. They'll never let you in."

"No need for you to worry. Christos and his club are no longer relevant. There are better opportunities, and with the right connections and arrangements, the golden goose will be ours."

"But I can't go back to Mykonos. Not after the murder."

Sergey shook his head. "I know. It is a shame. And, as I said, a great waste." He leaned in, kissed Anna hard on the lips, and pulled back. He ran his fingers lightly along her wet skin down to her breasts, cupped them in his hands and squeezed the nipples. "Yes, yes, yes…a terrible waste."

He looked into her eyes, smiled, slid his hands up to around her throat and squeezed again, forcing her head underwater as he did.

Chapter Five

Andreas carefully avoided touching anything in the briefcase with his fingers. He used the eraser end of a pencil to push around among ledgers, recording tapes, DVDs, CDs, flash drives, photographs and dozens of sealed envelopes.

"What's all this?" said Andreas?

"Like I said, the contents of Christos' second safe."

Andreas spoke through taut lips. "Why didn't you mention any of this in your report?"

Tassos tapped his fingers along the open lid of the case, his face angry. "My friend, if you're thinking what I think you're thinking…" He paused and gave a broad smile, "I completely understand why. But I assure you those days are behind me. Besides, if I were intent on, shall we say, an unofficial confiscation, the last cops I'd bring in on the deal would be The Lone Ranger and his sidekick."

"I thought you didn't like American western movies," said Kouros.

Tassos shot the open palm equivalent of a middle finger in Kouros' direction but kept his eyes on Andreas. "Do you get my point?"

Andreas' face relaxed. "Okay, but what's in there that's so important you have us acting like spooks in a B movie."

"Fair question. With the aid of a pair of latex gloves I saw enough in the ledgers to explain how Christos managed to keep so many of Greece's major players and public officials on his side for decades."

"If you're saying you've found evidence of corruption, I'm shocked." Andreas raised his hands as if surprised. "Greek government officials taking bribes? My, my, what is our country coming to?"

"No one's going to care," said Kouros. "All the world knows they're goddamned crooks."

"*Thinks* they're crooks," said Andreas. "But good luck on getting a prosecution. I spend more time trying to light fires under prosecutors than chasing bad guys."

"Fellas, give me some credit. If this were just about payoffs we wouldn't be having this conversation. Yes, the ledgers show a lot of bribes to a lot of important people, but bribes only guaranteed their loyalty until someone else offered the corrupt bastards more than Christos did.

"Christos' real influence was what he had on virtually every politician and family in Greece that's mattered over the last forty years. It's all described in the ledgers. Enough toxic events and transactions to have them all by the balls."

"Come on," said Andreas. "You can't be saying that every prominent person in Greece has something that serious to hide?"

"No, I'm not, but virtually all of them have at least some family member who does. And that's all the leverage Christos needed. After all, he wasn't asking to get away with murder or rob the National Gallery. All he wanted them to do was make sure he could run his club without complications or competition."

"I wonder if that's what drew all the movers and shakers to his club?" said Kouros.

Tassos nodded. "Because they knew if you wanted to be indiscreet, Christos' place was where you could do your thing and get away with it."

"As long as you protected him," said Andreas.

"Smart guy," said Kouros.

"Dead guy," said Andreas.

"Some of his 'friends,'" Tassos accented the word with finger quotes, "were pretty fucking kinky. Those folks preferred to use his house. From what I could make out from the ledgers, the Marquis de Sade would have been proud."

"Do you think he was murdered because of what's in the briefcase?" said Kouros.

"Don't know, but my instincts tell me it's a hell of a lot more likely he was killed because of what's in there than because Christos' girlfriend and her buddies botched a robbery.

"If I had to guess, I'd say he was supposed to die and the reason for his death is answered by something in the briefcase. As for just what that might be or how it all ties together," Tassos gestured no with his head, "I don't have a clue. But one thing I know for sure. If what's described in that ledger ever gets out, it will bring on an international media shit storm like this country's never seen before."

"Terrific, just what we need. More international press stories screaming about our 'national character.'" This time it was Kouros using finger quotes.

"Bad press might be the least of our worries if the blackmail value of what's in there is as powerful as you say," said Andreas.

Kouros smiled. "You mean like a tape recording of our prime minister lip-locked in an intimate cell phone conversation with his lover?"

"Joke all you want about that old bit of political gossip, but don't underestimate what the right sort of pressure applied to a politician's vulnerabilities can achieve in knowledgeable hands." Andreas nodded at the case. "Did you find anything else interesting in there?"

"I only looked at the ledgers. Didn't touch anything else." He smiled. "I thought it best that I wait for you. But I assume it's supporting proof for what's in the ledgers, because next to each ledger entry are categories labeled, 'dates,' 'times,' 'names,' 'places,' and 'storage media.'"

"Seems pretty well organized," said Kouros.

"Looks like Christos recorded or at least made detailed notes of every conversation he ever had with someone of importance. Plus, I've a feeling there's proof in there that people who should have known better did a lot of very stupid things in public at the end of a long night of partying."

"Like I said, he was one smart guy. So, where do we go from here?" said Kouros.

"One place we definitely won't be going is to Spiros. At least not now," said Andreas. "He'll have an orgasm at the thought of how many favors he'll be owed if he *handles* things right. The arrogant bastard will blame it all on a robbery gone sour, and with an easy conviction of the girlfriend and her accomplices, close the case without ever mentioning the contents of the second safe. Then he'll spend the rest of his days reminding the rich and powerful that he was their savior."

"Or worse," said Tassos. "There's enough blackmail material in here to make him a very, very rich man."

"Let's hope he's not gone completely over to the dark side," said Andreas. "But I get your point."

"The eleventh commandment. Thou shalt not lead thy boss into temptation," said Kouros.

"The first thing we need to do is find out exactly what's in this massive pile of shit you so kindly dumped in our laps."

"That's going to take a lot of time and we can't do it here. My friend will be back any minute."

"Assuming you don't mind turning the briefcase over to me, we can do it back in my office in Athens. At least I know that small part of police headquarters is secure."

Tassos shut the lid, pressed the locks closed, scrambled the tumblers, and pushed the case across the table toward Andreas. "Done. This mess is now officially yours. Uhh, make that unofficially. By the way, the combination is Tassaki's birthday."

"Nice touch."

"I did it in the hope that by the time his next birthday rolls around we might have some idea of what the hell's going on here."

"His birthday is almost a year away."

"You're right. That's not enough time, I should have said—" Tassos reached for a police radio on his belt. "It's vibrating." He tinkered with a dial and brought the communicator up to his ear.

"What is it?" said Andreas.

"Three men just robbed the national bank on the ring road. They escaped on motorcycles."

"Descriptions?" said Andreas.

"Foreigners."

"That's a big help," said Kouros.

"All approximately six feet tall, Caucasian, muscular, each wearing jeans, long sleeve grey work shirts, light blue windbreakers, work boots and ski masks."

"So, what's the foreigner tie-in?" said Andreas.

"The one who did all the talking had an Eastern European accent."

"What about the bikes?" said Kouros.

"All yellow, and fast. Probably stolen. They took off north in the direction of the new port."

"They've probably hooked up with a fast boat and are on their way to who knows where by now," said Kouros. "The only one with any chance of catching them now is the coast guard."

"Don't be so sure," said Tassos. "Are you two Athenian desk jockeys up for a bit of old fashioned, down home police work?"

Andreas looked at Kouros, then back at Tassos. "Why not?" He picked up the briefcase and headed toward the door, "The Lone Ranger and Tonto are always up for a little adventure."

What locals called the "ring" or "new" road was finished in the late 1990s and enclosed a much older inner road that marked the land-based perimeter of the old port area of Mykonos. Beyond the north and south edges of the original town the old road hugged the sea as it made its way north to the villages of Tourlos, San Stefanos, and Houlakia, and south to the village of Ornos. At a turnoff to Ornos Beach the old road split, continuing south to the area of Agios Ioannis of *Shirley Valentine* film fame, and west, past the island's soccer stadium, to the steep rocky hills of

Canalia peninsula, a modern construction miracle or a development curse, depending upon your point of view.

The new and old roads connected south of Mykonos town at Ornos, and north of the town at the sea midway between the old port and the new port in Tourlos. Between those two junctures, and out of sight of the old town, the new road ran up and down hills for approximately two miles in three unequal north, central, and south sections, separated by rotaries at the north and south ends of the central section.

At the north rotary a road to the west snaked down to meet the old road just above the town, along the way offering the island's most spectacular views of the majestic old town below. The road east from the rotary passed by the Mykonos hospital, cultural center, and a gauntlet of businesses as it wound its way around brown-beige hills toward the town of Ano Mera three miles away at the heart of Mykonos' agrarian roots.

At the south rotary, the road off to the west entered the old town in an area known as the bus station, and with an abrupt left, turned into a flagstone lane that narrowed down over a quarter mile until ending close by the six windmills symbolizing Mykonos. The road to the east led to the airport and police station. Professional and business services, notably banks, clustered around the south rotary, possibly in the belief that proximity to the police station might minimize robberies.

The new road was a godsend for those seeking relief from choking summer traffic along the old inner road, but to others it was the devil's work in disguise. The new road offered easy access for armies of heavy construction equipment and building supplies streaming off of ships on their way to undeveloped parts of the island.

In less than two decades Mykonos went from being a quaint Greek island to a world-class summer playground with an international reputation for a free-wheeling 24/7 seasonal lifestyle and a vibrant tourist-driven economy. As for the traffic, some said it was worse than ever.

Many saw a golden lining in all the changes. They were the ones who believed that regardless of what might happen to the rest of Greece, Mykonos' jet set international reputation would continue to bring prosperity to their island. It did not matter what part the devil might have played in creating their modern paradise, for as the world knew, all were welcome to do their thing on Mykonos.

Except for bank robbers.

Chapter Six

Tassos turned left out of the airport onto a narrow road headed east.

"The new road is to the right," said Kouros.

"I thought I'd take the scenic route."

The road twisted east for a quarter mile until meeting up with a ten foot high chain link fence topped with razor wire marking the perimeter of the airport. From there the road and fence ran due east together for another quarter mile before turning sharply north for a half mile run parallel to the runway. Off to the right, roads led off to Agrari and Super Paradise beaches, and fields edged away from the side of the road onto steep hillsides filled with homes offering spectacular views to some of the island's most celebrated seasonal residents.

Halfway down the runway the road turned abruptly right and into a half mile-long series of S curves and straightaways. Tassos barely slowed down as he popped the police car out onto the main road headed east toward Ano Mera.

"And before you say it, Yianni, yes I know this isn't the way to the port." Tassos tapped a screen on the console of the police cruiser. "I'm following this."

"What's that?" said Kouros leaning over the front seat.

"Modern police legwork," said Tassos. "Each of the bank's money drawers contains a packet of money capable of transmitting a signal. Cashiers know to turn it over when there's a robbery."

"I thought the ministry's cutbacks killed that project?" said Andreas.

"They did," said Tassos. "But bankers on Mykonos thought that with less than twenty full-time cops spread out over three shifts during most of the year and only an additional fifty third-year police academy cadets assigned to help them out during tourist season, it might be good business to get together and fund the idea on their own. The technology is basically what's used to locate a missing iPhone."

Andreas shook his head and looked out the window. "We've got wolves descending on Greece in packs and all the government gives us to fight them are slingshots."

"And the bad guys know it," said Kouros. "The bastards have taken over parts of Athens."

"Hard to imagine that Greece once had the lowest crime rate in the EU," said Tassos.

"It's become so bad in some neighborhoods that vigilante groups are offering protection," said Kouros.

"For the price of your vote," said Tassos.

"It's working. Those neo-Nazi bastards are now in parliament," said Kouros.

"Let's not get into that political rats' nest," said Andreas. "We've three armed bank robbers to find before they get off the island."

"No problem," said Kouros. "Besides, they're a lot easier to catch than the miserable cocksuckers who steal us blind with campaign promises and a pen."

Andreas spun his right hand in the air.

Tassos pointed at the screen. "The money's stopped. Can't tell if the bad guys are with it. It's on the south shore between Kalifati and Kalo Livadi beaches, at the foot of two hills the locals call the 'mounds of Aphrodite.'"

"I know the place," said Kouros. "It's on an isolated peninsula about a quarter mile off the highway. The only way in by land is along a flat dirt road across a wide open space. Anyone coming is visible the whole time."

"So much for the element of surprise," said Andreas.

"It gets worse. The road turns east at the base of the first mound and runs between a gauntlet of one-story buildings on both sides. Mainly private homes, rooms to rent, and a couple of fish tavernas. Everything is owned by one family that likes its isolation."

"The perfect setting for a major shootout," said Andreas.

"They must plan on getting away by boat," said Tassos.

"Makes sense," said Kouros. "Just past the second taverna is a turn off to the left that brings you down to a cove behind the taverna. There's a tiny concrete pier with its far end and west side open to the sea. It's barely long enough for two small fishing boats to tie up alongside. Fishermen use it to unload their catch."

"Sounds like a boat's in their plan," said Andreas.

"What's ours?" said Kouros.

Andreas smiled. "The usual."

"I was afraid of that."

"Improvise?" said Tassos.

Andreas nodded. "And pray."

The distinctive, green three-wheel hauler with an extended truck bed hadn't seen a repair shop in decades. But its owner knew how to keep the tiny thing's 1300cc engine running. Those Mazda three-wheelers, with their generally oversized drivers crammed into tiny cabs up front, were once a staple of transport around the old port, but modern times and methods had made that form of hauler virtually extinct.

But this three-wheeler and the old man in the driver's seat with the steel gray fisherman's mustache, Greek fisherman's hat, and denim work shirt, were familiar figures in these parts. Everyday he'd drive his unmuffled hauler in along the same dirt road to pick up fish off his cousin's boat for delivery to nearby tavernas and hotels.

The old man noticed the three men in windbreakers standing by the first building on the left at the end of the dirt road. When he reached them he saw three yellow motorcycles tucked inside a shed on the far side of the building. The old man didn't recognize the men, but nodded to them. Two nodded back, the third kept yelling into a cell phone. He wasn't speaking Greek and wore a backpack.

The old man drove past the three and down toward the pier. He shouted greetings spiced with obscenities at his cousin unloading fish onto the far end out of a *caique* taking up practically the full length of the pier. The cousins exchanged waves as the old man backed his three-wheeler halfway onto the pier, getting it as close as he could against the wall. He slid across the seat and got out the passenger's door. He noticed one of the three men up by the tavern watching him and asked his cousin who the three strangers were.

The fisherman shrugged. "Tourists, I guess."

The old man kept talking to his cousin as he went to the back of his hauler, undid the tarp covering the two-foot high sideboards, and rolled it forward about a foot and a half. He began loading in fish from off the pier and, as he filled one section, he'd roll the tarp about a foot further toward the cab and load in more fish. He'd just about reached the rear of the cab when he heard the high whine of a fast boat sweeping into the cove from the open sea to the east, headed right for them and coming in quickly. The three strangers sprinted toward the pier. They squeezed past the hauler and old man, kicked through the fish still on the pier, and stood behind the hauler waving frantically at the boat.

The boat sidled up next to the pier facing into the cove and, as the first of the strangers leaped into it, the old man jumped into the *caique*. As the second stranger landed in the boat, two fish-covered men, one wielding a shotgun and the other an assault rifle, raised up from the hauler's truck bed shouting at the captain to cut his engines.

The stranger with the backpack still stood on the pier. He pulled a gun from his jacket, firing as he did at the two in the hauler.

The man with the shotgun instantly fired back, partially separating the gunman's head from his body and tumbling him backward off the pier and into the boat. His two companions in the boat jerked their hands above their heads but the captain ducked down, spun the wheel, and full-throttled the twin outboard engines in a dash back to open sea. A barrage of shotgun blasts and explosive automatic rifle rounds struck the engines, killing the boat dead in the water. The captain stood with his hands raised above his head.

By the time the three marked police cars made it to the pier, three live bad guys lay cuffed face-down on the concrete and the fast boat sat tied up alongside the *caique* with a dead bank robber still in it.

"Quite a mess you made here," said Tassos pointing at the body in the boat.

"Better him than us." Andreas gave a wave that included the old man and the fisherman. "I hope your friend with the hauler is okay."

"Petros? He's an old combat soldier. Loves a bit of action every once in a while. It was his idea for Yianni to use explosive rounds in the rifle. Said it's what the coast guard uses on boat engines when someone tried to run from them."

Petros smiled and cursed Tassos.

"I owe you one, my friend. You too." Tassos nodded at the fisherman. "I'm glad you listened when your cousin told you it was time to duck."

"What a cockamamie plan you came up with," said Andreas brushing fish parts out of his hair.

"Hey, it worked. When I saw Petros coming down the road, it all hit me."

"Next time you're inspired with a plan," said Kouros, "make sure you end up in the back with the fish."

"I'd have gladly partaken in the fun, but as Petros pointed out, he couldn't possibly hide me in the back of his truck, even covered with fish."

"We could have dressed you like a whale," said Kouros.

Tassos burst out laughing, hugged Kouros, and slapped Andreas on the back. "They'd have gotten away without your help. These guys have been robbing banks all over the Cyclades. First time on Mykonos though."

"Are they local?" said Andreas.

"Don't think so. One of my guys said they're speaking Russian to each other."

"Christ, don't tell me the Russians are getting into the crime business in the Cyclades, too," said Kouros.

"Why not? They go where the money is. Always have, always will," said Tassos. "Plus they love to party here. Who knows, it just might turn into their new romp and rob paradise."

"Catchy slogan. Maybe the Greek National Tourist Organization would like to borrow it?" said Kouros

Andreas shot him an open palm. "Do you think this crew had anything to do with Christos' murder?"

Tassos gestured no. "I doubt it. But we'll do whatever is necessary to make sure. He stared at the three on the ground. "And I mean *whatever*."

Andreas rolled his eyes.

"What we need is a break," said Kouros

"Europol is looking for the girl," said Tassos. "When they find her they'll watch her until she hooks up with her partners and arrest them all."

"Sounds like the sort of plan I like," said Kouros pulling a small fish out through the back of his shirt collar. "Let the other guys do it."

Tassos winked at Andreas. "My, my, I think our little boy's finally figured out this cop business."

Andreas shook his head. "I better get Yianni out of here and back to Athens before he starts thinking like you."

Tassos handed Andreas a set of car keys. "Leave the cruiser at the station. I've got a lot to do here. And don't forget the briefcase in the trunk."

"I was hoping you'd forget."

"Not a chance. And while we're on the subject of the briefcase, one more thing."

"What's that?" said Andreas.

Tassos smiled. "No exchanges, no returns."

Chapter Seven

Andreas' office sat on the fourth floor of Athens General Police Headquarters, next to a major hospital, across the street from the stadium of one of Greece's two most popular soccer teams, and down the block from Greece's Supreme Court. Better known as GADA, police headquarters lay at the heart of much of what affected the more than five million souls living in Athens. But Andreas' office looked away from all of that and its two long windows didn't offer much of a view. Andreas liked it that way. Fewer distractions. Besides, most of the time the blinds were closed. Too many prying eyes from up on high.

At the moment, his office looked like a clandestine peep show parlor. Andreas, Kouros, and Maggie sat huddled behind his desk staring at images flashing across a computer screen. It was compilation of film clips shot at different times and different locations.

"Jesus, Maggie, I'm embarrassed to be watching this stuff with you. It's like watching porn with my mother."

"Your mother would have better taste. Never saw so many naked, pot-bellied men in my life. In one place that is." She smiled.

"Pot-bellied is generous," said Kouros.

"We're not all in our twenties," said Maggie.

"Yeah, and neither are the girls. The oldest looks about eighteen," said Andreas.

"I wonder if they knew Christos was filming them?"

"I'd say not," said Maggie. "None of the men is trying to hold in his belly.

Andreas glanced at Maggie. "Women notice that sort of thing?"

She patted Andreas' belly. "Don't worry, Lila will tell you if it gets out of control."

Andreas looked down and squeezed his belly. "It's less than an inch."

"Two, but like I said, 'Lila will tell you.'"

"Uhh, folks, is that who I think it is making a grand appearance?" said Kouros.

A man in his fifties and a boy in his teens, alone in one of the bedrooms in Christos' house. The scene progressed to its inevitable, predictable conclusion.

"Jesus. I can't believe what I just saw," said Kouros.

"And we still have more than half the videos to watch," said Andreas.

"The photographs were bad enough, but these videos are…" Maggie shook her head. "I'm not a prude, guys. You know that. And I know men screw around, especially politicians, but what I'm seeing here is…"

Kouros finished her thought. "Disgusting."

"And it's not just politicians. We've got business leaders, academics, clerics—" Andreas tossed his hands up in front of his face and waved circles in the air.

"It's just what Tassos thought from the ledger entries. What's in here explains why Christos had them all…" Kouros paused… "literally 'by the balls.'"

"You just had to say that, didn't you?" Maggie smacked Kouros on the back of his head.

"Now you *are* acting like my mother."

The phone rang and Maggie picked it up. "Chief Inspector Kaldis' office."

She paused. "Hi, my love. I'm with the Chief and Yianni now. We're watching porn films. I'll put you on speakerphone."

Tassos' voice came bellowing through the speaker. "Glad to hear you guys are having such a fine time corrupting my girlfriend."

"We need her. She's the only one of us who keeps up on who's prominent in the news," said Andreas.

"With or without their clothes on," said Kouros.

Maggie smacked him again.

"Well, I'm back on Syros and just received pictures of another naked body. But you won't want to see this one."

"Of Christos?" said Andreas.

"No, his girlfriend. Polish police fished her body out of a pond yesterday in Bialystok. It wasn't really a pond, more like the cesspool for a toxic waste dump. They identified her from prints taken on a prostitution bust a few years back. The Poles notified Europol they'd found the girl Europol was looking for, and Europol called me."

"How'd she die?"

"Drowned and strangled. But not in the cesspool. Best guess from what they found in her lungs is a bathtub. Probably raped, too. And there was no effort to hide the body. It was thrown naked into the cesspool, not even weighted down."

"It has to tie into Christos' murder," said Kouros.

"The question is, 'How?'" said Andreas.

"Local police said she left Poland a few years back after her boyfriend was arrested for drug dealing. He spent two years in prison. Just got out six weeks ago."

"About the same time as the girlfriend's first trip back to Poland," said Kouros.

"Sounds like we have a suspect in two murders," said Andreas.

"Wish it were that easy. I've seen photographs of the boyfriend. He's about six-four, with blue eyes, light hair, and movie star good looks. He's definitely not one of the two guys we caught on security cameras with the girlfriend on Mykonos."

"What about those two? Any leads?" said Andreas.

"I sent photos taken off the security videos to the Polish police for an ID. Haven't heard back yet."

"We need a break," said Kouros.

"At least the Polish police know who they're looking for," said Maggie.

"But where?" said Andreas. "From the sloppy way they disposed of the girl's body I don't think they intended on hanging around Bialystok. Or Poland for that matter."

Tassos said, "If they headed east they could be in any of those ex-soviet peripheral satellites. It's the Wild West out there. No way Europol will find them if that's where they are."

Andreas rubbed at his eyes. "Somehow I don't think heading east is what they had in mind. Why kill the girl in a place where she could be identified if they were heading to a no-man's land? No one would have cared what they did to her there."

"And they could have sold her off to sex traders for fast cash," said Kouros.

"Maybe she didn't want to go and they were afraid she'd talk?" said Maggie.

"I don't think so, my love. From what Christos' maid overheard of the dead girl's conversation with her boyfriend, she'd have followed him anywhere."

"And she did," said Kouros.

"So, why did they kill her?" said Maggie.

"Don't know," said Tassos. "But my guess would be that she no longer figured in their plans."

"What plans?" said Kouros.

"Don't know that either," said Tassos.

Andreas shrugged. "Which means our best chance at finding a clue is likely in this briefcase."

"Sounds like you have an exciting evening ahead of you," said Tassos.

"Just a long one. The characters on these videos aren't exactly movie star quality," said Andreas.

"They even make you look good, Tassos," said Kouros.

"Says the kitten to the tiger," said Maggie.

"That's my girl. You tell him."

"Have the Polish police talked to the boyfriend?" said Andreas.

"Not yet. They can't find him. They went to the address in Bialystok he gave when released from prison but the person living there said he never showed up. They think by now he's out of the country."

"Then they have him on a parole violation," said Kouros.

"Nope. He served his full sentence. His debt to society is paid in full. And there's an application underway to expunge his record of the conviction based on newly discovered exculpatory evidence showing he was framed for the drug bust by a competitor."

"Why does that not make me feel comfortable?" said Andreas.

Maggie answered. "Because you're a cop. You know better."

"If the Polish police identify the dead girl's two companions, maybe we'll get lucky and they'll turn up somewhere they can be arrested," said Kouros.

"If you're into wishing, don't forget to have the boyfriend with them. He's the one I'd like to get my hands on," said Andreas.

"Careful what you wish for," said Maggie. "Sounds like a cold-blooded bastard to me."

"I'm not looking to make him my next-door neighbor, Maggie. I want to find out what the hell is going on."

"I'll just be happy to nail the two bastards who murdered Christos," said Tassos. "The rest of this is far too stressful for a man of my advanced years."

"In other words, you think it's a political hot potato," said Andreas.

"More like radioactive."

"Are you suggesting we end it with catching the two and forget about the boyfriend?"

"Would you listen if I did?" said Tassos.

"No."

"Good, we need cops like you to keep cops like me from corrupting Yianni with ideas like self-preservation."

"I love you."

"I assume that was Maggie."

"Yes, dear, and now if you'll excuse us we have a lot of hard work left to do tonight."

Kouros smiled. "Not so hard from what I've seen so far on the videos."

Maggie smacked him twice more.

It was after three in the morning when Andreas crept into the bedroom. He'd showered in a guest bathroom at the other end of the apartment, and left his clothes outside the bedroom door. The room was pitch black but he dared not turn on a light. Gently, he pulled back the covers on his side of the bed and carefully slid in on his back next to his wife.

"You're getting better at this, but still need some work on the cover pulling part."

"Sorry, I tried not to wake you."

"I'm just a light sleeper. I guess I've become a cop-wife. Always worried until her man is safely home."

Images of that afternoon's gunfight flashed though Andreas' mind. He rolled onto his side and kissed Lila on the cheek.

"Is that all I get for such a moment of life-realizing clarity?" said Lila.

"Put it on my account."

"You still owe me for the last time you said that."

He laughed.

Lila ran her hand along his belly, stopping to feather her fingers just below his navel before sliding down to grip his testicles gently with her fingers and wrap her thumb around the base of his penis. She drew her fingers up and around to join her thumb and began firmly pulling up and down.

Ten seconds later she stopped, dropping her hand as she did. "Am I doing something wrong? Do you want me to go down on you?"

Andreas stretched toward his nightstand and turned on the lamp.

"Sorry. It has nothing to do with you. I just spent the afternoon and most of the night looking at some of the kinkiest pornographic videos you could imagine."

"Are you telling me you spent all day surrounded by sex so you'd prefer not to get into it at home? When we agreed you should 'leave your work at the office,' that's not the part I meant."

"Trust me, if you saw what I saw you'd be off sex for a week. I'm just screwed up in the head tonight. But…"

Andreas rolled onto his side and slid his hand down under the sheet to between Lila's thighs. She squirmed for an instant, but relaxed as his fingers began moving in rhythm to her breathing. He knew where she liked to be touched. Andreas kissed first one, then the other breast, taking care to flick at her nipples with his tongue, all in time with the stroking of his fingers and Lila's moans. He slid his mouth down along her belly, and when he sensed she could stand no more his lips replaced his fingers between her thighs. She jerked at the sudden shift in pressure, but moaned again and again as he brought her to orgasm.

A minute passed. Andreas had not moved from between Lila's legs or stopped his caressing.

"How do you always know just what to do to me?"

Andreas slid up onto Lila's body and kissed her on the lips. "I can ask you the same question." He spread her legs with his knee and searched between them with his erection until he found where his mouth had just been. He moved his hips to enter her and she pushed hers up to take him. He moved slowly at first, but Lila put her hands upon the cheeks of his ass and pulled at him to move faster. He wrapped an arm around her back, and with his other hand squeezed her ass and pulled her up toward him.

Andreas thrust in pace with Lila's hands upon at his ass, and when she slid her hands down onto her own thighs, pulling them wider apart while urging him to drive harder and faster, he did until burying his face in her hair and moaning her name in his own release of rushing heat.

Neither moved for several minutes.

"Your account is now current."

Andreas' head lay buried in her hair. "Trust me, I'm laughing on the inside. There's just no energy left to show emotion on the outside."

Andreas pressed his hand on the mattress and rolled over onto his back. "Thank you for making me forget my day at the office."

"Any time." Lila patted his belly. "So what's with all the porn?"

Andreas had long ago given up keeping secrets from his wife. Initially he'd refused to talk about his cases, arguing that a decision to involve her in one almost cost Lila her life. But with the birth of their son it was clear Lila had no interest in putting both of Tassaki's parents at risk to bad guys.

And so he told her of his night watching decades of Athens' most prestigious and influential folks dangle their peccadilloes and other things in every which way and place imaginable.

"Sounds like stuff for an *avant garde* film festival," said Lila.

"More like outtakes from that American horror picture, *Night of the Living Dead*."

Lila laughed. "Did you find anything that might help you solve Christos' murder?"

"Anyone who knew what Christos had on them would qualify as a suspect. But there was nothing in the videos or on anything else in the safe that made one any more suspect than any other.

"We've got an open and shut case of murder against the now dead girlfriend and her two companions. What we don't know is whether anyone else was involved and, if so, why? I don't see how we'll ever get answers to those questions if we can't find her companions. And even if we do, I'd be surprised if they could finger anyone other than the dead girl's Russian boyfriend."

Andreas flicked his finger at one of Lila's nipples. She gave a light smack to his hand and pulled the sheet up over her breast.

Andreas kissed her cheek. "If it is someone on the videos, why now? There's nothing to indicate that Christos was using the videos to blackmail anyone for anything more than the same sort of protection he'd been getting for his business for years. Besides, having Christos killed before guaranteeing you'd get your hands on the incriminating evidence would be taking a hell of a risk."

"Yes, it might fall into the hands of the police," said Lila.

"Or worse."

"There's worse?"

"I see you're not quite yet a true 'cop-wife.'"

Lila shrugged. "Okay, so if what Tassos found in the safe threatened everyone involved to the point where each had a motive for murder, unless we're talking about some Agatha Christie they-all-did-it mystery, I'd say the likely culprit is someone who would benefit from having all that dirt on all those people."

Andreas smiled. "*Very good.* Tassos and I thought the same thing and we talked about interviewing everyone tied into what was in the safe to see if any of them might be that person. But we decided the most likely thing we'd learn from that exercise would be that our careers were over. After all, we'd be grilling the country's movers and shakers over things outside the apparent scope of solving a murder that has the actual killers virtually caught on video. We'd be hung out to dry if we tried to take it further."

"But shouldn't they be warned?"

"Warned of what? That there are videos out there showing them in compromising positions and that if someday someone gets their hands on them they might use them for blackmail? It would sound as if we were the ones looking for a payoff. After all, it's not as if anyone but us knows what's on those videos.

"The bottom line is, until whoever wanted what was in the safe makes a move, we have absolutely no idea who it might be. Assuming there is such a person. And the question isn't who could use all that information to their advantage, it's who couldn't?"

"So, what *do* you plan on doing?"

"Press Europol to find the girl's two companions and her boyfriend. We might get a different angle on things from one of them."

"How likely is it they'll be caught?"

Andreas shrugged. "If I were them, I'd be as far away from Greece and Poland as I could get, and stay there."

"Sounds like you have some time on your hands."

Andreas rolled over and turned off the light. "Yep."

Pause.

"Oh, no, not again…"

Chapter Eight

Sergey looked at his watch. He'd been waiting in the taverna for half an hour. Be cool, he thought to himself. It's just a test. She was like that. Always testing to see how you reacted under pressure. She couldn't help herself.

He ordered another coffee and looked just beyond the parking lot in front of the taverna at the section of harbor filled with small pleasure boats and a few larger fishing boats. A pier jutting straight out to sea on his left separated that side of the port from the larger part of the harbor filled with ferry boats waiting to load their cargoes of passengers and vehicles.

She'd told him to come here, to the port of Rafina east of Athens, to catch a high-speed catamaran to Mykonos, saying that she would meet him here thirty minutes ago. He had twenty-five minutes left until his boat left from that pier.

She's cutting it close, he thought. *Relax.* She's the one making everything possible. He'd let her play her games. He'd done all that she'd asked. She said to learn Greek and he was. She said to dispose of Christos and he did. She saw Anna as a problem and he resolved it. There was nothing she'd asked that he hadn't—

"Sergey. Come here." It came in a whisper from behind him, in Greek.

He turned and saw a dark-haired woman in mask-size sunglasses nodding at him as she sipped a coffee. She wore a black linen pantsuit and a high-neck, long sleeve, white silk blouse. He picked up his coffee, walked over to her table, and sat down.

The woman's hair drew back in a tight bun and she wore no makeup. Or at least she appeared not to be.

Sergey took the sunglasses as a good sign. Her eyes commanded attention. Fiery and black, they were hard to avoid and when she took off her sunglasses things tended to get serious. "How long have you been here?" he said in Greek.

She answered in Russian. "Speak Russian, your Greek needs a lot of work."

He looked at his watch.

"Don't worry, you won't miss your boat."

"'Your boat?' Aren't you coming with me?"

"I have no interest in visiting Mykonos. That's why I have you. I've made arrangements with friends. There will be people there to assist you with whatever you might need. And since your Greek is not yet good enough to transact the business that must be conducted, I have arranged for you to have a personal assistant who will be available to you twenty-four hours a day."

My keeper, he thought. "A he or a she?"

"Don't be cute, Sergey. This is serious business. If we don't take advantage of this opportunity quickly others will. We must establish ourselves on the island, *now*. No time for childish silliness."

"I know. I'm the one who brought the opportunity to you."

"People bring me opportunities all the time. I am well known in Eastern European prisons."

Legend would be the more appropriate word, he thought. If you had a big score and needed help to make it happen, the prison grapevine said, "Go to Teacher."

"What you brought to me was a gamble. I have no need to gamble. But I am making an exception. Because I see promise in you. On Mykonos you are to act as if I do not exist. Everyone is to believe that you are the boss, that you are responsible to no one. There is only one person who will know the truth."

She reached across the table with her right hand and patted his. With her left hand she removed her sunglasses and stared into Sergey's eyes. "*You*. Do not forget that. Ever."

Sergey forced his most relaxed smiled. "Don't worry, Teacher, I shall forever be your student."

"Good, then we shall never have a problem." She put her sunglasses back on and nodded toward the port. "You better hurry, your boat is about to sail."

Teacher didn't move from the table. She watched the catamaran maneuver away from the pier, make a deliberate 180-degree turn, and sail out of sight.

I shouldn't be involved in this. The man's an arrogant sociopath. Thinks he can con anyone. He probably thinks I'm attracted to him.

Then again, she was. But not in the way he thought. She looked down and studied her empty coffee cup. Perhaps growing older had her fixating on things out of a past that never was… at least not for long.

She thought she knew better than to imagine things differently than they were.

"Obviously not," she said aloud in Greek as she pushed herself up from the table and walked out the door without paying for her coffee. A burly man at an adjoining table wearing a gray tee-shirt, blue jeans, and a large black fanny pack immediately stood and followed her out the door, dropping a twenty euro note on her table as he passed by.

An all-black Range Rover pulled up to the curb in front of the taverna and the burly man pulled opened the rear door. As soon as Teacher stepped inside he closed the door and jumped in front next to the driver. The SUV moved quickly away from the curb.

"Back to the airport. And call ahead to make sure the plane is ready." She slid her sunglasses down the bridge of her nose to where she could stare over them through the deeply tinted windows. She saw tired commercial buildings filled with FOR RENT signs lining cramped, working-class streets. Other signs proclaimed, GREECE IS FOR GREEKS, offering free food to those who could prove their Greek lineage. Such ethnic hatred she'd seen before. It had fueled much of her success, driving the threatened into her arms. A lot was at play in Greece at the moment.

She smiled. *Which is why a sociopath is perfect for what I have in mind.*

◇◇◇

At the north end of Mykonos' old harbor a concrete pier jutted two-hundred yards out to sea. Close to shore the pier offered stern-first, long-term docking for large private yachts with the appropriate connections, and its far end provided parallel docking facilities for commercial catamarans loading and unloading passengers. Locals referred to the pier as "the old port." Between the pier and the old town was a parking lot used by Mykonians with special parking privileges and buses shuttling cruise boat passengers to and from ships anchored in the new port one mile away. To the north, on the other side of the pier, was the town's brand new municipal parking lot, most often used only by those who could not find more convenient illegal parking elsewhere.

Sergey was one of the first off the catamaran. He carried only a small backpack slung over one shoulder. Teacher told him there would be new clothes waiting for him on Mykonos and that he should bring nothing from his past. Even his conviction would be expunged. It would be a new beginning.

He walked along the pier between the boat and a stone wall toward a crowd of people waiting just beyond the end of the pier. He had no idea who would be meeting him. As he entered the crowd, someone tapped him on the shoulder from behind.

"Sergey?"

He turned toward the voice and saw a pockmarked sallow face, narrow angular nose, misaligned teeth, and greasy, gray-brown mid-length hair. *Rat* immediately came to mind. "Yes?"

The man flashed a toothy smile in a way undoubtedly thought by the man to be charming, but which only exaggerated his resemblance to a rodent. He was a head shorter than Sergey, gangly, and dressed in colors intended to draw attention.

Like a pimp, thought Sergey.

"Our mutual friend told me to take care of you. Follow me." He turned and walked toward a silver Mercedes taxi parked on the pier next to a private yacht. The man had spoken in Russian but not introduced himself, not offered to take Sergey's bag, nor said "please."

"*Boy*, take my bag."

The man froze. He turned his head and glared at Sergey. "I'm not your boy."

Sergey walked over, wrapped an arm around the man's shoulders, and smiled. "If you prefer being called my 'bitch,' that's okay with me, too. But start showing some respect to your boss." With that he swung the backpack off his shoulder and whipped it around into the man's belly. "Your choice."

The man caught the backpack before it fell to the ground. "I take my orders from Teacher."

"On this island I'm your boss, and if you don't like it, I suggest you leave it *now.* On that boat." Sergey nodded toward the catamaran.

The rodent's eyelids twitched wildly. "Sorry, I didn't mean to be rude." He held the backpack in his left hand and put out his right to shake Sergey's hand. "The name is Wacki."

"Wacki?"

"Yes, I know, sounds strange but it's a nickname I've had all my life. I think it suits me."

"I'm sure," said Sergey reaching out to shake Wacki's hand. "Speak Greek. I need the practice."

"Fine. I understand you speak some English."

"I speak a lot of English, plus Russian and Polish."

"Good, the English will come in handy until your Greek improves. But, of course, I will always be there if you need me."

"Of course."

"Do you prefer that I call you Sergey or something else?" He gave another toothy smile.

"'Boss' will be fine."

Wacki looked surprised, but quickly walked to the taxi, opened the rear door and motioned to Sergey. "If you please, Boss."

As Sergey got into the taxi he said, "I assume you prefer I call you Wacki."

As opposed to bitch, boy.

◇◇◇

A big attraction of Mykonos for the monied crowd was that with the right connections you could achieve virtually anything. But money alone wouldn't get you what you wanted. You needed juice. The island's powers-that-be could shut down anything and anyone if they weren't pleased. Courts offered little help if you hoped for relief within a decade, and even a judicial victory was likely only the first of many battles. The island powers had voting constituencies to satisfy, many of whom were members of large families whose support they needed to stay in power. If you didn't know whose toes you were stepping on—or how to dance around them—you were in for a nightmare of promises, compromising payments, and disappointments.

Those looking for a welcoming, good time experience in paradise should stay tourists. For those hoping to make money, the gloves came off the locals.

To most, Wacki would be an unlikely choice for doing knightly battle of the Camelot sort, but he was perfect for the rough and tumble world of Mykonos club-scene politics. He knew its dark side well, having spent half his life catering to the illegal and illicit wants and desires of visitors and islanders alike.

Wacki also knew the times were changing. Mykonos had been through more than a decade of extraordinary good fortune, with everyone profiting off high spending Athenian, American, and European tourists willing to pay whatever it took for a fun time. Those days were over, at least for this generation. But unlike virtually anywhere else in Greece, Mykonos' international reputation meant that some could still make a lot of money on the island. And Wacki had a pretty good idea where the new cash was coming from.

Russians were buying up the best seafront properties on the mainland. Prime homes near Athens in elegant areas on the way to ancient Sounion, some of the most desirable places along the Peloponnese coastline, and parts of the Halkidiki Aegean shore in northeastern Greece, close by the holy peninsula of Mount

Athos sacred to Russian and Greek Orthodox alike, had experienced a land rush of Russian investors.

Unlike British and Germans waiting for a "better price," Russians didn't care to wait. And Greeks welcomed them with open arms. Many Greeks had soured on the euro zone, and saw financial salvation in the arms of economic alliances with Russia. History had often shown the error of such thinking, but memories were short, especially for those in financial crisis.

With the introduction of direct flights between Moscow and Athens, it was only a matter of time until Russians fixed their eyes on Mykonos. Arabs were coming too, but Wacki's money was on Russians for the long term play, if only for their common Eastern Orthodox roots. Two hundred fifty thousand of the wealthiest Russians had already discovered and made Cyprus home.

Wacki didn't give a damn about the implications for Mykonos, his only interest was in getting a shot at Russians flush with cash. For that he needed a backer. Someone with money to lure more money. But bad times had eliminated the usual Mykonian suspects for such a venture. Wacki had even turned to lighting candles in church, hoping that would change his luck.

The answer to Wacki's prayers came in the form of a phone call on the day of Christos' funeral.

He'd heard rumors from Eastern European sex traffickers supplying girls to a dance club he once managed of a woman called "Teacher." As tough as those motherfuckers were, they spoke in reverential tones of a mysterious bankroller of some of the biggest criminal enterprises in Eastern Europe; ones that didn't have the good fortune of ex-KGB connections. Some said Teacher was ex-KGB, but that sort of thing was said about virtually everyone who made it big coming out of the former USSR. Besides, Wacki didn't care. He'd worked with that sort before.

The caller said Teacher needed a contact on Mykonos to help establish a "business presence" there, and he'd been recommended by "mutual acquaintances." Wacki jumped at the chance almost before it was offered.

In the Silicon Valley world of United States business, Teacher would be called an "angel investor" by the companies she helped. But in Teacher's world no one would couple that word with her name. Doing business with Teacher involved a lifetime commitment. There was no way out unless she ended it.

The story indelibly linked to the loyalty Teacher demanded involved an Albanian mafia chieftain who built a hugely successful digital pirating network using Teacher's money and contacts. One day he decided he'd shared enough of his profits and, relying on the protection of his small army of muscle, told her to go fuck herself. Less than a month later he watched as his wife and three children were doused with gasoline and burned to death. One by one. But he wasn't killed. Instead, his every other toe and finger were snipped off with pruning shears and his penis and tongue burned with a blowtorch.

The man now paid on time. And no one had crossed Teacher since.

Wacki wasn't worried about Sergey. He'd seen his kind before. Pretty boy tough guys who came to Mykonos thinking they'd show the island hicks how business was done in the big city. The lucky ones might get to open a small place, one that largely supported the landlord and a host of politicos with fingers up to their elbows in pretty boys' pockets. But the big clubs, the ones capable of pulling in 100,000 euros a night just to get in the door during peak season, were an off limits business to all but select locals and their political protectors.

How Teacher expected to get a foothold in that closed market was a mystery to Wacki. He'd just have to take care that whatever blame there was for failure—and he had no doubt there would be failure—fell on Sergey. He'd enjoy watching the arrogant prick get his balls fried.

The thought gave Wacki pause. He decided he better call Teacher and put some distance between himself and Sergey in her mind. Just to be sure she knew whom to blame when nut-frying time came to Mykonos.

Chapter Nine

Teacher stared at the computer screen as she listened to Wacki complain about the "asshole" she'd sent to replace him as "her man" on Mykonos.

They'd spoken only twice before. Once to satisfy herself that Wacki was the right person for what she had in mind and, later, to confirm the terms of their arrangement. Her conversations always used a secure teleconferencing hookup that allowed her to see the caller, but not the other way around.

It was obvious to Teacher that Wacki did more than dress the part of a pimp, he was one in every sense of the word. Pimps were quite useful in a world filled with johns, and for what she had in mind on Mykonos, an absolute necessity. But Wacki was no leader. For that role she had her Sergey. Wacki's part was as a humbled number two itching to report on number one's failings.

"So sorry to hear of your stumble on first meeting Sergey. I'm sure the two of you will soon be on fine terms."

"But why do you need him when you have me? He doesn't even speak Greek and knows nothing of how things are done on the island."

"If I recall, you are not native to Mykonos and had to learn its ways. I hired you to help Sergey learn what you know. Not to question my judgments."

"Oh, no, I wouldn't dare question your judgment. I was just curious." There was a decided quaver to Wacki's voice.

"Good. Because I'm relying on both of you for the success of the project."

"Thank you for your confidence in me."

"Just understand that Sergey is your boss."

There was a momentary pause before Teacher heard, "Yes, absolutely, I understand."

"I'm glad to hear that. I certainly wouldn't want there to be any misunderstandings that might jeopardize my plans. And if you ever feel the need to contact me again, you know how to reach me."

"Thank you."

"You're welcome. Good day."

The screen went blank. Teacher stared at it for a moment before looking at a photograph on her desk of a young girl in a first communion dress wearing spring flowers in her hair. Everyone who saw it on her desk thought it was of Teacher. But she knew better. She had no idea who the little girl was. Nor did she care. It served only as the symbol of a life she never lived.

Whenever she thought her life was good and she could relax, she'd look at that photograph and remembered the truth.

Teacher picked up the photograph.

She hadn't chosen her life. Even now, when she was free to do as she wished, it was not hers. She was on a course set long before she had any say. No matter how she looked, no matter what or whom she knew, indeed no matter how eloquent her words, she would always be that Eastern European child stolen away from parents of whom she retained not a single memory. She'd been very young and whoever *that* child was or might have become died that day.

She was reborn to a different life, where no one cared if she lived or died as long as she produced. Her first memories were of her tiny hands making knots for rugs, her body serving the much larger hands of others. It did not matter if she were three or four or five—and to this day she did not know her age—she was touched by so many she no longer cared or noticed. Unless there was pain. But that was not often. As long as she did as she was told.

Teacher shut her eyes and squeezed the photograph.

She was a trafficked slave and learned as a child to avoid beatings by understanding orders in whatever language they were given. She could not read more than a few hundred words, and not all in the same language, but she could do her sort of commerce in a dozen languages. She was the interpreter for those who did not understand the requests, the demands, the orders of their owners and customers.

But she became more than that. She grew to be ruler of her peers. Her slight, incorrect translation of a requested act would lead to a beating. A more serious error on a vital direction could lead to death. It did not take many such mistakes for the others to realize she must be obeyed. And those who understood that her words were wrong dared not intervene to correct. They appreciated her power and the simple principle by which she ruled: Do as she said or surely die.

It was no different a rule than all enslaved lived by. It was as she was taught, and she followed that teaching by whatever means required to better her horrible life. She became the unquestioned leader of her tiny captives' universe, but never allowed a hint of her power to reach those who truly ruled her life, for they would have ended hers at once. She ordered others to abuse her in the presence of her captors, so they thought her weak and bullied. It was a dangerous game she played, but it was how she survived—and thrived.

Still, she knew it wouldn't last, it never did. She was a chattel, no more no less, and all that would keep her safe was her *own* power. She could not let that fade. She found lieutenants with no desire to command but who relished executing their master's orders as ruthlessly as necessary to maintain power.

From those she controlled who knew how to read, and magazines left by those they served, she learned to read French, Italian, German, Russian, and English.

And she was lucky, too, for she was not one of those girls forced to lie upon a cot in a shantytown taking on all comers until she died, or lost her value as a whore and ended up a laborer in some other's hands, until she died.

Yes, lucky because she was attractive and desirable to men of great wealth and power. She knew how to communicate with them, to be obeyed, and to please them. She earned large sums and favors for her captors. And they let her travel to places she knew existed only from the magazines. They never feared her return because if she ran away she knew they would find her, and death would be the most merciful end she could expect for such a foolish act. But as long as she pleased her clients she lived a life beyond her dreams.

She had another bit of luck. She did not menstruate until almost seventeen. Otherwise she'd have been a mother by no later than fourteen. She remembered the moment she first bled. She cried, for she knew what it meant. It was the first sign of her imminent fall from grace. She'd seen so many children birthing children in captivity lose whatever vestige of unreasoned hope they still held for their lives.

The fate of a child was a particularly effective means for controlling the mother. Many, certainly all who cared, soon turned into old women, not so much at first in their bodies but most definitely in their souls, watching helplessly as their captors plucked and priced their children for market as any commodity. But she was free of that manipulation, at least until then.

Teacher opened her eyes and put the photograph back on the desk.

I knew what I had to do, I had no choice.

He was a policeman. A widower. He said he was in his forties, but she knew he was older. He protected the men who owned her and many of those who paid for her company. She knew he liked her. She let him think that she liked him too. Nothing sexual, that would have been too easy and ended his attraction to her with an orgasm. No, she interested him with her mind, listening to every word he said, commenting on his every thought in the most flattering of ways, and making sure to refer back to other things he'd said in other conversations.

Three months of this led to a weekend away together. Three more weekends led to a marriage proposal. She told him there was no way her captors would let her go. He told her not to worry.

The wedding was private but her captors attended, smiling as if they'd been family. She had escaped. She was free.

He was a kind man. He encouraged her to learn. She went to school, and she graduated. She attended college. Never did she look at another man. She was committed to her husband and their two children. Yes, she'd become the mother of two beautiful sons.

Teacher closed her eyes and pressed her fingertips against them.

Vladimir. And his rambunctious, mischievous brother.

She pressed harder.

My lovely Sergey.

She was in a class when they came to her home. Her husband had many enemies. They cut his throat, severed his genitals, and stuck them in his mouth. They did the same to her two beautiful boys. She did not know who did it. It could have been any of many.

She found them when she came home. She sat among them only for minutes, then packed her bag and left. There was nothing more she could do for them. She did not attend their funerals, for by then she was no longer in that city or that country.

She fled to lose herself, leaving behind all her papers and whatever else she thought could be used to trace her.

She became a nameless refugee in a foreign land. And, in time, experienced a revolutionary new emotion. Freedom. She no longer feared death, and with that discovered liberty, took absolute control over her life for the very first time.

She dropped her hands to her lap and looked again at the photograph.

She made friends among the many like her that she met in shelters and on the streets. She'd lived their lives, spoke their languages, and they bonded. They shared their pasts, spoke of future hopes, and did what they could to protect themselves in the present. They stood shoulder to shoulder. They spoke up. They organized against those who would harm them. They made things happen.

She taught them how to overcome and unite, weaned their fears into strength and their innocence into power. In return they called her "Teacher." That was far more than this once stolen child ever dreamed of achieving.

Then came the money.

Chapter Ten

Wacki would have chosen any number of hotels on the island over the one Teacher picked for Sergey. There wasn't anything particularly wrong with the place; it just seemed out of touch with the vibe Wacki saw as Mykonos.

The Asteria was among the first hotels built on Mykonos after World War II and one of many across the country financed by public funds in an effort to promote Greece's tourist economy. It remained government owned but operated under a lease between a Mykonian and the ministry of tourism. The building was of Greek government design not traditional to Mykonos, most notably in its balconies and three-story height. But the hotel sat at the rear of the property and, painted all white with traditional Mykonian blue trim, blended in relatively well with its surroundings.

Like most post-war, government-funded hotels, the Asteria had been built at one of the best locations in its community. The entrance stood along the broad flagstone road walked by virtually everyone coming into the old town off a boat or from a car parked in one of old port's municipal lots. During tourist season, except for those in taxis or locals on business requiring a vehicle in town, everyone had to pass by the Asteria on foot.

A seven-foot high, whitewashed stone wall separated the hotel grounds from the road. Across the road sat a tiny beach used largely by cruise boat visitors sunning themselves during the day, and by cats and dogs for doing their thing at night.

Rarely did one see a local on that beach…except in amorous pursuit of a tourist.

Sergey had a suite on the hotel's top floor overlooking an acre of well-maintained gardens, a poolside dining area, and the old harbor. It was the best room the Asteria had to offer, yet compared to what else was available on the island, Wacki thought the accommodations spartan. But he dared not question Teacher's judgment.

Sergey stood with his back to Wacki, looking out the window as he spoke. "I want to meet the owner of this hotel."

"You mean the Mykonian who has the lease?"

"Yes. What's his name?"

"Lefteris, but he's not in town as much as he used to be. He leaves the operation of the hotel to his son. Would you like to speak to the son?"

"No. I want to speak to the owner."

"Okay. Let me find him and see when he's available."

"Where does he live?"

"Out by the lighthouse on the northwest tip of the island."

"I want to see him now."

"He might not be home. He could be anywhere. If there's something wrong with the room let me know and I'll get it fixed without bothering Lefteris."

"The room is fine. Just get me a meeting with him *now*."

"May I ask why?"

"No."

Wacki nodded and forced a smile. "Yes, boss. I'll make some calls and make it happen."

Sergey didn't turn away from the window. "Good."

An hour later Wacki and Sergey bounced along in a Jeep winding along a ridgeline road high above the island's northwest coastline. The road ended at the island's only lighthouse and, in keeping with the practical way islanders tended to name places after their geographical peculiarities, this area was known as *Fanaria*, the Greek word for lighthouse.

As with virtually all secondary roads in Mykonos, repaving schedules largely coincided with the four-year mayoral election cycle and, as the next election wasn't for a year, the Jeep's off road capabilities were getting a workout.

"Quite a view from up here, isn't it?" Wacki spoke as his eyes darted between the road and Sergey in the passenger's seat.

"Yes."

"Over there to the left is Delos. It's a holy island, second in importance only to Delphi. Next to it is Rhenia, the locals call it 'Big Delos' and straight ahead is the island of Tinos. It's famous for—"

"How much longer until we get to Lefteris' house?"

"A couple more minutes. It's on the left, facing west. Terrific view of the sunset. Maybe the best on the island. He moved here from town a couple of years back. A lot of Mykonians have moved out of town. Practically abandoned parts of the old town to Albanians."

"You don't say," said Sergey.

"Now we've got Pakistanis and Bangladeshis moving in. The whole place is changing."

"I'm sure."

At a long, white-stuccoed wall Wacki turned left through a blue, halfway-open sliding gate. He parked on a flagstone driveway next to the wall and led Sergey through an archway into an entrance foyer. The house stood on the right and a large, semi-enclosed terrace opened off to the left, each done in the same all-white with blue trim motif as the hotel. They went out onto the terrace.

Lefteris' home, like his hotel, had an unobstructed view of the sea, though from this height the Aegean seemed a sapphire tabletop peppered with colorful toy boats sliding by puffs of white cotton.

Wacki waved to a gray-haired man of about Wacki's height, but at least twice his girth. He sat on a beach chair next to a swimming pool that looked to fall off into the sea.

"It's windy, Lefteris," said Wacki.

"Always is this time of day this stage of summer. Sit over here. It's protected from the wind." He spoke in Greek and pointed to two chairs facing his. As the men approached, Lefteris struggled to his feet and extended his hand to Sergey.

"Welcome. I'm Lefteris."

Sergey shook his hand. "Sergey."

Lefteris motioned to the chairs again. "Please, sit. Would you like anything to drink?"

"No, thank you," said Sergey.

"Water?"

Wacki gestured no.

Lefteris switched to English, "Please forgive my English, it is not very good but I understand you do not speak Greek."

Sergey nodded. "I'm trying to learn."

"Good. I'm sure we will find some way to communicate." Lefteris sat down. "So, what can I do for you?"

Sergey sat down, crossed his legs, and pulled a cigarette and a lighter out of his shirt pocket. "May I smoke?"

Lefteris smiled. "Of course, this is Greece. We're civilized."

The men laughed.

"Thank you for seeing me on such short notice." Sergey lit the cigarette and put the lighter back in his pocket.

"You are a guest of the hotel." He waved toward Wacki. "And a friend of Wacki's. How could I refuse?" Lefteris smiled.

"I don't know what Wacki has told you about me or—"

"Nothing," said Lefteris in a bit too quick of answer.

"As I was saying, *or* the purpose of my business on Mykonos."

"Business?" He looked at Wacki then back at Sergey. "What business?"

"One that will be highly profitable for both of us."

"I already have a highly profitable business, I need no other."

Sergey smiled. He was holding the cigarette but had not yet taken a puff. "We both know that's not true. You, like every other hotelier on this island, are suffering. Hotels offering far more to guests than yours can possibly match are cutting rates to the point where you cannot compete on price and still make a profit. You'll be lucky if you make enough to cover your expenses for the season. And with all that you owe to the banks I doubt you'll make it another season, certainly not two. Crossing your fingers won't work either. It will take at least a decade for Greece to get back on its feet."

"You don't know what you're talking about. I lease the hotel. I'm not an owner. I'm not worried about the banks."

Sergey laughed. "I like your style. But we both know that not owning the hotel is a decided disadvantage, because the only time a hotel on Mykonos is likely to make any real money for its owner is when it's sold. And that's an opportunity you'll never have."

Lefteris stared at Sergey. "You seem to know a lot about my business."

"Enough to know that what you said about your debt situation isn't true. You borrowed a lot to cover renovations required by your lease, and even more to cover this season's estimated operating costs. With the way things are going, how do you possibly expect to meet your bank payments? *And*, with what you'll owe in lease payments to the government…" Sergey shook his head.

Lefteris didn't answer.

Sergey continued. "I'm sure I don't have to tell you that in the current political climate the ministry isn't about to cut you any slack. It's a new crew in there. Not like the old days. You'll be in default on the lease and, if someone with money comes along willing to take over your lease, *bye-bye,* you're history. You'll end up with no hotel and a lot of debts you can't possibly pay."

Sergey pointed at the house and pool. "My guess is you'll lose this place, too."

Lefteris stared at Sergey. "I assume you didn't come here to lecture me on hotel economics. What's your point?"

Sergey stared back. "I want to buy your hotel."

Lefteris leaned forward in his chair. "Are you, crazy?" He wagged his right hand in front of his own face. "In the first place, as you just said, it's not mine to sell. All I have is a lease. Besides, I have no interest in selling."

"No interest in selling your lease? At any price?"

"At any price that you or your partner here could meet." Lefteris turned and ranted at Wacki rapidly in Greek.

Sergey waited until he had finished.

"Wacki, tell me exactly what he just said, word for word."

Wacki started to stammer.

"I said, 'word for word.'"

Lefteris spoke. "I said that you and your asshole of a partner, Wacki, couldn't possibly come up with enough to pay me what I would want to give up the hotel. It's my baby. I'll nurse it to my death. So stop wasting my time."

Sergey nodded. "I understand your commitment to a place you created, but on reflection, perhaps the time has come to consider moving on and enjoying the fruits of your life in luxury and peace."

"Like I said, the two of you are wasting my time." He tried to stand.

Sergey barked, "*Please*, don't get up before you've heard my offer." He softened his voice. "That would be very rude."

Lefteris dropped back into the chair.

"First of all, sir, Wacki is not my partner. He is just one of my many paid employees."

Sergey fixed his eyes on Wacki. "Isn't that right, *boy*?"

Wacki looked at his feet. "Yes, boss."

Lefteris looked at Wacki. "You told me he was your partner."

"You must have misunderstood," said Wacki still looking at his feet.

Sergey turned to Lefteris. "Well, now that we've cleared up that little misunderstanding, perhaps we can get down to business."

Lefteris raised and dropped his hands. "Why not? After all, it's bad business to turn down a deal you haven't been offered. So, what do you have in mind?"

Sergey pulled a piece of paper out of his shirt pocket and waved it at Lefteris. "I'd prefer that my employee not know the amount I'm offering you. It's written out on this, and as soon as the ministry of tourism approves the lease transfer that amount will be paid to you in full. I assume you'd prefer for as much of the purchase price as possible to be paid off the books, but I'm afraid with all the regulatory scrutiny these days I can't risk losing the license by doing it that way. So, to compensate you for that inconvenience,each year I will pay you five percent of the hotel's annual net profits for as long as I have an interest in it."

Sergey handed the paper to Lefteris and watched as Lefteris tried to hide his surprise. He wasn't a very good poker player.

"There must be something else you want from me," said Lefteris.

"Yes. In order to ease our transition into the community, for a reasonable period of time I expect you to make yourself available to me as a consultant, all expenses paid of course."

Lefteris shook his head from side to side. "I don't get it. Like I said before, you must be crazy. We both know your offer makes no sense. The hotel isn't worth anything near what you've offered. Why are you offering so much?"

"I assume that means my offer is acceptable on the terms I've outlined?"

Lefteris looked at the paper again, drew in and let out a breath. He nodded. "Yes. But I'll have to check with my attorneys. As soon as I get their okay I'll have them prepare a memorandum of understanding to submit to the ministry."

"No problem. As long as I have your word that we have a deal."

Lefteris stood and extended his hand. "We have a deal. But I'd appreciate it if you didn't tell anyone what you're paying me. No reason to start attracting hungry relatives and long lost friends."

Sergey laughed. He put down the cigarette he had not smoked, stood up, and shook Lefteris' hand.

Teacher would be pleased.

On the way back to town, Sergey listened as Wacki rambled on about how Lefteris must be losing it to have thought that Wacki would ever suggest he was Sergey's partner. As they pulled up in front of the hotel, Sergey leaned over and patted Wacki's thigh.

"I assume Lefteris and the recently departed Christos Vasilakis were friends?"

"Yes, very close friends."

"And you were as well?"

"Yes, I'd worked for Christos for a while a few years back."

Sergey shook his head. "Horrible what happened to that old man. Beaten to death in his home during a robbery. He was a legend on this island. Probably almost as much of one as you think you are." Sergey laughed and gave a gentle slap to Wacki's thigh.

Wacki forced a grin.

"Just so there's no confusion, my friend, about the degree of loyalty and confidentiality I expect from you, if I think you're even mumbling in your sleep about anything having to do with me or any of my business, let alone talking about such things to another human being, I can assure you that you'll look a hell of lot worse at your funeral than poor Christos did at his."

Sergey squeezed Wacki's thigh hard enough to make him jump. "Remember that always."

Teacher smiled as she listened to Sergey tell the story of his negotiations with the hotelier. He sounded as enthusiastic as a young boy reciting the details of his first day at school. He had so much more to learn, but this was not the moment to make that point. This was a time to praise and encourage him, and to savor an emotion she never thought she'd sense again: a loving mother listening to her child.

It was a lifetime since she'd felt that way. *No, two child-lifetimes.*

Teacher had tens of thousands of followers gladly willing to die to execute her orders and she truly loved them, but not with a mother's love. Her love for them was born out of the camaraderie they shared as ignored and undervalued human beings united by a common lack of faith in governments and endless suffering at the hands of society's empty promises. They were the disenchanted, the crazies, the betrayed, the outcasts, the exploited.

Teacher used the skills she'd developed as a trafficked child to harness their rage and focused it in violent attacks on those she presented as symbols of their oppression. She offered her followers a simple satisfaction for otherwise belittled lives: revenge.

It did not take long before prospective targets saw the wisdom in paying Teacher for protection from her followers' ire. That's when money started rolling in and Teacher's life became infinitely more complicated.

The money was far more than necessary to care for her followers, and deciding what to do with it led to bankers, lawyers, and investment advisers. Teacher had become part of the very system her followers despised. But they saw her as different, for she brought them a better life; something no government had ever done. In exchange, they ruthlessly spread her methods of doing business across Eastern Europe, taking advantage of power vacuums that accompanied distracted, corrupt governments. And those who went to prison found new followers for her there. No opportunity was missed, and all knew her simple rule: Those loyal to her were lavishly rewarded and those not were mercilessly destroyed. Teacher had become the quintessential, multi-national corporate leader.

She smiled again as Sergey described how "Lefteris' eyes popped wide open when I gave him our offer."

She thought how very different things would have been had her sons lived to succeed to all that she'd achieved in her life.

Her smile vanished. *I never would have permitted them my life. They were gentle, open souls who loved, not harmed.*

No. Her life demanded a very different sort of successor.

Chapter Eleven

In mid-afternoon Andreas received a call from Europol informing him that a man traveling as Sergey Tishchenko had arrived that morning in Greece on a flight into Athens' Venizelos International Airport. They had no further details, except that the name matched that of a man the Greek police were looking for in connection with a murder investigation. Andreas thanked the agent for the information and gently put down the receiver before letting out a roar of curses at the ineptitude of Greek bureaucrats.

Maggie opened the door to his office. "Are you calling me?"

"Some goddamned idiot at immigration couldn't spot a polar bear in a Santa Claus suit in August. But I bet the bastard's damn good at finding a reason to wreck a tourist's holiday. Can you believe it took *Europol* to tell me what's in Greece's immigration database? Had the asshole bothered to check the same alerts we'd given Europol we could have snatched the boyfriend at immigration."

He slammed his hand on the desk. "Now he could be anywhere." Andreas ran his hand across his face. "Have Yianni check the passenger list for every flight out of Athens today. Let's see if he's on one of those."

"Will do, but he could have taken a boat and, as loose as ticket agents are on checking IDs before issuing a boat ticket, no telling what name he could have used."

"Good point. But if this Sergey is our boyfriend, I don't think he's hiding if he flew into Greece using his real name. Check out the boats, too."

"There are a lot of boats in Greece this time of year, some with thousands of passengers and crew, and not all their records are available on computers."

Andreas picked up a pencil.

"Is this a tapping or breaking moment?"

Andreas smiled and began tapping the eraser end on his desk as he stared out the window. "Start with the boats leaving today for Mykonos. See if we get a match on a ticket issued in his name."

"You don't actually believe he'd be insane enough to go to Mykonos if he had anything to do with Christos' murder?"

"I find it hard to believe that he'd come to Greece under any name at all, let alone his real one."

"I know you're the cop, not me, but even assuming he has no idea we have his girlfriend on video at the scene of Christos' murder, wouldn't he have to be a complete idiot not to realize that once his girlfriend turned up dead in the same Polish town where he lived, that she and he would be prime suspects in Christos' murder if for no other reason than coincidence?"

"You're absolutely right, and whether he's sane, insane or an idiot, it's precisely because of what you just said that all my instincts tell me that whatever reason was strong enough to bring him to Greece to face that risk must have something to do with Mykonos."

"In other words…"

Andreas smiled. "Humor me."

Less than an hour later Maggie burst into Andreas' office followed by Kouros. "We found our boy. He was on a Sea Jet that arrived on Mykonos around noon out of Rafina."

"Makes sense," said Andreas. "He probably took a taxi from Venizelos. It's a closer port to the airport than Piraeus. Any idea where he's staying on Mykonos?"

"I called Tassos," said Kouros. "He's making discreet inquiries. Sergey just arrived, and hotels don't have to turn over information on new guests to the police until tonight."

"Heaven forbid they were required to submit in real time by computer," said Andreas.

"If he's staying in a rented room rather than a hotel his name may never turn up," said Kouros.

Andreas stood up. "Grab your toothbrush, Yianni. I'm betting Tassos will find him. But even if he doesn't, we'll comb the island until we do. Alert the coast guard and airport police that if they let this bastard off the island before I say he can leave I'll have them all transferred to where there's no more beaches, no more nightlife—"

"No more nookie," said Kouros.

"In other words," said Maggie, "you'll cut their balls off."

"Precisely. Including those who don't have any."

Andreas and Kouros just made the seven o'clock flight to Mykonos. No helicopter was available and even if one were, with all the economic cutbacks Andreas would need ministry-level approval to use it. It was a lot less hassle to fly commercial and, in this case, quicker. Tassos met them as they stepped off the stairs from the plane onto the tarmac.

Tassos pointed at an unmarked police car off to the left and walked toward it. "I found Sergey. He's ensconced as a VIP in the best suite at the Asteria."

"So much for trying to hide," said Andreas.

"And rumors are flying all over the island that he's a big-time Russian with lots of money to spend."

"How the hell did those start?" said Kouros.

"My guess is from him," said Tassos.

Tassos slid onto the driver's seat, Andreas sat next to him, Kouros in the back. "Before we start to drive, I think we should decide where we're headed with this guy. He's not behaving like a suspect in a murder investigation. He hired one of the most connected pieces of nightlife scum on the island as his assistant and they've already met with the owner of the Asteria in what I understand was a command performance ordered by Sergey. At least that's what I heard from the hotel concierge who tracked down the owner and set up the meeting at the urgent request of one very anxious Wacki."

"Wacki? Is that jerk-off Sergey's assistant?" said Kouros. "He's been involved in every sort of dirty deal on the island, from hookers and drugs through election rigging."

Andreas nodded. "Yeah, I know him. He's everything you say and more. But he's also clever enough to go where the money is."

"So, how does a guy less than two months out of a Polish prison manage to show up acting like an anointed king?" said Kouros.

"Tassos is right. This isn't adding up."

"The part about coming to Mykonos fresh out of prison to make a score isn't a new story," said Tassos. "But with this guy it's the other way around. He's bringing serious money here. My guess is, unless he's hit the lottery, the money's not his."

"Yianni, check out what Europol, Interpol, CIA, MI6, and anybody else has on Sergey. I want to know everything there is on this guy."

"I assume that means we're not paying him a visit tonight," said Tassos.

Andreas nodded. "Not until I have a better idea of whom we're dealing with. Just make sure the local cops are watching him like a hawk. I don't want our boy taking a piss without us knowing about it."

"Some of my guys from Syros are on him 24/7. There aren't enough cops on Mykonos to do the job right."

"Terrific," said Andreas.

"So, where to?" said Kouros.

"Dinner. Tassos, you pick the place."

"Ahh, the kind of police work I can sink my teeth into."

Kouros groaned. Tassos smiled.

Tassos turned right out of the airport, drove down the hill, went straight through the south rotary, and a couple minutes later slowed to turn left at the road's intersection with the old road by the bus station. In high season this was the most hectic intersection on the island, if not in all the Cyclades.

To the left, the old road stood lined on both sides with car and motorbike rental agencies clogging the already narrow two lanes down to one and a half with their rows of double and triple parked motorbikes and four-wheel ATVs. Pedestrians, finding no sidewalks, had no choice but to dodge and weave among the madness, ever alert for less than accommodating drivers coming at them from all directions.

Tassos sat stuck in the middle of his left turn between a Jeep facing him at a stop sign on his left and a phalanx of motorbikes parked on the right. He could have squeezed the unmarked car between the Jeep and the four wheelers but a big guy in a sleeveless t-shirt, sitting on a motorbike outside the first rental shop and chatting with the owner, blocked what was left of Tassos' side of the road.

To make things worse, another turning car now blocked Tassos from behind and the intersection was in total gridlock. All because of the idiot on the motorbike. A third-year cadet out of the police academy was too busy flirting with a pretty tourist girl to do his job directing traffic.

"How the hell do these rental places get away with tying up this intersection with their shit?" said Tassos.

"They're protected," said Kouros.

"Not by me." Tassos hit the horn but the guy on the bike ignored him. Tassos honked again. The guy still didn't turn around, but flipped an open hand curse gesture over his shoulder at whoever was honking. Tassos, took his foot off the brake and allowed the car to coast forward until it nudged the rear wheel of the motorbike, sending driver and bike spilling lightly onto the road. The driver jumped up cursing and ran at Tassos' window. He reached in awkwardly for Tassos' throat.

Tassos grabbed the man's wrist, pulled, grabbed the man's elbow and pulled some more until the man's head slammed into the top of the doorframe.

"Whoops, so sorry," said Tassos allowing the man to pull away. Before the man could make another run at the car the cadet was at Tassos' window yelling at him to get out. The owner of the rental agency was screaming to the cadet about what the "fat asshole" in the car had done to one of his motorbikes.

"Need help?" said Andreas.

"You must be kidding." Tassos got out but didn't say a word until the rental guy had finished his rant. The cadet asked for Tassos' identification.

"You're a newbie here, aren't you?" said Tassos showing his badge to the cadet.

The cadet jerked to attention. "Please, sir, continue on. Sorry for the inconvenience."

Now the owner started cursing Tassos *and* the cadet.

Tassos smiled at the owner as he said to the cadet, "I want you to call your sergeant and tell him I said to get his ass over here right away with enough trucks to confiscate all of this guy's four-wheelers."

Tassos pointed to a turn down the road. "All the way to there. And what the hell, while they're at it, have them pick up his two-wheelers, too. They're all illegally parked, and probably a hell of a lot more than his license authorizes him to rent."

The rental owner was screaming at the top of his lungs with threats of what he'd do to the "fat man who thinks he's a big shot" if the cadet weren't there.

Tassos kept smiling as he walked over to the owner. He stuck his credentials in the owner's face and said, "Do you want to go home or do you want to go to jail?"

The man didn't say a word.

"I said, 'Do you—'"

"Home."

"Then shut the fuck up." Tassos got back in the car and blew the rental owner a kiss.

"Very nicely done," said Kouros. "I've had wet dreams about doing something like that to some of those assholes. They're out of control."

Tassos pulled away, smiling as he did at the man he'd knocked off the bike.

"You can get away with just about anything on this island if you pay the right people" said Kouros.

"Didn't use to be that way," said Tassos.

"Well, it sure seems that way today," said Kouros.

"It isn't quite that bad," said Andreas.

"Probably only because the limit hasn't been tested yet," said Kouros.

Fifty yards past the intersection, where a ramp to the left led up to a classic Mykonian hotel, the craziness of the intersection turned into sea views and old stone walls overlooking the sandy cove of Megali Ammos at the bottom of the hill. At the near end of the cove sat one of the last, and certainly most enchanting, old time beach tavernas on the island.

"Perfect choice," said Andreas. Tassos nestled the car up against a fence on the left side of the road. "But I don't think you can open your door."

"No problem, I'll slide across and get out on your side." Tassos looked at Kouros in the back seat. "What, no wisecracks?"

Kouros opened his door. "Not after I saw what you did to that guy on the motorcycle...old man."

Chapter Twelve

The bamboo-capped, white stone shack known as Joanna's Place sat perched on the bottom of a waning crescent moon beach. Charming during the day, it turned downright ethereal at night in the silver moonlight reflected off the water.

The three cops made their way across the road to a narrow archway in a solid white wall forming the rear of the taverna. On each end of the taverna the wall dropped down to serve as the low border for the seaward side of the road, and together they wound away in both directions until out of sight.

Eight steps down from the road brought you back fifty years, to a time before the world had discovered Mykonos and Mykonians had not yet made dozens of other beaches readily accessible to visitors. Back then this was the place to come, and come they did. Even the Beatles and Pink Floyd ate here, though the music they heard—or one might hear on a chance evening today—was quite different from their own.

Off to the right stood a bar lined with wooden stools arranged so that patrons had to turn to get a peek of the sea through windows cut in walls. On the left sat the primary reasons for coming here: a huge kitchen and massive outdoor grill.

The half-dozen tables spread about inside were mostly empty, for here you came to sit outside on a covered stone patio running the length of the place, twenty feet from the edge of the sea. You could dip your feet in the water between courses.

Tassos embraced a smiling woman with short dark hair and a staunchly British accent. She promptly kissed and hugged Andreas and Kouros.

"Ah, the three musketeers have returned to Mykonos," said Joanna.

"All evil should quake in its boots," said Kouros.

"Let's hope not," she said. "On Mykonos that would bring on a major earthquake."

They all laughed, and she led them to a table in the corner at the enclosed right end of the patio. "This should give you privacy and you'll still have a great view of sunset."

"Every table has a great view of sunset," said Tassos.

Joanna smiled and patted Tassos on the shoulder. A young woman brought them water, a bottle of wine, and menus. "The wine is with my compliments. I'll be back in a minute for your orders."

All that separated the tables from the beach were a low white masonry wall running parallel to the sea and a few hand-hewn wooden pillars supporting the bamboo roof. A dozen handwoven wicker baskets from the nearby island of Tinos hung upside down from the ceiling, each fitted with a single bulb capable of casting just enough light to bring a pale glow to the room once sunlight was gone.

The only sound was the lapping of the sea against the shore. None of the incessant, pounding club music of virtually every other beach taverna at this sunset hour.

The sea shimmered in combinations of gun-metal blue, silver, and gold against a backdrop of vermilion skies and shadowy forms of distant islands. Except for a lone white church with a blood-red roof on the tiny island of Baou at the entrance to the bay, nothing in view suggested that the hand of man had played a part in any of this—unless of course you looked sharply to the left or right. But no one here did that. This was a place for remembering simpler times as you watched a glowing orange ball fade below the horizon.

Tassos broke the silence. "I first came here forty years ago. I was with my wife. In my mind, this place hasn't changed that much." He paused. "Come to think of it, my wife hasn't either."

He poured wine for the others and himself. "*Yamas.*"

"You still think of her?" said Kouros.

Tassos smiled. "You're only asking that question because you haven't yet found the love of your life. Otherwise you'd know the answer." He took a sip of wine. "My memories of my wife are like that ring you wear of your father's. With you always, even if you don't think about it. Then comes a time when you notice…and remember…and forget again…until the next time."

Kouros spun the ring on his finger. "Sorry, I didn't mean to sound insensitive. I just thought what with you and Maggie…" He let his voice trail off.

Tassos smiled. "No offense taken. I understand. And yes, Maggie is very special to me, but my wife will always remain in my thoughts as that young woman she was on the day that she died." Tassos gulped down the rest of the wine and smacked the glass on the table. "*Theos singhorese tin.*"

Kouros and Andreas did the same, "God forgive her soul."

Tassos filled the glasses again, and lifted his, "And to Yianni's father."

"*Theos singhorese tin.*" They toasted and went back to staring in silence at the sunset.

"What's more, these days Joanna's is just about the only place on the island where I can afford to eat. That is, if I were paying." Tassos winked at Andreas.

"The island's changed so much since I first came here," said Kouros. "I can't imagine how different it must seem to you."

Tassos nodded. "Some say it's changed for the better, others for the worse. But it's definitely changed a lot. Especially after the sun goes down. In mid-summer I don't recognize this place at night anymore."

"And with the likes of Sergey showing up, it's in for a hell of a lot more changes," said Andreas.

Tassos picked up his wineglass. "Foreigners aren't responsible for what's happened on Mykonos. Mykonians control it, they get the credit as well as the blame."

"Maybe," said Andreas. "But if they let Russian mob types get a foothold here, they're in for a whole different kind of grief. Things won't run the same way. It will be bloody."

"Yeah, but who's going to be dumb enough to let them in?" said Kouros.

Tassos smirked. "With so many big time property owners in deep shit with their banks, unpaid taxes, and loan sharks, it's only a matter of time before some of them start accepting offers they think will make them healthy again. And from past experience, for sure some of them won't give a damn about what it might mean for the future of the island as long as it puts money in their pockets."

"Hey, if you really want to play the cynic, my friend, be a real one," said Andreas. "Why should any oligarch with big ideas and a bank account to match waste his time negotiating with property owners? No matter how bad a jam they're in or lousy the economy, they think their property is worth whatever they say it is. The smart move is forget about them, buy up some nearly bankrupt bank that holds their mortgages and start foreclosing. Soon you'll own half the island. *Yamas*."

The men clinked glasses.

"From what I've been reading in the papers, I think the technical term for that sort of financial situation is a 'fucking mess,'" said Kouros.

"Depends," said Tassos. "Others would call it 'opportunity.'"

"Sorry to interrupt, gentlemen," said Joanna armed with a pen and pad in hand, "but have you decided yet?"

"Uhh, no, we've been too busy taking in the view," said Tassos.

"And holding hands," said Kouros.

"No problem. Happens all the time. Besides, I've taken the liberty of ordering the appetizers. You just have to figure out what else you want."

"Fish," said Tassos.

"*Barbouni*," said Andreas.

"And octopus," added Kouros.

"The octopus is already coming. I'll get the red mullet on the grill and we'll keep going from there. Okay?"

"Okay," said a trio of hungry men.

"Be right back," she said.

"I love it here," said Andreas.

"Me too," said Kouros.

"To tradition," said Tassos raising his glass.

"And kicking the butts of those who don't get it," said Kouros.

"Until they do," said Andreas.

"Yamas!"

The reflective, neon green and yellow athletic shoes tied in very nicely with the just as brightly colored green linen pants and yellow Hawaiian shirt embroidered with silver and gold sequin images of buxom nude women in profile. Sergey couldn't see Wacki's eyes because they were covered in white-frame, oversize Chanel sunglasses, but he assumed the pupils were the size of donuts.

Wacki was standing just inside the hotel lobby, and a young American couple talking with the concierge couldn't take their eyes off of him.

"I thought you said tonight was casual," said Sergey.

"It is casual. This is my look of the night." Wacki waved his hand at Sergey as if it were a magic wand. "And I think you look perfect as a boss out for a night on Mykonos."

Sergey was wearing Dolce & Gabbana black jeans, a white Giorgio Armani tee-shirt, and black Louis Vuitton loafers. A black elastic band held his long silver hair in a tight knot. He'd found the clothes in his closet in a box marked "casual." He wondered, but didn't ask, whether Wacki was his mysterious personal shopper.

"So, where to?"

"It's only midnight, boss, and too early for the sort of night life you're interested in seeing. I thought I'd show you Matogianni Street. It's what gets most of the big spender tourists shopping."

Like Alice after her rabbit, Sergey followed Wacki out the hotel door and through its gardens toward an archway into Wonderland.

"For years that place to the right, on the edge of the harbor just past the beach, was the closest bit of competition to Christos' place in town."

They stood directly in front of the hotel, swarmed by mainly thirty-year-olds and younger headed into town and older folk headed out.

"But its business died when Athenian black money dried up. Too much cheaper competition elsewhere for the booze and other things it offered. Rumor has it that some connected locals are planning to open a titty-bar there, offering lap dances and all that goes with it."

"That should give tourists an interesting first impression of 'magical Mykonos.'"

"Yeah, I was surprised, too. But a club like that a couple of miles outside of town is making a hell of a lot of money, so it was only a matter of time before someone copied it. That's how things work here."

"So, the key is to come up with something that can't be copied."

"Yeah, but what's unique? Titties are titties. Besides, if you come up with a big money-making idea the Mykonian mafia will find some way to take a cut of it or open their own place."

"Mafia?"

"No, not the sort you're used to. This mafia isn't leg breakers. They use connections to destroy your business if you don't play ball."

"But, it's still a titty bar at the entrance to the historic old harbor."

Wacki shrugged. "Most Mykonians avoid town at night during the busy season, and know only what they hear. Those who run the night make sure that whatever shit a few might raise is drowned out in promises of how much money it will make the town from foreigners. And with Greece in the middle of financial meltdown, that sort of talk is music to voters' ears, even though most should know by now that very little of that money will ever find its way into any one's pockets but those in control and their patrons.

"The bottom line is most don't care what happens during tourist season and those who do are afraid that if they take a stand the mafia will retaliate against their businesses or property."

"Sounds like a terrific place to do business."

Wacki smiled. "I thought you'd like that."

As they walked toward town, Wacki nodded at a building on the right at the end of the beach. "That's the original hotel on the island. The same family opened the first hotel outside of town. Their new one's on a large piece of property overlooking the new port in Tourlos. I thought you might like to know. Just in case you're interested in buying another hotel."

Wacki smiled.

Sergey did not.

"And up ahead begin the jewelry stores. I sometimes think there must be more of them per square foot in the old town than anywhere else on earth."

The road funneled down between buildings until it was only inches wider than the taxis forced to creep along at the pace of the crowds in front of them. Sergey stopped to look at a jewelry store on the right, three doors before the taxi stand.

"This one's the most famous jeweler in Greece. The shop draws a high-end, world-class clientele."

Sergey looked in windows filled with bowls, candlesticks, and other objects of hammered silver, and finely detailed works of art expressed in gold: necklaces, earrings, and rings. He recognized a necklace as one Anna had worn when she first came to see him.

He moved on.

Ten paces later the road opened into the town's main square. It sat at the north end of the harbor, on the other side of town from the bus station, and though officially named Manto Matogianni Square in honor of the island's Greek War of Independence heroine, everyone called it the "taxi square." Here you stood in line and prayed for one of the island's thirty or so taxis to come quickly.

They crossed down through the square behind the statue of Manto and onto a lane between a kiosk on the right selling breath mints, cigarettes, and condoms, and the Greek equivalent of a fast food place on the left. A quick right and another left had them in a tiny square filled with mostly empty chairs and tables, bordered by two bars on the left and a church straight ahead.

"This is a good place to start our tour. The church is Saint Kiriake, it's one of the three main ones in the town of Mykonos. If you lived in town you belonged to one of them, unless you're Catholic. Their church is in Little Venice."

Wacki turned away from the church to face the bars. "But that's not why this square is famous. It's famous because of what once was over there." He pointed at the bar on the left.

The place had a porch big enough for a dozen to sit comfortably, three-dozen when crammed. Inside the bar looked hardly big enough to hold more than a hundred.

"That's where Mykonos' famed international gay nightlife scene got its start. The tables here used to be packed all night with customers of Alberto's."

"Does Mykonos still draw a lot of gays?"

"You better believe it. By far most of its tourists are straight, but without the gay influence this island would go into cardiac arrest. They're big spenders and bring style to the island. The places they like are always the busiest in town."

Wacki waved at the square. "But the scene's not happening here anymore. A few years back you couldn't squeeze through this square between now and four in the morning."

He shook his head. "It's all gone except for a tiny mention of its name beneath a sign on the bar next to where Alberto's used to be."

"What happened?"

"The same as happened to a lot of places in Greece. Landlords blinded by memories of extraordinary good times didn't appreciate the financial realities of a country in crisis and refused to reduce skyrocketed rents. That gave inventive, connected competition with lower overhead a chance. It shouldn't come as a surprise what happened on a party island where the loyalty of most tourists to even their favorite places is best described as, 'The king is dead, long live the new king.'"

"Is there a new king in town?"

"Yes, on the other side of the harbor. We'll get there when it's jumping. But that won't be for a couple more hours. The magic starts building up in town after sunset but doesn't really get pumping until around two and keeps on rolling straight through dawn."

Matogianni was more like a stone path than a street, varying between six and twelve feet wide. Beyond the church an array of shops lined both sides of the lane, and for as far as the eye could see the path was packed with people studying shop windows and each other.

Color, style, practicality, fashion sense meant nothing. If there were a perceptible dress code it was that anything goes, except for those women and their imitators who followed another rule: Do whatever it takes to emphasize your boobs and butt. If it shimmers, stretches, shakes, or shines, sooner or later you'd see it strut by on Matogianni.

Wacki didn't bother to stop as he walked past the shops. "The bars along here aren't a big draw. Hit or miss. No real followings except for friends of people who work in them and, if the place happens to be tied to a bar in Athens, customers from Athens who come here."

They passed a jewelry shop on the right advertising the world's most expensive brands of watches. "This place does a huge business. A lot of people off cruise boats and yachts come to Mykonos just to buy their watches here."

Sergey studied the name above the door.

"The island's high-end places are still making money. More and more wealthy Arabs are coming each year and they like to shop. Louis Vuitton just opened a place and is doing very well, mainly off the cruise boats. Tour groups from Asia head straight for it."

It's all true, thought Sergey. This is an island paradise with a monied, holiday-minded crowd prepared to spend big on high-end jewelry, expensive watches, and pricey clothing; a rapidly growing Arab and Asian clientele; and a civic ethos where the guiding moral principle was "Will it make us money?"

"Come on, boss, there's a lot more to see. The evening hasn't even started."

I've found heaven.

Chapter Thirteen

Andreas knew tomorrow would be a long day. That's why he made sure Tassos and Kouros understood that their requested "quick drink in town" would be just that. He'd made his point three hours ago.

They'd parked at the base of the six windmills, overlooking a bay on the backside of the old harbor. The dozen or so multicolored, three-story former pirate-captain homes along the bay—virtually the only such structures in otherwise mandatory white, two-stories maximum Mykonos—gave the area its name: Little Venice. At sunset its bars and restaurants were packed with tourists staring west across the water. And from then until sunrise with partiers seeking a less spiritual sort of satisfaction.

They'd headed toward one of the old captain's houses, and a local hangout on the ground floor known for its traditional Greek music; but Tassos made them stop first at a piano bar next door. The bar was gay, but filled with a mixed crowd, as were most of the gay bars in this area of town. Tassos said he loved the singer and every time he was in town he made a point of going there.

Tassos found a seat next to the piano and sat mesmerized through two sets. Andreas and Kouros stayed at the bar talking with the owners and a neighboring bar owner who'd popped in to listen to a couple of songs but stayed when he recognized Andreas. Their conversation was the same as everywhere else in Greece: Damn the politicians and how can our country get out of the mess it's in without them.

By the time they dragged Tassos out of the bar it was after one, but the owner of another bar saw them and insisted they come in for a drink in his place. It was filled with locals anxious to give the three cops an earful on what they should do to fight the increasing crime rate. Kouros' suggestion that they hire more cops, double the starting salary of eight hundred euros a month, and stop asking for favors every time one of their relatives was arrested, didn't go over well.

But it did get them out of the place, and Andreas steered them back toward the car. The street was crowded with drunken kids, so Andreas cut through a bar on the right out onto a slightly less crowded stone path running between the bars and the sea. They'd made it as far as the narrowest part of the path when waves brought on by some distant passing cruise ship splashed up onto the path ahead, forcing them to pause.

Just as the way was passable again Tassos tapped Andreas in the middle of his back and whispered. "Coming right at us, that's him. The big one with silver hair. The one behind him is Wacki."

Andreas stepped back to let the men pass. He smiled at them as they went by. Sergey stared straight ahead as if he hadn't seen him, Wacki nodded and said, "Thank you."

"Silver head's a friendly guy," said Kouros.

"Big guy," said Andreas. "And he looks in shape."

"Prison gives you a lot of time to work out," said Tassos.

"Looks like Wacki's showing him the town," said Kouros as he stared at the legs of a tall, young blond woman coming from the same direction as Sergey and Wacki. She wore a denim micro-skirt, white tank top, and platform sandals, and clung to a thin, swarthy Greek boy in his twenties wearing a white tee-shirt, torn jeans, and dirty athletic shoes.

"Looks like that sucker's going to get lucky," said Kouros.

"I doubt it," said Tassos. "He didn't want to work tonight. It's his wife's birthday."

"What are you talking about?"

"That's not his wife. They're cops. They work for me and they're tailing Sergey."

"Son of a bitch." Kouros looked at Andreas. "How come I never draw that kind of duty?"

Andreas smiled. "If you'd like, I'm sure we could substitute you for the blonde."

Tassos nodded. "From where they look to be headed, you two would make a far less conspicuous couple."

They watched Sergey stroll off into the heart of Little Venice as if he had not a care in the world.

"I really want to nail that guy," said Tassos.

"*Avrio*," said Kouros.

"It's already 'tomorrow,'" said Andreas looking at his watch. "As of two hours ago."

Sergey and Wacki had spent an hour amid the coffee shops and bars at the T-shape end of Matogianni. "To give you an idea of the type of people on the island," according to Wacki.

It was the heart of Mykonos' late-night café society and hosted a number of world-class restaurants tucked away in the branching warren of narrow lanes. Barely thirty yards long, that tiny bit of Matogianni still managed to attract everyone who wanted to see or be seen at some point during the evening.

The next stretch of road offered additional expensive fashion shops, high-end jewelers, and clustered bars trying to offer something unique to passersby.

Wacki walked by them all and stopped at a garden-like setting on the right, just beyond two churches bordering the lane. It was separated from the street by a velvet rope guarded by two attractive, well-dressed women. One immediately lifted the rope. "Good evening, Mr. Wacki."

"This is the monied crowd's primary hangout. Inside the music's deafening, outside the talk and hustle is nonstop. Everyone wants one of those tables on top of the steps by the door. It means you're a big shot. Or willing to spend like one. All you'll see here are beautiful people." Wacki smiled, "And those who can afford to pay for them."

They sat at a table closest to the front door. Women kept passing by to say hello to Wacki and smile at Sergey. Sergey ignored them. His mind was on all the money the island attracted.

Twenty minutes later they were off to Little Venice and what Wacki called, "the wilder side of town."

The street into Little Venice was about as wide as Matogianni but here the shops were more attuned to the tastes and needs of locals and the more practical-minded tourist. It was not of interest to Sergey.

Wacki took a left just beyond a large church and then a right into a crowd of what looked to be high school and college kids. "This area has a lot of bars, mainly down along the water. It gets action all night, mostly from the young, straight crowd." He went through a doorway to the left and through another into an enclosed patio next to a bar crammed with people.

"This one gets partiers of all ages. It gets so crowded in there late at night that a fart could blow out the windows." He pointed at a door opening to the sea.

"That way, it's less crowded. Take a right outside and keep going all the way to the end."

Sergey went first and reached the doorway just as a wave hit the path in front of the bar, soaking everyone on the path. He waited for the waves to subside, then squeezed past three men who had also been waiting to cross in front of the bar.

He saw nothing to distinguish one bar from another. All were geared to marketing the same great view and nightlife vibe to twenty-something-year-olds who'd downed bottles of cheap booze in their hotel rooms in the hope of getting on a buzz that would keep them high enough to nurse one purchased drink in the bar as they worked their routines to get laid.

This wasn't the way Sergey planned on making his fortune.

At the first captain's house the path veered away from the sea. Wacki led the way along a lane winding behind the houses up to a large, all-white domed-church off to the right. It sat overlooking the sea just beyond the last captain's house. Wacki stopped in front of the church to tie his shoelace.

"This is the most photographed church in the Cyclades, the Fifteenth-Century Paraportiani. It's really five churches in one. Its roots go back to service as part of a gate to a thirteenth century castle that once stood here. That's why they call this area the *Kastro*, for castle."

Sergey kept walking but stopped where the path took a sharp right at the far side of the church. Beyond that point the path and church sat masked in darkness. He looked back at Wacki but a flash of light on his left made him instinctively swing toward it.

Framed in the glow of a cigarette lighter stood a boy of no more than nineteen in a black tank top. He smiled at Sergey.

"I wouldn't stand there too long unless you're looking for action," said Wacki coming up beside Sergey. "For as long as I've been on the island this area's been the place to come for anonymous gay sex. Though it's toned down somewhat from the old days."

Wacki stared at the boy still holding the lighter and smiling. "My guess is that's because there's a lot more foot traffic through here these nights. Straights and gays on their way down to the new clubs along the harbor on the other side of this hill.

"Most people coming through here these days aren't looking for action." Wacki smiled. "Unless they stop."

Sergey turned and walked past the boy to the top of the hill. He heard music coming from a street in front of him. But the buildings were dark and beyond them stood a long, solid concrete wall. He thought the music must come from the buildings along the harbor below.

Past the church they turned left toward a twenty-yard patch of badly poured concrete that dropped abruptly from a height of two stories to sea level. The drop began at the entrance to a patio off to the right enclosed by a low stone wall. To the left a boulder-strewn jut of land reached out and down to the sea.

As they made their way down the hill between the patio and boulders, Wacki waved his hand off to the right. "One of those buildings next to the patio is the Folklore Museum. Care to imagine the sort of shit the *ya-yas* with brooms find around here every morning?"

"Doesn't *ya-ya* mean grandmother?"

"Yeah. Maybe what they find turns them on." Wacki practically cackled.

"I'm certain if anyone would know what turns a grandmother on it's you."

Wacki seemed unsure whether or not to take the comment as a compliment.

Sergey was not surprised.

At the bottom of the hill they turned right toward a mass of people crowded in front of three bars. Bodies were packed onto virtually every inch of the thirty feet of concrete running between the front of the bars and a low stone wall marking the edge of the sea wall.

"The wind's not blowing hard tonight so there's a big crowd outside. They'd all be pounded with seawater if the wind were up." Wacki pointed at the middle bar. "In there. The one with the white doors is the place I was talking about. It's the new king of late night in town."

They squeezed in between a small stage the size of a narrow desktop on the right, and the edge of a bar on the left running the length of the place. They'd just about made it around the corner of the bar when a blaring whistle and a sudden change of music made Wacki tug on Sergey's arm.

"We're never going to make it back there. The show is about to start. Just stay where you are. It will be over in five minutes."

The lights went out except for a spotlight focused on the stage. Into it stepped the drag world's personification of a mature Eva Peron, all aglitter in a sleeveless red sequin gown and doing his/her lip synching bawdy interpretation of a song from *Evita*.

The audience went wild, but by far the most fascinated were the women. They hooted and hollered louder than the men. Sergey studied the crowd, a mixed bag of partiers sharing one significant trait: Virtually all had spent serious money trying to look fashionably understated.

When the song ended, Wacki gestured toward the back. Sergey shook his head no, and pushed toward the front door.

Outside, he turned right and walked past the public toilets on the left toward a sign marked, BOATS TO DELOS HERE. He stared across the harbor at his hotel on the other side.

Wacki ran to catch up with him. "I wanted you to see the upstairs, they did a great job."

"No need to. I can tell their crowd has a lot of money to spend. That's all I needed to see. So, are we done?"

"Not yet, I've been saving the big money-making operations for last. One's in town, two others are on a beach about fifteen minutes away by taxi. We'll take the backstreets, it's faster."

They walked behind the town hall and passed by a small square shared by two bars of the same name. Wacki called it the island's "meat market" for young straights. After the square, they wove through a maze of four- and five-foot-wide, virtually deserted lanes. There was barely a sound. It was as if they'd gone back in time.

Or to a different island.

They popped back into the crowds on the same street as they'd taken into Little Venice, but this time headed in the opposite direction. As they passed a schoolyard on the left, the street opened into a large square.

"That's it on the left."

Wacki pointed at a psychedelic pink marquee looming above a long red carpet, cordoned in half lengthwise by silver-color metal stanchions and a red velvet rope. The carpet ran from the square up to a large grey metal door.

On a Cycladic island long known for its simple, tasteful architecture, Sergey thought the entrance a comic self-parody of what must lay inside. But two massive bouncers by the door, and enticingly clad women collecting euros from a long line of twenty-somethings queued up to get in, made it clear that this was anything but funny. It was a serious, highly profitable business capitalizing on arousing the fantasies that drew so many to Mykonos.

Thirty yards or so beyond the entrance, the square faded off into an outdoor basketball court and playground. Men milled around in the shadows at the far end.

Sergey nodded in their direction. "Is that this side of town's equivalent of Paraportiani?"

Wacki laughed. "The police station used to be in this square. Today it's where you come if you want to do business with the Albanian mob. It's their hangout."

Sergey pointed at a group of provocatively dressed young women and men outside the entrance to the club hustling passersby to come inside. "What's with them?"

"All the big clubs have hot looking tourist kids running around passing out handbills and chatting up whoever they can to fill up the places. It's all about body count, and the kids shill for the clubs by sticking ads on cars parked at the beaches during the day and pounding out their messages in town at night until the last bus leaves for the out-of-town clubs."

"What do they get paid?"

"Five euros or so an hour, plus free admission and a drink."

As soon as the bouncers saw Wacki coming toward them they nodded and one opened the door. Inside the place was ablaze with noise and lights and music. The downstairs was one big dance floor and bar, pumped along by very hot-looking women perched strategically above the crowd in places where they could perform their craft, colloquially known as pole dancing.

Overlooking it all was a balcony circling most of the dance floor and filled with more people, some sitting at tables.

"Up there is for VIPs. It's a more refined crowd."

From what Sergey could see of the crowd, by "refined" he assumed Wacki was referring to their choice of stimulants.

"Let's go. I've seen enough."

Outside Wacki pointed at a taxi waiting in front of the club. "Hop in. Only two more places to see, they're at the same beach."

It took the taxi five minutes to crawl the two hundred yards up from the club to the bus station. Getting through the crowds was like swimming head-on through a frenzied rush of hot-to-spawn salmon.

At the bus station Wacki pointed to a long line of young people boarding two municipal buses. "We're all headed to the same place. They'll have a lot of catching up to do when they get there. By now the clubs are packed with wild ones from the beach tavernas who've been going at the same crazy pace since late afternoon."

The drive took longer than Wacki said it would. Mainly because the taxi driver kept slowing down to avoid motorbikes flying up and down the road to the beach.

The driver said, "I think they call this 'the road to Paradise' not because of the beach, but because that's where crazy tourists who drive like that are likely to end up. If they can, locals avoid this road like the plague between dark and a few hours after sunrise."

"If locals are afraid to drive on their own roads, why don't the cops do something about it?" asked Sergey.

The driver laughed. "The cops don't care. The only ones who care are the club owners. And they don't want anyone messing with the image of Mykonos as a place where you can do anything you want and be protected by the gods of Delos from harm. Which includes arrest.

"You should see the medical clinic the morning after a busy night. Looks like a combat zone, but you'll never hear a word about any of that. All's always perfect on this island."

And looking to be more so every moment, thought Sergey.

At the beach the taxi turned left, climbed up onto a rise, and stopped by a large stone building overlooking the sea.

"Here we are."

Again a long line at the door, money changing hands, and Wacki waved in through a VIP entrance, this one on the left. This club was much bigger than the first, but just as packed and looked like it could handle five thousand customers. They entered past a bar onto the dance floor. In front of them was the VIP section, and off to the right a pool. The place packed in thousands of celebrants of every imaginable shape, size, color, sex, and dress, all pumping along in rhythm to the music and lights, accompanied by stimulants of their choice, and all aiming to make it through to watching the sunrise over the sea.

The last club on Wacki's tour sat on the beach and was smaller than the one above it. A massive glass wall separated the place from the sand. Here, too, the bar was the first thing you saw, next came a pool with the dance floor beyond it, and a VIP section farther along terracing up a hillside. The music and light show seemed a bit more sophisticated, and the place looked to attract a slightly older, somewhat more upscale crowd than the others, but to Sergey its bottom line was the same: Do whatever it takes to bring in the bodies and make the money.

It was a philosophy he knew well.

He'd run these kinds of clubs before. Smaller, yes, but the crowds were the same and so were the problems.

He doubted any of them had the proper licenses, but they obviously had the juice to stay in business, and that was all that mattered.

In the taxi on the way back to town Wacki said, "Now that you've seen our magical island at night, what's next?"

"I want to meet your mayor."

Chapter Fourteen

The sun came up the same as it always did, though for late night partiers with shuttered windows it wasn't that big a deal. But Andreas liked to sleep with his windows open when on the island. He loved the smells of wild rosemary and thyme scented by sea breezes. There was nothing like that in air conditioned Athens where he slept behind rolled down steel shutters. None of that here. At least not yet.

Andreas' in-laws were in Athens so he stayed at their summer place on Mykonos' north central coast. It was a rare location, having its own cove. Though by law no beach was private, since Lila's family owned the land surrounding the cove, for all practical purposes the beach was theirs alone to share with the sea.

Mykonos was a different island out there away from the craziness of the season. A true paradise.

Lila loved sitting on the beach in the morning as Aegean sunlight danced upon the water casting the sea in hues of silver, rose, and gold, popped distant islands into sight, and bounced shades of blue across the sky to fire up a splash of green along a light brown hillside, a shot of pink amid oleander green, a beige lizard against a gray wall, or a cresting wave of white against a deep blue sea.

Andreas' favorite time of day was late afternoon, watching light range across fields of ochre, gray, and black—framed in the stones and shadows of ancient walls lumbering up onto hillsides or sliding down toward the sea. For Andreas, those tranquil moments eased away his memories of places forever lost to modern times; and led him to wonder how akin his own thoughts might be to those of ancients who looked out upon those same hills, seas, and sunsets so many thousands of years before.

But today was not one for musing about the beach or ancient times. Tassos and Kouros had crashed in the guest bedroom and there was a busy day ahead. Andreas pushed himself out of bed, went to the bathroom, threw some water on his face, and headed for the kitchen to start the coffee.

Tassos and Kouros were already there, cups in hand.

"Morning, Chief. Sleep well?"

"Are you trying to impress me? I can't remember the last morning I saw you in the office on time."

Kouros smiled. "That's because I spend my first waking hours at home doing paperwork, and sometimes I get so distracted I forget what time it is."

Andreas held out his left arm and used his right hand to feign playing a violin.

"Well, for this morning at least I can vouch that the boy has been working." Tassos poured a cup of coffee and handed it to Andreas.

"Thanks. On what? Too early to be his suntan."

Kouros handed Andreas a half-dozen sheets of paper. "It's everything the agencies had on Sergey Tishchenko. Aside from the arrest in Poland that put him away for two years, he has no criminal record. That might be because up until he moved to Poland he was in the Russian military. One report said he was thought to be part of a military drug and sex trafficking operation that got its start during the first Chechen War in 1994, and kept up at it until they lost their patron's protection. That fits time-wise, because the ring fell apart about the time Sergey left Russia for Poland."

"Where was he born? How old is he?" said Andreas.

"Not sure. Records say he was an orphan, but nothing about when, where, or how. He gave a birthdate when he joined the military that made him old enough to enlist. That would make him around thirty-seven, today. He listed his parents as deceased, that he didn't know their names, and had no next of kin."

"Sounds like someone trying to hide from something," said Andreas.

"Or escape. Possibly from a foster home or orphanage," said Tassos.

"Maybe. What else do you have on him?"

"He was heavily decorated in the military and went from enlisted man to major. The military even sent him to university."

"He's a man who knew how to please his superiors," said Tassos.

"And, if I recall correctly, pleasing one's superiors in Chechnya meant doing some pretty nasty things," said Andreas.

"Like drowning your girlfriend in a bathtub?" said Kouros.

"How was he in prison?" said Andreas.

"A model prisoner. So much so that they let him grow his hair as a reward for good behavior. Only incident even mentioning him was the suicide of a cellmate. And Sergey was nowhere around when it went down."

"What happened?" said Tassos.

"The report says a guard found the cellmate alone in his cell hanging by his neck from shoe laces tied to the railing at the foot of the upper bunk. He'd made a noose on one end and let his knees drop until he passed out. He suffocated."

"Christ, he could have stood up anytime to save himself," said Kouros.

"You really have to hate your life to end it that way," said Tassos.

Andreas picked up his coffee and took a sip. "Or be a lot more afraid of living it."

"Do you think Sergey might have driven him to it?" said Kouros.

Andreas shrugged. "We'll never know." He took another sip. "If what's in those records is the true story of Sergey's life, I don't see how he has the money to buy a hotel on Mykonos."

"Perhaps he's back in business with his old Russian military buddies?" said Tassos.

"But why a hotel on Mykonos? All their connections are in Russia," said Kouros.

"The island is getting a lot more Russian tourists. Maybe they want their own hotel?" said Tassos.

"That would make a lot of Mykonian hoteliers and their guests very happy," said Kouros.

Andreas put down his cup. "I think it's time we introduce ourselves to Mister Tishchenko."

◇◇◇

The mayor's office was on the second floor of the late eighteenth century, two-and-a-half-story municipal building at the south edge of the old harbor. It was the only structure on the harbor with terra-cotta roof tiles.

The place had seen a lot of changes over the centuries, most recently a new mayor. The old one had been in power for two decades and likely would have remained so for another two had he not surprised everyone by abruptly resigning in midterm as ruinous financial crises loomed on the horizon.

The office of Mykonos' mayor controlled virtually everything that happened on the island. If the mayor was not pleased, he could shut you down in a heartbeat. The island's new mayor was of short stature, mustache, and hair, but long on charm and political instincts. He'd been in local politics his entire adult life and knew how things worked on his island: money talked.

So, when Wacki called him to say big Russian money wanted to see him ASAP, the mayor passed on his usual early morning coffee in the port with cronies to meet with Sergey in his office.

When Sergey and Wacki walked into his office the mayor jumped up from behind his desk, came around to the other side, and, with arms spread wide open and a broad smile across his face, said in Russian, "Welcome home!"

Sergey was surprised. "You speak Russian?" he said in Russian.

The mayor said in Greek, "I have no idea what you just said, my friend, because I just exhausted my knowledge of Russian in welcoming you home, but please, sit." Wacki translated into English as the mayor shook each man's hand and pointed to three chairs at a small round conference table next to a window overlooking the harbor. Once his guests were seated, the mayor took the empty chair.

"What did you mean by 'Welcome home?'" said Sergey in Greek.

"No need to struggle with Greek, said the mayor. "I see you speak English."

"Yes."

"My English is not so good, but I think it would be better if we try to speak in English. Okay?"

"Okay."

"What I meant was that this building was built by a Russian count and it served as his residence. We're sitting in a place where you and your countrymen should feel as much at home as we do. Our home is your home!"

Sergey smiled. "Thank you. That is very kind of you to say."

The mayor nodded. "I'm sure you're very busy, so why don't you tell me how I can be of assistance to you?"

"I assume by now you've heard of my interest in acquiring a hotel on the island?"

"Yes, Lefteris is a dear friend. He said you made a very generous offer and assured him that things would continue as they always have."

"That was very kind of him to say, and yes, I understand there are certain interests that must be protected."

"We are a very small island with simple, poor people. It would not be fair if we allowed foreign wealth to come in and disrupt a way of life that has existed for generations."

"I can assure you I have no interest in causing harm to any business falling under your protection as mayor. My wish is to bring new people with new money to your island."

"New business is always appreciated. As long as it does not come at the expense of the old."

"There is no business on this island that will suffer because of my plans for the hotel. In fact, everyone will benefit because what I have in mind will draw guests to the island all year round, not just during the brief summer season."

"That would be an extraordinary achievement. But how do you expect to do that? Other hotels have tried to do the same thing with ideas like conference centers and spas, but all failed. People come to Mykonos for the beaches and fun of summer. There is no other significant draw."

"With all due respect, Mayor, I think there are other ways."

"What sorts of ways?"

Sergey smiled. "Walls have ears. I wouldn't want a competitor learning what I have in mind before I have the chance to try them out myself."

The mayor shrugged. "Suit yourself, but if your plans require town approval, and it's hard to imagine they would not, sooner or later you'll have to tell us what you 'have in mind.'" He emphasized the last three words with finger quotes.

"And as much as I don't want to upset your deal with my good friend, Lefteris, I cannot guarantee you'll get approvals for such 'other ways' if they conflict with what the ministry of tourism allows under its lease of the hotel."

"Thank you for your candor, Mayor. But I can assure you what I have in mind will bring great riches to the town and all who assist in making my project a success."

"That is a philosophy I share. In business it is important to be nice to those who are nice to you."

"You will find me to be very nice."

The mayor nodded.

"There is one slight favor I'd like to ask of you, if I may," said Sergey.

"Please, ask. If I can help I will."

"I would like an introduction to your police chief. I have a delicate matter to discuss with him, and with your introduction I'm sure I'd get his absolute cooperation."

The mayor stood up, walked across the room, picked up his mobile phone, and pressed a speed-dial key.

"Hello, Mihalis. I'd like to see you in my office as soon as you can get here. It's about a 'delicate matter.'" He paused. "Great." And hung up.

The mayor smiled at Sergey. "He'll be right over."

"Please, I don't want to impose on your time. Perhaps there's another office we could use?"

The mayor waved his hand. "I won't hear of it. It will be my pleasure to help out. After all, my *casa* is your *casa*." He smiled again.

Sergey smiled, too, but for a different reason. The mayor's curiosity had him taking the bait. Sergey knew his only chance at getting the police chief to cooperate was if the mayor were on board. And the only way for that to happen was to make his pitch when they were all together in the same room.

Step one accomplished. On to step two.

Being police chief on Mykonos was much like a minister trying to keep order in a brothel when the fleet was in. The best method was pray and duck.

Mihalis knew his job depended on keeping locals who mattered happy and that this gig was way better than most. With any luck he might be able to hang onto it for the couple of years left until his pension.

He parked the blue-and-white police car beneath the overhang of the municipal building and walked toward the steps on the left leading up to the second floor. A young woman stood in the entrance to a bar at the base of the stairs.

"Opening a bit early aren't you, Stella?"

"Just closing. It was quite a night last night." The bar was hers and, as the last traditional Greek dance place on the island, it was a favorite hangout for locals and traditionally minded tourists ending a late night of celebrating.

As Mihalis made his way up the steps he wondered what sort of shit storm the mayor had in store for him now. On this island there was always something.

◇◇◇

The moment the police chief entered the room Sergey stood up and held out his hand. "Thank you for coming, Chief." He spoke in English.

"My English not very good," said the Chief.

"I'll speak slowly but if you don't understand something Wacki will translate. Again, thank you for coming."

"Anything to help our mayor."

"Thank you, Mihalis," said the mayor."

"As the mayor will tell you, I am about to buy a hotel on your island."

The mayor nodded.

"I am concerned only about one thing. Security."

The mayor's face tightened at the question, and the Chief asked for a translation.

"I just want to know if I will be safe?"

The mayor answered. "Of course you will be safe. Why would you think otherwise?"

"I heard that a prominent businessman was recently robbed and beaten to death."

"Exaggeration. It was a crime of passion."

The police chief asked Wacki to translate what Sergey and the mayor had said.

Sergey talked over Wacki's translation.

"What do you mean 'a crime of passion?'"

"It was the man's girlfriend and a couple of men who did it. It wasn't a random robbery," said the mayor.

The chief spoke in Greek. "Mister Mayor, you shouldn't be telling him this. That is not publicly disclosed information."

Wacki translated for Sergey.

"Don't worry, I won't tell anyone," said Sergey. "I just wanted to be assured there wasn't some organized criminal element operating on the island."

"Absolutely nothing like that to worry about here," said the mayor. "Right, Mihalis?"

The chief shook his head and tried to speak in English. "Please, do not talk about this. It is not my case. It is on Syros. We are not to discuss the case."

"Have the killers been arrested?" said Sergey.

The chief gestured no.

"If you know who did it, why aren't they in jail?"

"They're in Poland," said the mayor.

The chief shook his head. "Please, Mister Mayor."

Sergey shrugged. "I guess the lesson in all of this is not to keep a lot of money at home?"

"This wasn't about money," said the mayor. "Christos had opened his safe and given them everything in it. There was nothing left to steal. They killed him out of passion. Isn't that right, Mihalis?"

The chief looked beaten. "Yes, Mister Mayor."

"Good." He looked at Sergey. "I hope our little discussion was helpful."

"Yes, very. Thank you."

Chapter Fifteen

Once out of the mayor's office, Sergey hurried down the steps and walked straight for a blue dome church across the harborfront road from the municipal building. It sat on the edge of the sea at the beginning of a concrete pier running about a quarter of the way across the middle of the old harbor. The pier's seaward side was filled with large motor yachts tied up stern first, and its other side with smaller pleasure craft and colorful fishermen's *caiques*.

Sergey stopped in front of the church.

"The blue dome means it's a church to Saint Nicholas, patron saint of sailors." It was Wacki coming up from behind him. "Some like to think of him as Santa Claus."

Then I should light a candle to thank him for the mayor's gift to me, thought Sergey.

"What was it with those questions about 'security?' I could have told you there was nothing to worry about. Everybody knows it was Christos' girlfriend who did it. It's the worst kept secret on the island."

"I wanted to hear it from the police chief."

Wacki shrugged. "I told you the mayor would play ball. But it was a good idea to reassure him that his friends wouldn't be hurt. They can be very nasty."

Their time will come. "I want to take a look at those boats next to the pier. I'll see you back at the hotel."

"Fine, I'll let you know what gossip I pick up from the locals about you." Wacki smiled.

Sergey walked out onto the pier as if he'd not heard him. A fisherman mending nets on a *caique* nodded hello. Sergey returned the nod and squeezed past a tourist couple trying to snatch a peek of life among the yachting crowd. He stopped at the end of the pier and stared across the water toward the hotel.

Teacher was right to say Anna had to go. If they'd found her she would have talked. He better get word to the other two. No, he'd better get rid of them. Couldn't chance blowing this opportunity. It would be tough enough once that mayor learned what he had in mind. The mayor and his cronies would try to take it for themselves or fuck him if they couldn't.

Shit.

If he didn't get his hands on Christos' information his plans were ruined. The police didn't have it or else that ass-kissing police chief would have told the mayor, and from the way the mayor was blabbing on about Christos' safe there's no way he knew anything about Christos' leverage.

Maybe it's still in Christos' house? *Goddamn bitch. If she'd gotten Christos to tell her where he'd hidden the stuff I wouldn't have this problem.*

Sergey turned and headed back to the church. Once on the road, he turned left and walked past a row of farmers selling fresh produce out of small vans and trucks. On the beach behind them, fishermen stood around a long marble table aimed back toward the sea displaying their morning catch for sale.

Wacki was sitting in a taverna across from the market with a man in a panama hat. Sergey didn't stop. He had to figure out a way to get his hands on Christos' files.

Damn, I forgot to light that candle.

Andreas watched the man walk up to the hotel desk and ask the clerk for his room key.

"Mister Tishchenko."

Sergey swung around in the direction of the voice.

"Yes?"

"My name is Andreas Kaldis." He pointed to the two men with him in the lobby. "We're with the Greek police."

Sergey answered in broken Greek. "I'm sorry, I don't understand Greek."

Andreas switched to English. "Is this better?"

"Yes, but who are you?"

"We're with the Greek police."

"What can I do for you?"

"We have some questions we'd like to ask of you."

"Here?"

"No, let's go upstairs to the dining room. It should be empty now."

"Please." Sergey waved his hand for Andreas to lead the way.

The dining room was one flight up and they sat at a table by a window overlooking the sea.

"Do you mind if I see your identification?" said Sergey.

"Not at all." Andreas pulled his ID out from around his neck.

Sergey smiled. "It certainly looks official, but I have no idea what it says."

"I'm Chief Inspector for Special Crimes based in Athens. Detective Kouros is my assistant, and—"

"I'm Tassos Stamatos, Chief Homicide Inspector for the Cyclades, based on Syros."

Sergey's face showed no emotion. "Thank you. So, how can I help you?"

Andreas said, "We understand you're new on the island."

"Yes, just arrived yesterday."

"And that you're buying this hotel."

"Word travels fast."

"All the way from Bialystok," said Andreas.

Still no emotion.

"What has us wondering, Sergey...You don't mind if I call you Sergey, do you?" said Andreas.

Sergey gestured no with his head.

"Ah, I see you're already picking up our language," said Tassos in Greek.

Sergey showed no reaction.

"What has us wondering is where you got the money to buy this place?" said Andreas.

"That's none of your business."

"It is when someone with your background shows up here spending big-time money."

"Greece isn't a laundromat," said Kouros.

"If you know my history, then you know that I've paid my debt to society on that false charge. And that it soon will be expunged from my record. I've also served my country honorably. I've come here to establish a legitimate business."

"Will your girlfriend be joining you?" said Kouros.

"I don't know who you're talking about."

"Of course you do," said Andreas.He nodded at Kouros. "Show him the photograph."

Kouros pulled an 8x10 out of an envelope and slid it across the table to Sergey.

Sergey stared at the photo but said nothing. "A dead woman on a gurney. Is that supposed to mean something to me?"

"Polish police fished her out of a cesspool in the town you gave as your address when you got out of prison."

"Like I said, is that supposed to mean something to me?"

"She did to Christos Vasilakis," said Andreas.

Sergey blinked. "Who's that?"

"Come on, Sergey," said Andreas. "If you're on this island ten minutes you'd have heard the story of the club owner bludgeoned to death and robbed."

Sergey swallowed. "I did not know his name. Yes, I've heard of that terrible tragedy."

"Did you also hear who killed him?" said Kouros.

"I didn't know that was public knowledge," said Sergey.

Andreas tapped the photograph. "This dead girlfriend you shared with the victim. She did it with the help of some men."

"Well, if you know the three who did it, your case is solved so why hassle me?"

"Three? Did I say three?" said Andreas.

"I thought there were four," smiled Kouros.

"I thought you said it wasn't public knowledge?" said Andreas.

"I just came from a meeting with the mayor. He told me it was the girlfriend and two others."

"I wonder how that subject came up?" said Andreas.

"He was trying to reassure me that Mykonos was a safe place to do business."

"What did he tell you about the murder?"

"That it was a crime of passion, not robbery."

"But the safe was wide open. Sure sounds like robbery to me," said Andreas staring into Sergey's eyes. "Maybe they didn't find what they were looking for."

Sergey didn't blink. "I wouldn't know anything about that."

Andreas kept up his stare. "But if they didn't, maybe they're still looking for it?"

Sergey shrugged. "Maybe."

Kouros reached over, picked up the photograph and held it up in front of Sergey's face. "You still don't recognize her?"

"Are you suggesting I'm a suspect?"

"For the moment let's just say that you're a series of unexplained coincidences," said Andreas.

"Well then, if you're done with me for now, do you mind if I go to my room? I've a lot of work to do."

Sergey stood but the cops did not. "So, may I go?"

"As long as you don't leave the island," said Andreas.

"Don't worry. I have no reason to." Sergey walked toward the stairs and said without turning around, "I love it here."

"What do you think?" said Andreas when Sergey had disappeared.

"Is it okay to talk here?" said Kouros.

"Yeah, he's gone," said Tassos. "I sure wish I understood English better. I couldn't follow everything."

"Don't worry. I got to play your hard ass part," said Kouros.

"He doesn't rattle easily," said Andreas.

"Smart ex-cons learn to be that way around cops," said Tassos.

Andreas explained to Tassos what Sergey had said, then shook his head. "I don't get it. If all he wanted was to buy this hotel, why murder Christos?"

"Jealousy?" said Kouros.

"What, kill the lover, kill the girl, then try to become a big man in the very place where cops are most likely to be looking for you? Sounds more like a psychopathic egotist to me."

"Maybe he didn't think we'd find out about his connection to the girl?" said Kouros.

"Then he's stupid, and we'll nail him. But somehow I don't think that's the answer. Tassos, do you think you could find out if Sergey was telling the truth about his meeting with the mayor in a way that doesn't raise suspicion? For the time being, we want to keep gossip to a minimum."

"I'm not on the best of terms with his Honor the Mayor, but the police chief might know something. I'll try him first."

"Good. So, I'm back to what I said before. Why kill Christos if all Sergey wanted to do was run a hotel? I can't imagine he needed the ammunition in Christos' second safe to get permission to take over the lease. Sure, maybe he'd have to bribe a few people to get some permits, but that's business as usual for a guy like Sergey. It's not like he's trying to cut in on the Mykonos nightlife mafia's action by opening a club. It's just a goddamned hotel. There are one-hundred sixty-two of them on the island."

"Maybe he's thinking of tearing the hotel down and building condos?" said Kouros

"If he killed two people just to do that he really is insane. First, of all, in this real estate market he's better off renting rooms, and second, like Andreas said, why kill someone when all you have to do is pass around some bribes? That guy's done this sort of thing before, he has to know that."

"So, how do we find out what he really has in mind?" said Kouros.

"I'd start with Wacki," said Tassos. "He's a weak sister when it comes to dealing with cops."

"You mean honest cops," said Kouros.

"Tassos, see what you can find out about that meeting with the mayor. Yianni and I will talk to Wacki. If Sergey's dirty, I want him to know we're out to nail his ass."

"I wonder how he'll react to that sort of pressure," said Kouros.

"Can't wait to find out," said Andreas.

◇◇◇

Sergey sat at a table in his hotel room and stared toward the harbor.

Those cops knew nothing of his plans. They knew about Anna so they suspected him. But she was a dead end. The others soon would be too.

He wondered if he should call Teacher to make the arrangements. She could find the two easily. But she'd want to know why. No, he'd better handle this himself. He could never seem rattled or unsure to Teacher. That would be dangerous.

He'd use the same mutual friend from his prison days who'd put him together with the two men to find them. And, for the right price, to get rid of them, too.

Sergey poured himself a glass of water from a bottle on the table. Those cops had to know about Christos' files. It all fit. The cop from Syros was in charge of murder investigations and the police chief said it wasn't his case, it was "on Syros."

They must have found the files and figured that's what the robbery was about. That's why they came to him. They weren't interested in solving the murder, they wanted him to know what cards they held and, if he were interested, that he'd have to pay for them.

He took a sip of water. That could be arranged. He'd get Wacki to do it.

Chapter Sixteen

Wacki got up the moment Andreas and Kouros sat down at his table.

"Please, no reason to leave. It's a beautiful day to be sitting with old friends in a taverna along the harbor." Andreas pointed at Wacki's chair. "Stay."

Two other men at the table looked at each other as if unsure what to do.

"You two may leave," said Andreas.

They quickly did.

"I thought you worked in Athens," said Wacki.

"Missed me, huh?"

Wacki smiled.

"We just had a most interesting chat with your employer."

"Who's that?"

"Come on, Wacki, don't make this hard on us." Kouros gave him a quick smack on the arm that was slightly more painful than friendly. "Because we'll have to make it hard on you."

"I'm just showing the guy around town and acting as his translator."

"Since when have you become a tour guide?" said Andreas.

"Since the economy cratered. Just in case you public payroll guys haven't noticed."

"Play nice," said Kouros, feigning another run at Wacki's arm.

Wacki winced. "What do you guys want with me? I'm working for someone who's interested in taking over a hotel. He's trying to help Greece by making money for everyone."

"I've heard that money pitch before. It can justify a lot of things," said Andreas.

"Like I said, he's into 'making money for everyone.'" Wacki paused and dropped his head until his eyes were visible over the top of his sunglasses. "That is, for everyone who *wants* to make money."

Andreas leaned in to six inches from Wacki's face. "Some things never change. You're still a rat-faced, crooked son of a bitch who thinks everyone can be bought. Congratulations, asshole, you just made the top of my shit list. You want off it? Tell me what your boss is really up to."

Wacki jerked back in his chair. "Honest, all I know about is the hotel. I'm his employee, not his confidant."

"Were you with him at his meeting with the mayor?"

"Yes."

"What did you talk about?"

"Things?"

"What sorts of things," said Kouros, patting him lightly on the arm.

"He wanted to know if the town was safe."

"For that he went to the mayor?" said Andreas.

"The police chief was there. He told him the town was safe."

"Anything else?"

"Not that I can remember?"

"Are you sure?"

"Yes."

Andreas motioned with his finger for Wacki to lean in toward him. "I want to make myself perfectly clear. If I find out you're holding out on me about what Sergey's really up to, you and all your island buddies will become my number one targets in what I can assure you will be ironclad, big-time, jail-time investigations. And I'll personally let each one of them know it's all coming down on them because of you."

Andreas smiled. "Do we understand each other?"

Wacki nodded.

"Good. Now run along."

And he did. Straight back to the hotel.

Tassos walked past the cop at the reception desk and up the stairs to the second floor of the police station. He stopped at a door around and to the left of the top of the stairs, knocked once, and opened the door.

"Hi, Mihalis."

The police chief looked surprised. "Tassos, what are you doing here?"

"Just thought I'd stop bye to say, 'Hi.'"

Tassos plopped onto an overstuffed chair alongside Mihalis' desk. "I understand your distinguished mayor is running his mouth off about *my* investigation into Christos' murder."

"How the hell do you know that?"

"Never mind how I know, how does the mayor know about my case?"

"Christ, Tassos, he's the mayor, how do I know?"

"Because you're the only one in this goddamn sieve of a police station that I told about the girl and her two accomplices."

Mihalis ran his hand through his hair. "Honest, I didn't expect him to tell the Russian."

Tassos hoped his surprise didn't show. "You were there?"

"Yes, the Mayor said he had a 'delicate matter' to discuss and when I showed up the Russian and Wacki were there."

"What did the mayor tell them?"

"It was hard to follow, they were speaking in English and Wacki was translating."

"Did the Mayor mention the girl and the accomplices?"

"Yes."

"How many men did he say were with her?"

"I think he said 'a couple,' but not sure."

"What other cats did your esteemed mayor let out of the bag?"

"Nothing. Just that it was a crime of passion. Not robbery."

"How did he come to that conclusion?"

"The mayor said there was nothing left in the safe to steal. Everything had been taken." Mihalis paused. "Sort of makes you wonder if it wasn't a crime of passion what were they looking for?"

"Sure does. Thanks, Mihalis." Tassos pulled himself out of the chair. "And I'd appreciate it if you didn't pass along this little chat of ours to the mayor."

At least not until I'm out of the building.

Wacki sat at the table in Sergey's room, repeating word for word his conversation with the two cops.

Sergey listened patiently until Wacki finished. "Interesting. I assume this means those police cannot be bribed."

"Kaldis? Not a chance. He's a legend on a mission. And he has a rich, socially prominent wife. Doesn't need the money."

Sergey flicked his index finger against his lips. "I guess we must find another way to get what we need from him and his colleagues."

"Good luck with that," said Wacki.

Sergey smiled. "Thank you."

Chapter Seventeen

Andreas, Kouros, and Tassos sat outside a *cafenion* next to the entrance to the airport, two buildings up from the police station.

"Is your plane on time?" said Tassos.

"Far as I know," said Andreas.

"We'll see it coming in from Athens. It drops off one load of passengers, fills up with another, and heads straight back," said Kouros.

"I've heard the Athens-Mykonos trip is the most profitable per mile airline route in Europe," said Andreas.

"Everyone tries to find a way to get rich off of Mykonos. It's like a curse," said Tassos. "Whether honest or dishonest, they all come here to make money from its tourists."

"My bet is whatever Sergey has in mind it won't be honest." Andreas raised his coffee cup. "Here's to hoping we figure out what that is before he does it." He took a sip and put the cup back on the table. "Wish we could stay, but I've got to get back to the office."

"Yeah, Chief, if you stay away too long people might start to realize who really runs the office."

Andreas smiled, "Are you trying to get Tassos to put in a good word for you with Maggie?"

"Wouldn't hurt."

"You're wasting your time, she'd never believe me anyway," said Tassos.

"Let's just keep an eye on Sergey. And let Wacki know we're watching him so he doesn't get cocky," said Andreas.

Tassos nodded. "But, as you said, I'm afraid we won't know what Sergey's next move is until he makes it."

"You don't think Wacki might talk?" said Kouros.

Tassos gestured no. "Even if he would, I think Sergey's smart enough not to trust him with anything that really mattered."

"I think the only real shot we have at finding out what he's up to is through the two guys with the girl who killed Christos," said Andreas.

"Sergey must know that, too," said Kouros.

Andreas nodded. "Which means if Europol doesn't find them first Sergey is home free."

"Damnit," said Kouros. "I wish I knew what the son-of-a-bitch was up to."

"We will," said Andreas. "The only question is 'when?'"

"And 'how?'" said Tassos

Andreas stood up and nodded toward the sky. "Let's go, Yianni, here comes our plane. Athens awaits our return."

"As Mykonos mourns."

◇◇◇

The call came into the police station in the early afternoon and the caller asked to speak to the chief of police.

Mihalis answered on the first ring. "Yes?"

"Is this the chief of police?"

"Yes."

"This is Wacki. I'm calling on behalf of my employer, Sergey Tishchenko. You met him this morning in the mayor's office."

Now what? thought Mihalis. "What can I do for you?"

"As you know, my employer doesn't speak Greek so he asked me to pass along something you might find interesting in connection with the investigation of the murder of Christos."

"It's not my case."

"I know, but you are the only one he knows to contact."

"Have him call Tassos Stamatos on Syros."

"That might be a problem."

"Problem? What sort of problem."

"Well, right after my employer left the meeting with you and the mayor he was confronted at his hotel by Tassos Stamatos, Andreas Kaldis, and a detective Kouros. From his conversation with them, he had the distinct impression there was something else the killers were after."

"So?"

"And those police had whatever it was."

"Why would they tell that to your employer?"

"I don't know. But, like you, my employer thought it strange for them to think he would have an interest in what they had. It may be an innocent remark that he misunderstood, and whatever they were talking about was part of the official file on the investigation. He just didn't want there to be any misunderstandings with you or the mayor on his commitment to being a legitimate businessman in this community. He had an unfair scrape with the law before and doesn't want that being used by anyone to imply he's not pursuing this opportunity on the up and up."

Jesus, thought Mihalis. *Was that why Tassos showed up here this morning? If he was fishing for what the mayor knew about whatever the killers were looking for...* "Thank you. I appreciate your call."

"You're welcome. Always happy to help."

Mihalis hung up the phone. There were always rumors that Christos must have had something on a lot of people to be able to run his club as he did for so long. *Shit, if Tassos found it... and didn't turn it in.*

He shook his head. He hated going after cops. And if super-clean Kaldis was involved, this was a problem way above Mihalis' pay grade.

Before he breathed a word about this to anyone, he better make damn sure there's something to it. Otherwise, goodbye pension.

◇◇◇

"Keria."

The maid turned to face the man's voice. Mihalis stood inside the doorway of a large living area she was cleaning. Next to him stood the maid's boss.

"Excuse me for bothering you at work. I tried you at home but you weren't there and it's urgent I speak with you immediately."

The boss shook her finger at the maid."He won't tell me what this is about. If you're in any sort of trouble you can take your things and get out of here right now."

"I can assure you this is not about her or anyone in her family. Now if you'd please excuse us, I'd like to speak to her alone."

"I'm not used to being told what to do in my own home," she snarled.

Mihalis smiled. "If you'd prefer I can spend the time checking whether or not that stairway I saw when I came in leads to an illegal basement."

She glared at the maid. "If my husband is fined because you brought the police into our house, you're fired!" She spun around and walked out of the room.

"Seems like a real charmer to work for."

The maid did not respond.

Mihalis nodded. "I understand. You need this job. Times are tough. Let me get to the point. It's about your former employer, Christos Vasilakis."

"I told everything I know to the other policemen."

He nodded again. "I'm sure. But I just want to go over a few things to make certain that they didn't miss anything. Please, sit down." He motioned toward a chair.

She gestured no. "Madam does not allow me to sit on her furniture."

"Very well." He cleared his throat. "What I want to go over is what you told the policeman from Syros."

"You mean the older man?"

"Yes, the older fat man."

"I told him the same things I told the other police. I came into the house, saw Mister Christos on the floor, called the police, and sat with him until they arrived."

"Did he ask if you knew where Christos kept things in his house?"

"What sort of things?"

"Valuables."

"I told him, in the safe."

"The one in the bedroom?"

The maid hesitated for an instant. "Yes."

He paused. "Was there another place Christos kept valuable things?"

One of her eyes began to twitch. "I don't know what you mean?"

He walked to a couch next to where the maid stood and sat down. For thirty seconds he stared directly up and into her eyes without saying a word.

"Unless you want me to tell your employer you're withholding evidence in connection with the robbery and murder of your former employer, I suggest you tell me *now* precisely what you told the Syros cop about any other place where Christos kept his valuables."

She shut her eyes and dropped her head. "In the wall next to the living room fireplace. Under white marble tiles."

"Hi, honey, I'm home," Andreas yelled from the entry foyer of their apartment.

He heard a loud whine coming at him from the next room. It sounded like a missile. Around the corner it came, headed straight at him. He bent down, waited until it was right upon him, and swooped it into the air, spinning it round and round above his head. The whine turned to laugher and spurts of, "Daddy home, daddy home."

"You sure know how to draw a crowd, my darling," said Lila walking into the foyer. "But be careful, I was in the middle of changing Tassaki's diaper. He's likely armed and dangerous."

"So, what else is new?"

"Was Mykonos that bad?"

"Just business as usual. Bad guys and bizarre behavior." Andreas kissed Tassaki on the cheek, nibbled at his belly, and put him down on the floor. Tassaki shot off in the direction of his mother but went right by her.

"Marietta will intercept him before he can do much damage."

Andreas put his hands on Lila's waist and kissed her on the lips.

"The kid gets a whole spin in the air and the mother just a peck?"

Andreas smiled. "He came at me naked."

Lila laughed. "Any news on finding Christos' killers?"

Andreas gestured no. "Just that the Russian guy I'm convinced must be behind it all turned up bold as brass on Mykonos looking to buy the Asteria hotel."

"Did Christos have anything to do with that hotel?"

"Nothing."

"Is the Russian trying to take over Christos' club?"

"Not that I know of."

"Then why do you think he had anything to do with Christos murder?"

"He shared the same girlfriend with Christos and we know the girlfriend was involved in his murder. She went to visit someone in Poland a couple of times right after this guy, Sergey, got out of a Polish prison. On her last visit, and a few days after Christos murder, she turned up dead in Sergey's city. Too many coincidences."

"Are you sure she went to visit him?"

He gestured no. "But Christos' maid once overheard her talking to someone named Sergey as if he were a boyfriend about arrangements to visit him in the same town in Poland where our Sergey lived."

"That's it?"

"What are you, a prosecutor? I'm talking police instincts here. Yes, I know we don't have a case yet. But we will. When things start to break they'll break quickly. You'll see."

Lila, shrugged. "You know best about those sorts of things." She kissed him on the cheek and whispered in his ear. "Marietta is watching Tassaki. Follow me and I'll show you where your baby boy learned how to greet his daddy."

Andreas ran his hand along Lila's bottom. "I thought you'd never ask."

Chapter Eighteen

Some said that between Greece's financial crisis and a nearly ten dollars per gallon price of gas, Athens traffic was much lighter than it once was. But to Andreas this morning's commute was as bad as ever. Perhaps he was only anxious to get back to his office. His unit was terrific, but he was the engine that drove the investigations, and things piled up whenever he was away, even for a few days.

His phone rang. It was Maggie.

"Yes, my love, what can I do for you?"

"Where are you?"

"Almost at headquarters. Traffic's a bitch. Can this wait until I get there?"

"No, turn around and head to the ministry. The minister wants to see you right away."

What the hell does Spiros want now? Always with the drama. "Did he say what it's about?"

"No, he just sounded nervous."

"In other words it has to do with the press. His whole world is driven by what the media says about him."

"Well, whatever it is, there's nothing in the papers or on television about it yet."

Maggie had a 24/7 ear for the news. If she didn't know about it, it wasn't out there.

"Well, then, so far so good."

◇◇◇

It took Andreas another twenty minutes of weaving through traffic to reach the ministry. His lights and siren were practically useless.

When he finally reached the ministry he went straight to the minister's office and the secretary showed him right in.

"Chief Kaldis is here."

"Thank you. Please, leave us and hold all my calls. No matter who it may be."

When she left Andreas said, "Sounds serious."

Spiros pointed to the chair in front of his desk. "You have no idea. Or at least I hope you don't."

Andreas sat in the chair. "What the hell was that supposed to mean?"

Spiros bit at his lip. A sure sign he was frightened.

"Come on, Spiros, it can't be that bad. We've been through a lot worse."

Spiros ran his hands through his color-enhanced, thinning, jet-black hair. "It's about your friend, Tassos."

"Tassos?"

"He's gone rogue."

"What the hell are you talking about?"

"Andreas, I know how close you are to him. But we all know his history. A little business on the side to enhance his lifestyle is wellknown."

"Not to me it isn't." *At least not since we've been friends.*

"I'm afraid he's been caught red-handed. And, frankly…" Spiros reached into his desk, took a pill from a bottle, and swallowed it without water. "Frankly, circumstantial evidence has you and Kouros involved in it with him."

Andreas drew a deep breath. He did not want to respond in anger. "Why don't you just tell me what you're talking about?"

"Early this morning I received a call from the chief of police on Mykonos. Tassos had paid him a visit yesterday about the Christos Vasilakis murder."

Andreas shrugged. "Why wouldn't he? It's his case."

Spiros nodded. "Later that same day the police chief received a call from someone representing…" Spiros looked at some notes on his desk, "Sergey Tishchenko, who said you and Kouros had spoken with him about the same case."

"He's a potential suspect."

"But why would you, the Athens-based head of Special Crimes, be involved with an investigation into a murder on Mykonos where everyone knows who did it and one of the killers is already dead?"

"If you know so much about the case, then you should also know that Sergey Tishchenko was the dead girl's ex-boyfriend."

"Yes, I know all about that, and his prison record, and that she went to visit someone in Bialystok. The same town Tishchenko gave as his address when he got out of prison and where she turned up murdered."

"How do you know that?"

Spiros raised his voice. "In case you've forgotten, I'm the minister of this department." He swallowed. "The police chief tracked down the maid who'd found the body. She told him about the girlfriend's phone call. He also interviewed Sergey, who disclosed his record saying he had nothing to hide from the police."

"Did he also say the girlfriend came to see *him* in Poland?"

"He said the last time he saw her was before he went to prison, and that she had a lot of boyfriends in Bialystok. She was a prostitute there and her arrest record confirms that. She could have gone to see any of them. Or all of them."

"And just by coincidence he happens to end up on Mykonos with enough money to buy a hotel?"

"He said everybody in Poland knows Mykonos is the place to come to make a fortune, and that he'd mentioned the possibility of his moving to Mykonos to her before he was arrested. She went to Mykonos because of him, not the other way around. As far as the money goes, these days who are we to ask where money comes from if people are willing to invest in Greece? As long, of course, as it isn't tied into Christos' murder. Do you have any reason to think that it is?"

"What does all this have to do with Tassos?"

"And you."

Andreas leaned forward in the chair. "You're beginning to piss me off."

Spiros held up his hands. "Andreas, I think of us like brothers. I am having this conversation with you because of that. If you're going to be your normal belligerent self it will only make things worse."

Andreas squeezed the arms of the chair. "Make what worse?"

"The maid told the police chief there was a second safe in Christos' house. Tassos' report made no mention of that second safe. And the maid said he told her to 'keep that second safe just between us.'"

Andreas' hands froze to the chair.

"Does that come as a surprise to you?"

"I repeat my question, Spiros, 'What does this have to do with Tassos?'" He paused. "And me?"

"Come on Andreas, if Tassos emptied that safe and didn't report it…" Spiros waved his hand in the air. "Everybody knows the rumor that Christos was blackmailing a lot of important people, and if Tassos found what Christos had on them, why wouldn't he use it to do the same?"

Andreas wanted to defend Tassos, tell Spiros the truth about what he'd found and why they hadn't disclosed it. But Spiros could be a tricky bastard. No telling how he might play that. He could keep the files for his own use, make himself look good by telling the press that he'd uncovered corruption in his own department and purged it, or just hold Andreas' admission of complicity over his head for the rest of his life.

"Andreas, did you hear me? Do you have anything to say?"

Perhaps I should just say the obvious, he thought. That it was Tassos' word against the maid's as to whether she ever told him about a second safe.

"I think there are some nuances here that you're missing, Spiros. For example—"

Spiros yelled, "You and your buddy are in deep shit, Andreas! Don't lecture me about 'nuances.' Yes or no, did the maid tell Tassos about that second safe?"

An alarm went off in Andreas' head. It was time to play defense. "I think you should ask Tassos."

"Why can't *you* answer that question?"

"Because I don't know."

Spiros shook his head. "I'm so sorry you said that. I'd hoped to help you. But I see you're just as guilty as Tassos."

Andreas said nothing.

"The police chief had the safe opened. It was empty." He paused as if waiting for Andreas to say something.

Andreas sat quietly.

"You have nothing to say?"

"Just listening."

"Well maybe you'd like to read something instead."

Spiros handed him a forensic report. It described what was found inside the safe. No contents and no prints, except for a thumb at the inside top of the door and a partial on fingers along the door's top edge.

"As you'll see, the safe was wiped clean except for where it appears whoever wiped it down held onto the top of the door, perhaps to help himself up."

Spiros handed Andreas a second report. "This ID on the prints came in this morning just before I called your office. Guess whose they are?"

Andreas didn't have to ask.

"We have your buddy tied up in a neat little bundle all ready for the prosecutor. And you, too, if you don't cooperate and tell me all about this scam you're running."

Andreas stood. "With all due respect, Minister, I think I'll leave now."

"Don't you dare leave. I have you on tape saying you knew nothing about the second safe."

"I don't know what you're talking about, Minister. You asked if 'the maid told Tassos about the second safe.' How would

I possibly know that? I wasn't there. I think you owe me an apology."

Spiros' face turned bright red.

"You better take another pill. You don't look well."

"Kaldis, you are suspended as of this minute!"

Andreas stared Spiros directly in the eyes and spoke without emotion. "You're the minister, you can do that. Just be careful what you say to the press. There may not be enough pills in your drawer to cover what could happen if you said the wrong things."

Andreas walked out of Spiros' office and through the ministry's halls as if alone in a soundless tunnel. He heard none of the hellos or saw any of the waves of those he passed. His focus was on reaching the car, getting inside, and driving. Anywhere. Just driving.

He tried not to think about his father. He thought about his mother, about his wife, about his son, and about his sister. But not about his father.

A half hour passed until he pulled over and parked. It was a quiet street and Andreas sat staring straight ahead for a few minutes before opening the door. He got out and walked to a tree-shaded knoll. The sun was brilliant yellow and the sky ablaze in blue. Andreas dropped his head and stared down at a grave.

"I never forgave you for taking your life, for leaving us alone. I blamed myself for not being able to stop you. But what could I have done as an eight-year-old? But now I'm a man. And I've failed you again."

He drew in and let out a deep breath.

"Is this how you felt, Dad? Set up and called corrupt for bribes to someone else when all you'd ever tried to do was the right thing for your country and family?

"Is this how you felt when betrayed and destroyed by your own? Does it matter that your assassin was a crooked, scheming minister, while mine is just an arrogant, disloyal coward? I'll end up in the same place as you, destroyed by the press in a rush of 'LIKE FATHER LIKE SON' headlines."

He drew in another deep breath. "How will mother be able to stand it again? How will Lila…Tassaki." Tears welled up in his eyes.

"I tried so hard to make you proud, Dad. To redeem your name." He struggled to contain the tears, but they came just the same. "I've failed you. I've failed everyone."

Andreas stood by the grave staring off toward the horizon when his phone rang. He didn't want to answer it. There was no one he wanted to talk to. He let it ring until it went into voice mail. It rang again. He ignored it again. Once more it rang and once more he ignored it, but this time he pulled it out of his pocket to shut it off. It rang in his hand. It was Maggie. He paused, and pressed ANSWER.

"Yes."

"Andreas, I don't know what's going on, and there's no time to ask you. Three goons just showed up to take possession of all our files on the Christos Vasilakis murder investigation."

Andreas felt his heart sink. Spiros was doing what he had to do to crucify him. *I'd do the same thing.*

"Andreas, are you there?"

"Yes."

"I told them no one gets access to anything in Special Crimes' files without your permission. They said they had the permission of the minister and that you were suspended. I said, 'I didn't give a shit, I wasn't suspended and without permission from Chief Kaldis, no one gets to see those files.'"

Andreas almost felt a smile. "What happened?"

"They tried to get into your office but I blocked the door and yelled at them to leave."

"They left?"

"No, they tried to push me out of the way."

"Are you okay?"

"Me yes, them no."

"What happened?"

"Yianni heard me yelling and came out of his office like a bull. I almost felt sorry for the three assholes. Two of them had to carry the third one away. They said they'd be back with warrants."

"How's Yianni?"

"Fine. He told them real cops don't push women around. And if they come back they better know how to fly out a window."

Andreas did smile. "Maggie—"

"Don't bother saying a thing. We figured it out. It's all taken care of. Take care of yourself. We know you'll straighten things out. You're our chief and we're all behind you one hundred percent, no matter what you decide."

Tears welled again in Andreas' eyes.

"Thank you."

"We love you. Now call your wife."

Chapter Nineteen

Lila was waiting for Andreas when the elevator door opened in their apartment's entry foyer. "I told the doorman to let me know the moment you were home. Maggie called. Are you okay?"

Andreas gestured no. "Sorry I didn't call. I decided it was better to come home and tell you the news in person. I've been outthought, outflanked, set up, and, to put it succinctly, royally fucked by that bastard Sergey."

"Maggie said you're suspended?"

He nodded yes. "Spiros, jumped to a conclusion that is reasonable but idiotic if he actually trusted me. He's trying to make a case against Tassos, and now me, of stealing information that could blackmail virtually every powerful person in Greece."

"Maybe you should use some of it to blackmail him?"

"The thought did pass through my mind, but even if I could, things are too far along for that. I'm just waiting for the story to break in the press. Which reminds me. I need to tell my mother, prepare her for all of this." He shook his head.

Lila took his arm and led him into the living room. They sat on a couch facing the Acropolis. She put her head against his chest.

"Darling, your mother loves you. She's very proud of you. Tassaki and I are, too, this will change nothing."

"Of course it will. I'll be vilified worse than my father. It will destroy her. It will destroy all of us. I don't even want to think about what it will do to your reputation."

"Think about it all you want. I couldn't care less what those small-minded, jealous bastards think. They live for bad news about other people's lives. Jealousy is the Greek national curse. None of that matters to me."

"Yeah, but what if he makes a case and I go to prison?"

"I'll bake cookies."

"Cute, but I'm being serious."

"So am I. If Greece doesn't want you we'll go somewhere that does."

He paused. "There is something else you should know, because my decision affects your life at least as much as it does mine. At one point Spiros offered me a way out, and it's probably still available."

"What do you have to do?"

"Turn on Tassos."

Lila lifted her head off of Andreas' chest and leaned away from him.

"You're not thinking of doing that, are you?"

"No, but I wanted you to know that the offer was made."

"Good, because if you did I could never live with you."

"That makes both of us who couldn't live with me."

"What are you going to do?"

"I don't know yet. First thing is to speak to Tassos and Yianni."

"What about a lawyer?"

"That, too, I guess. Damnit. I'm not used to playing defense. It makes me feel helpless. I've got to come up with a plan before Spiros goes public with this."

"What about your suspension? It's bound to get out to the press."

"Until Spiros has proof to make the charges stick, he'll be too afraid to say anything that might embarrass him if he ends up with no one to prosecute. All he has now are Tassos' prints on an empty safe and nothing to corroborate there ever was anything inside.

"What I'm worried about are television crews chasing after me for video. They'll run the same loop of me over and over on the nightly news while sanctimonious, talking-head anchors demand that the ministry stop 'covering up a scandal' involving the head of Special Crimes. That's the sort of pressure that could get Spiros defensive enough to say something stupid and ignite a media frenzy that would ruin my reputation no matter what comes of any prosecution."

"Sounds like you should hide out. Some place where you can be alone with your thoughts and come up with a plan. No need to worry about us. We'll be fine."

"But if I disappear the media might say I took off because I'm guilty."

"If the press wants to call you guilty they'll do it anyway, but at least they won't be stalking you with cameras. And if Spiros wants to find you, he knows he can reach you through me."

Andreas nodded, "Aren't you worried about my being alone? That I might need a suicide watch?"

She gestured no, her face expressionless. "Never even entered my mind. How many times have you told me you've been haunted all your life, wondering how different your life might have been if your father had lived, if he'd stood up to the 'bastard' who set him up to look corrupt?"

Lila shook her head. "No, the man I married would never subject his son to that same lifetime ordeal."

Andreas pulled her back against his chest and kissed her forehead. "Have I told you how much I love you?"

Lila stood up and tugged on Andreas' arm. "Me too. Come. It's time to wake your son. He misses his daddy."

It was late afternoon when Tassos and Kouros arrived at Andreas' apartment.

"I was wondering when you'd get here. Couldn't reach either of you all day."

"We decided not to call you," said Tassos. "Our phones might be tapped now that we've lost our security clearances with the ministry."

"You've been suspended, too?"

Tassos nodded. "I was summoned back to Athens this morning. Spiros even sent a helicopter for me. It was a really bullshit presentation. He actually expected me to believe that you and Yianni had turned on me."

"He tried," said Kouros. "Even promised not to prosecute me for what I did to those three pricks who went after Maggie. I told him, 'Go right ahead. It should make great press that on the ministry's orders a little old lady was brutally attacked by three men trying to force their way into her boss' office and the only person prosecuted was a cop who came to her assistance.'"

"I suggest you leave out the 'little old lady' bit if you ever tell that story to Maggie," said Andreas.

"Why? Maggie's the one who told me to say it. She's as angry as a mama bear protecting her cubs. God protect Spiros from her wrath."

Andreas nodded. "He tried to get me to turn, too."

"Of course he tried. And, frankly, if either of you think testifying against me might save your careers I want you to do it. You're both a lot younger than I am and have your families to consider. Besides, with what I have on every judge and prosecutor I'll never get any jail time. The most I'd lose is my pension, and from the haircuts the government keeps giving them, there's not much left to lose there."

Andreas stared at Tassos. "My friend, I know you're upset that your declining years caused you to leave those prints on the safe, but you're not going to get off so easy for that screw-up. Yianni and I intend to remind you of it every time you say how dumb some bad guy is."

"Yeah, I can't wait to start, old man." Kouros smiled.

Tassos lowered his eyes and shook his head. "I really did screw up. Sorry."

"Hell, look at the bright side," said Andreas. "Now Sergey has us all really angry at him."

"So what are we going to do about it?" said Kouros.

"Not sure yet, but whatever it is we better act fast. It's only a matter of time until Spiros gets someone who can testify about what was in that safe," said Andreas.

"And who would that be?" said Tassos.

"The coroner, the guy you had open the safe, anyone who was there when it was opened. You can't expect them all to cover for you," said Andreas.

Tassos smiled, "You're right, I couldn't. That's why there was nobody with me when I opened it. As soon as the safe was unlocked I had everyone leave. I'm the only one who saw the contents." Tassos smiled. "I'm not that dumb. Just too weak in the knees to get up out of a crouch without hanging onto something."

"Son of a bitch," said Kouros.

"I've learned over the years that certain aspects of police work require a 'protect your own ass' approach."

"Where's the stuff now?" said Andreas.

"Where not even my mother could find it," said Kouros. "And Lord knows I've had enough practice hiding things from her. Maggie threw everything into a backpack, gave it to me, and told me get the hell out of the office before Spiros' reinforcements arrived."

"The only way I see to get Spiros off our backs is by proving Sergey was behind Christos' murder," said Tassos. "And that means finding the two guys who killed him before Sergey does."

"Europol's working on it," said Andreas.

"I'll put out word on the Eastern European bad guy grapevine and see what that turns up," said Tassos.

"What are you talking about?" said Kouros.

"Drug and human traffickers are always passing through Greece from the Balkans and further east. And they're constantly exchanging information with their contacts and business partners here. It's vital for their personal and business health to know who's doing what in their spheres of interest. We just have to hope that somehow the two killers are known to someone on that web so that we can get a line on them."

"Couldn't Sergey find them the same way?" said Kouros.

"If he has the right connections, yes."

"And you do?" said Kouros.

"Let me worry about that."

"What do you want me to do, Chief?"

"Go fishing."

"Huh?"

"Pack a bag and meet me here at midnight. We're taking off for parts unknown."

"And where exactly is that?"

"'I could tell you, but then I'd have to kill you,'" said Andreas.

"Tom Cruise in *Top Gun*," said Kouros.

Tassos smiled, "Better that than *Mission Impossible*."

Things were going quite nicely, thought Sergey. The hotel owner agreed to sell, the memorandum of understanding was signed and submitted to the ministry of tourism, and the mayor was on board as much as Sergey could hope for.

He took a sip of water and studied the grounds surrounding his table in the hotel's poolside garden restaurant. There were a lot of changes to make here. But once he had the right politicians on board this place would be a gold mine. No, a diamond mine. It would change Mykonos forever.

He looked at his watch. It was almost midnight. Wacki was supposed to be here by now with news on whether the cops had a line on the two guys he'd sent with Anna to kill Christos. Sergey's own contact had turned up nothing.

He didn't want to have to ask Teacher for help on this. She only wanted to hear good news. And that's all he intended to give her.

"Hi, Boss." Wacki dropped into the chair across from Sergey and waved at a waitress for a drink.

"What did you find out?"

"Nothing about the two guys. The police have no idea where they are. Europol traced them to Bialystok but lost them when the girl turned up dead. Their best guess is they had a falling out, and the two guys iced her and took off."

Damn, thought Sergey.

"I understand why you might be concerned that your old girlfriend and her buddies are killers, but there's no way they're coming back to this island. So, if I were you I'd relax."

Sergey stared at Wacki until Wacki fidgeted in his chair.

"But I do have some good news. Your idea on that call to the police chief worked wonders."

"Tell me."

"Rumor is that all three cops have been suspended."

"Why?"

"There was a second safe in Christos' house, one that wasn't mentioned in that Syros cop's report."

"What was inside?"

"No one knows."

Good, thought Sergey.

"But now the safe's empty."

Even better news.

"Sounds like Stamatos and his buddies are facing jail time. Cops are afraid of prison. Too many enemies inside looking to settle a score. They'll be too busy trying to save their own asses to be any more trouble for us."

All I have to do is find a way to squeeze those cops until they realize the only move left for them is to turn over Christos' files to me.

Sergey took another sip of water. Things, indeed, were going quite nicely.

Wacki had called Teacher twice today. All was going according to plan though she wondered why Sergey had Wacki checking up on the two men who murdered Christos. If he were worried the police might find them, the two should be killed.

She looked at the photograph of the young girl on her desk. "I pray for the day there no longer will be a need for violent acts. But violence is the nature of the godless creatures with which we grapple every day. It is ironic, it is tragic, but to do battle with the devil you must be prepared to do what even the devil dare not consider. Then the devil will deal."

She reached out and stroked the girl's face. Sergey knows all of that, she thought. He has since he was five. It was how he survived the violence of the orphanage and his years of abuse at the hands of slave-masters who called themselves foster parents. They were much alike in many ways.

My escape was a marriage. His was the army.

Teacher withdrew her hand from the photograph.

He did not know she was aware of his past. But she hoped he realized a new road was open to him. One that could lead to harmony in his life, allow him to achieve great things, and be acknowledged for his deeds. It was a step of destiny that only he could take. No matter how he suffered in his youth or sinned thereafter to survive, this was his chance at a blessed future.

She cleared her throat. "We shall see."

Chapter Twenty

Andreas and Kouros made it from the apartment to the harbor town of Vouliagmeni south of Athens in thirty minutes. This was Greece's most exclusive marina, where the rich and mega-rich kept their private yachts. The forty-eight-foot Uniesse's engines roared to life the moment the two cops stepped out of the taxi. The two jumped on board, cast off the mooring lines, and were underway.

"It should take us less than three hours to reach Lia," said the captain.

"I really appreciate this, Zanni," said Andreas.

"Appreciate what? An excuse for me to get out of the house for a moonlight, full-throttle sprint across a calm sea? I'm the one who should be thanking you."

Andreas laughed and smacked him on the back. "I also appreciate your keeping this just between us."

"No problem. Like I said, I should be thanking you."

The nearly full moon had turned the sea to silver glass, spewed out as diamonds in the breaking wake of the ship.

Andreas whispered to Kouros. "When you see the world looking as serenely at peace as it does tonight, it's pretty hard to imagine all the deep shit we're in."

"Yeah, but did I hear him right? Are we headed to Lia beach, on *Mykonos*? We may as well have stayed in Athens."

"Relax. Lia's on the island's southeast corner, far away from all the late night craziness, and with any luck we'll be in and out of there long before any early risers are around to notice us."

"But Mykonos is the first place the press will look for you when they can't find you in Athens."

"We're not staying at Lila's parents' house. That's where they'll look. We're using the home of American friends. They won't be back until September. Their house is isolated at the top of a rutted, dirt mountain road far away from any beach. No tourist ever goes up there except by mistake, and the neighbors can't see a thing over the walls surrounding the place."

"Sounds like Meteora."

Kouros was referring to the community of soaring, massive gray stone pillars in central Greece where for more than a thousand years many sought monastic seclusion among its virtually inaccessible heights.

"Not quite, we won't have to hoist ourselves up in baskets. Lila arranged for one of her parents' cars to be left by the beach."

"I sure hope this works."

"The house has television, so if it doesn't, I'm sure the networks will tell us."

◇◇◇

The house sat high above the sea, facing south across the relatively undeveloped far southeastern shoreline of Mykonos. Centuries-old walls ran down from the property toward the sea, marking boundaries, holding back erosion, shading goats from the sun, and offering sanctuary to lizards from predators.

Its owners had taken great care to build in keeping with the habitat. The gardens were desert-like, with natural stone and unpainted wood featured in everything they built. The property literally faded into the mountain, and to find it even those who knew where it was often had to think, "Look just below and to the right of the mountaintop radar station."

The sun was still low in the eastern sky, and Andreas sat outside having coffee on a stone terrace spanning the south side of the house.

"Couldn't sleep?" asked Kouros coming out onto the terrace with a cup of coffee in his hand.

"I'm a bit wound up."

"I bet."

Kouros stared at a span of islands spread out across a rose-blue sea running off to the horizon. "What a view."

"Sure is. Makes it worthwhile getting up at dawn." Andreas took a sip of coffee. "I've been trying to figure out which ones they are. I recognize Naxos and Paros off to the west."

"I was in the navy and used to know that stuff. Let me see if I still remember them." Kouros stared east for about a half minute.

"Okay, the one way off in the distance to the left is Ikaria. It gets a lot of play in the foreign press about a relaxed lifestyle that has quite a few Ikarians living to be over a hundred."

"Mykonians say that's because they're just too bored on Ikaria to bother to die."

Kouros laughed. "The next one is only about six or seven miles from here. It's uninhabited, all rock and cliffs, and the locals call it Stapodia. Beyond it is Donousa, and off to its right but so far away it's hard to make out even on a clear day is Amorgos. You were right about the last two, Naxos is across from us and Paros is next to it on the right."

"Well done, sailor. Now, could you tell me when that rash of white overrunning those beaches to the right of us is going to spread over here and kill this view."

Kouros pointed to some dots of white along the beaches directly below them. "The infection has already started." He took a sip of coffee. "Build, build, build."

"That's been our countrymen's mantra since the eighties. It's all about the money. Either having it or giving the impression that you do. And for those with that mindset, building a house on Mykonos was a surefire way of showing yourself part of the in-crowd, or able to spend as if you were."

"Tell me about it. The other night I met a woman in a nightclub and when I told her I was a cop who spent time on Mykonos she thought I was loaded. But as soon as I told her I was an honest cop she walked out on me."

Andreas laughed. "I assume you wanted her to go."

"Well, to be honest, I told her that last part *after*."

Andreas shook his head and grinned. "What the hell has happened to us, my friend. 'Nothing in excess' once was Greece's guiding principle. Now it's, 'Nothing is ever enough.'"

"I wonder what the Mykonian perspective is on all this?" Kouros spread out his arms and waved them in the direction of the beaches below.

"I'm not sure there is a 'Mykonian perspective' on things these days beyond one they share with the rest of Greece over how this financial catastrophe will end."

Andreas sipped his coffee and stared at the sea. "But Lila once told me something about Mykonos that might help answer your question."

"Go for it."

"For most of their history Mykonians were an overlooked people living in poverty under a range of different foreign occupiers, some good, some not. They saw their families slaughtered, carried off as slaves, die from strange diseases brought to their island from foreign lands, and starve to death.

"They also witnessed the rise of the greatest civilization of its time within a mile of their island, on a place one twenty-fifth Mykonos' size, where hundreds of years before the birth of Christ more than twice as many people lived as currently do on Mykonos. In its day Delos was the place to be and to party, filled with lavish homes, temples, theaters, athletic facilities and places of commerce far outstripping any comparable lifestyle on Mykonos today.

"But in the blink of an eye it all was gone. Leveled, destroyed, wiped off the face of the earth for having made an unwise political choice.

"As Mykonians, they live amid constant reminders of that precipitous past, for the marble and much of the carved stone that embellishes their homes and churches today comes from Delos' razed civilization of two thousand years ago.

"So, I guess if there is a 'Mykonian perspective' to be applied to our times it's that although their island has prospered and will likely survive our nation's current crisis far better than anywhere else in Greece, '*all fame is fleeting, all glory fades*.' In time, new occupiers will come to their island bringing new ideas and different methods. When that will occur and whether the transition will be glorious or not, who can say? But it will happen. Always has, always will."

Kouros nodded. "That's a bit heavy for this early in the morning. I could have used more coffee. But if you want my opinion on what drives this place it's simple. The locals may bitch and moan about what's happened to their island but they've let it happen for one very simple reason."

"Which is?"

"Precisely what we were talking about before. They like the money. Period. End of story."

Andreas looked back at the sea. "I see things somewhat differently. But you have a point. One that makes me think perhaps we're going at Sergey the wrong way."

"What do you mean?"

"We're focused on finding the two guys who murdered Christos, but even if we do and they finger Sergey, it's their word against his. It might screw up his plans for going into business here, because whether he's guilty or not, once accused, the locals will drive him off the island, but it won't put him away. To really hurt that bastard we have to reach the core of what's driving him."

"And how do we do that?"

"Follow the money. It can't be Sergey's. There must be somebody bankrolling him. If we find where the money's coming from, we might have a better idea of where it's headed."

"We already know he's buying the hotel."

Andreas shook his head. "Not nearly enough of a return for all the shit he's stirring up. It's got to be something else. Something much bigger."

"So, where do we start?"

"With another cup of coffee and more staring at the sea. Not quite sure yet how we'll get there without access to the Europol resources I had as Chief."

Kouros smiled. "We still have Tassos."

"And Maggie."

"Wonder what they're up to?"

"Hopefully, something a lot more productive than we are," said Andreas.

"Speak for yourself. I intend on spending the afternoon working on my tan."

"Probably about as good a plan as any while we wait for the next round of shit to hit the fan." Andreas put down his coffee cup. "I just wish I knew who the hell was going to throw it."

Sergey sat eating breakfast in his room. He would liked to have had it in a taverna or *cafenion* along the port, but even with his poor Greek he could tell that the moment he walked into one he instantly became the topic of conversation. It was to be expected. Small towns and islands were like that, always looking for new subjects of interest for the gossip mill.

But he figured the less he showed his face around town the less talk his presence stimulated. They could talk as much as they wanted later, after he had his hands on those files.

He was pissed. The two men with Anna had done just as he'd told them to do: disappear off the face of the earth. No way to find them without Teacher's help. But if he asked for her help she'd definitely ask, "Why?" Might even want to know when he expected to have Christos' files.

He couldn't risk that. He must have them before she asked. They were necessary for the next step, to do the magic that would make it all come together.

He shook his head. No way he dared do anything that might start Teacher thinking he was less than perfect.

Those two sons of bitches just better stay hidden until after he had the files. Once he did, Teacher probably would want to find the two herself, just to clear up loose ends.

He heard a knock on the door.

"Come in. It's open."

Wacki entered wearing fire engine red jeans, a different florescent yellow Hawaiian shirt, white Louis Vuitton beach sandals, and red-frame sunglasses.

"Is there any other man on the island who dresses like you?"

"There's nobody, man or woman, who dresses like Wacki."

Sergey suppressed a smile. "So, what has you up and about before noon?"

"The files you're interested in. I've been asking around. About the fat cop. And whether anybody knew anything about him and some files. I told folks there was money in it."

"And?"

"A Bulgarian cleaning lady who works at the airport called me this morning. Bitch woke me up."

"Just get to the point."

"Okay, okay. A few mornings ago she was cleaning up the baggage area to get it ready for the first flight of the day in from Athens when she heard someone forcing open the sliding doors leading into the baggage area from the terminal. It's illegal to do that but sometimes locals who don't want to wait outside for their friends do it anyway.

"It was a fat guy with a briefcase and she told him he shouldn't be in there. He thanked her for being a 'concerned citizen' but said he was a cop on official business and continued walking toward the doors leading out to the runway.

"He stood by the doors until the plane landed, then went out onto the tarmac to meet two other men coming off the plane. She recognized the other two as cops who used to work on Mykonos."

"Kaldis and Kouros?"

Wacki nodded. "Anyway, she stopped paying attention once she realized the fat man must have been a cop, too."

"That's it?"

"Not quite. An hour or so later she was working on the second floor when she saw the same three cops come out of the director of operation's office. It surprised her, because she knew the director was out of the building."

"And the briefcase?"

"Still with them."

"When did all this happen?"

Wacki smiled. "The morning after Christos' body was discovered and Tassos Stamatos conducted an investigation of the scene."

And emptied the safe, thought Sergey. "I want to meet with that Syros cop right away. But let's make it a surprise."

Chapter Twenty-one

Syros lay forty-five minutes due west of Mykonos by fast boat, in the north central region of the Cyclades. The island's architecture varied from town to town, but was heavily influenced by romantic classicism and differed substantially from traditional Cycladic forms, as did the muted, slight peach cast to its capital city of Ermoupoli.

The Zodiac entered Syros' harbor at Ermoupoli from the east, aiming toward a long concrete dock running in front of the customs house and port authority headquarters on the right side. Off to the left loomed shipyards that once were the busiest in Greece, but that was long ago. So, too, were the island's modern glory days.

Phoenicians were the first known inhabitants of Syros, naming the island from their word for "wealth," and later occupiers, pirates, and Syriots seeking precisely that same prize brought boom and bust times to the millennia that followed. Syros' last great aristocratic run, as Greece's nineteenth century ship building and repair center, ended at the close of that century with the opening of the Corinth Canal and the harbor and shipyards at Athens' port city of Piraeus.

Syros still had its stunning neo-classical buildings, streets paved with marble, and opera house—some said the first in Greece—but there was no question the glory had faded. No more than four hundred of the island's twenty-five thousand residents still worked in its shipyards and though known for agriculture, the island's main role now was as the political center of the Cyclades.

Wacki pointed beyond the shipyards at the shell of a building all the way across the semicircular harbor. "That building is *Lazaretta.* It was built in the 1840s to quarantine anyone arriving by sea who might be carrying plague. Later it was used as a prison but hasn't been in a hundred years. Maybe they'll re-open it for Stamatos and his buddies. It's probably the only prison in Greece with no one inside who wants a piece of them." He laughed.

"Where does Stamatos live?" asked Sergey.

"On the sea on the other side of the island, about four miles outside of town. It's a village called Kini. But he won't be there. My people told me that if he's not in his office at police headquarters up on that hill," Wacki pointed at building on a bluff above and to the right of the customs house, "he's usually in a taverna on a side street just off the harbor."

They tied up in front of port authority headquarters and walked toward a line of cafe umbrellas, chairs, and tables perched off to the left along a narrow concrete apron between the sea and a two-lane harborfront road. Directly across the road were the tavernas, bars, and cafes servicing those who chose to sit outdoors by the sea. Waiters darted back and forth among the two-way traffic carrying trays filled with food, drink, and the remains of both.

They crossed at a small square, turned left and walked along the harbor road for a few blocks before turning right. Dead ahead and four blocks away was City Hall. It was by far the island's most dominant building, a football field-size neoclassical beauty, sitting behind an even larger town square.

Wacki stopped at a seven-foot wide alley on the left. "Police headquarters used to be up by city hall until the government moved it onto that hill I pointed out from the harbor. But Stamatos still hangs out down here."

They turned into the alley and walked about twenty yards before Wacki stopped. "That's it. The next taverna on the left."

It was a cozy looking place set off from the quiet, white and gray marble-paved street by a line of potted oleander and tamarind.

Sergey peeked through the leaves. Three old men sat drinking coffee at a table near the front watching two younger men at a table next to them play backgammon. Toward the rear, next to the kitchen, two men at a table were talking. One looked to be a cook. The other was Tassos.

Sergey took a deep breath. "Translate *exactly* what I say, word for word. And do precisely the same thing for whatever comes out of his cop mouth, no matter what it is, even a cough. Do you understand?"

Wacki nodded.

"I said, '*Do you understand*?' "

"Yes, I understand."

"Good. Just translate. *Don't think.*"

Sergey reached behind his head, pulled out the elastic band holding his hair in a bun, and shook his head. He ran his fingers quickly through his hair and headed for the entrance to the taverna.

Tassos' eyes were fixed on Sergey from the moment he came through the taverna door headed straight at him. When Tassos saw Wacki he said, "Ah, sorry there, Sergey, didn't recognize you with your hair down."

Sergey said in English. "I would like to speak to you."

"I don't speak English very well."

"That's why Wacki is here."

"This should be fun. Okay, guys, sit down." Tassos looked at the other man at his table. "Could you excuse us, Niko?"

Niko got up and went into the kitchen.

"So, what can I do for you?" said Tassos.

Sergey leaned in and fixed his stare on Tassos' eyes. "You have something I want."

Wacki translated.

"Good choice. The coffee's terrific here. Shall I call a waiter?"

Wacki translated.

"Don't play games with me, I may be the only friend you have left in Greece."

"Thanks to you no doubt."

"Don't blame the messenger. You're the one who took what did not belong to you. Is it my fault that your police colleagues are prepared to ruin you and your two friends over something they're not even certain exists?"

"But you're certain."

"Let us say I have more faith in you than do your comrades. I do not think you would have allowed things to go this far if there wasn't something important in that briefcase."

Sergey studied Tassos' face for any change of expression as Wacki translated 'briefcase.' There was none.

"What briefcase?"

Sergey smiled. "The one you brought out onto the runway to meet your friends, Kaldis and Kouros, the morning after you found what you carried in that case."

Tassos shrugged. "I don't know what you're talking about."

"The same briefcase you and your friends spent an hour together with alone in the airport director's office."

Tassos shrugged again. "Is there a point to all this? Or are you just trying to impress me with how interested you are in my luggage? I can give you the name of the store where I bought it. It's right around the corner from here."

"I don't think you realize just how valuable an asset you possess."

Tassos smiled. "My girlfriend tells me the same thing all the time."

Sergey kept staring. "I have a serious business proposition. One that will make your girlfriend even happier. It is the kind of offer that will set you for life."

Tassos shook his head. "I hate those kinds of offers. The deal usually includes a dramatically shortened life span. In my experience people who make those sorts of offers don't like having extra partners around once they get what they want."

"I am talking about a one-time, up front payment."

"My, my, you must really want whatever you think I have. After all, I could say that I had it, take your money, and never deliver."

"You would not be so foolish as to do anything like that if you knew whose money you would be taking."

Tassos threw his hands up in front of his face. "Whoa, you mean it's not your money?"

"Does it matter? Your country is in ruins. Everyone is taking from anyone who will give. You should know that by now. If not, you must learn."

"And I bet you have the perfect teacher in mind." said Tassos.

Wacki's face turned white, and he hesitated.

"What's the matter, Wacki, don't you know the English word? It's '*teacher*.'" Tassos said his emphasized word in English.

Sergey switched his stare to Wacki. "What is he saying? And why are you talking about Teacher?"

Wacki swallowed. "He said, 'And I bet you have the perfect teacher in mind.'"

Sergey quickly refocused on Tassos. "You and your countrymen must learn to accommodate a new world order. Greece no longer has the unconditional support of the West. It must now look to the East for help. My purpose in coming here is to do great good for the people of Mykonos, to help them through difficult financial times such as they've not experienced in decades."

"Save your speech for the mayor, Sergey. Even if I were interested, I don't have what you want. And I have no idea where it is, assuming it even exists."

"I am so sorry you feel that way. Things will only get worse. You do know that, don't you?"

"What's that supposed to mean?"

Sergey looked away. "You and your friends are outcasts. You're dirty cops. And once the media is done with you, no one will do you any favors. Even your friend here will make you pay for coffee. And when you come to me later begging to make a deal, the price will be much less."

Tassos nodded and stared down at his coffee cup. "I lied before."

Sergey refixed his stare on Tassos. "How so?"

"The coffee's not that good. I won't miss it." He looked up and smiled at Sergey.

Sergey stood up from the table. "I swear on my mother that you will." He turned and stormed toward the door.

"Hey!" Tassos yelled to Wacki as he hurried to catch up with Sergey. "Tell your boss I didn't know he had a mother. But I'm sure she must be very proud."

Sergey said not a word as he marched from the taverna toward the boat. Wacki kept trying to get him to speak.

"I don't think he meant our Teacher. I was just startled when he used the word. I mean, how could he possibly know about Teacher? Who would have told him?"

Sergey glanced at Wacki. "For your sake, pray that you're right."

Wacki nodded, shut up, and concentrated on trying to keep in step with Sergey.

As they neared the boat Sergey said, "I want you to set up a meeting for me as soon as I get back to Mykonos. It has to be an out-of-the-way place where no one will see us."

"Sure, who are we meeting?"

"*We're* not meeting anyone. Just me and whoever heads the Albanian mob on Mykonos. I want a one-on-one, no witnesses meeting. Understand?"

Wacki swallowed hard. And prayed the meeting wouldn't be about him.

◇◇◇

"I hope you boys are enjoying your holiday," said Tassos.

"I think Yianni is beginning to find life as a suntan lotion tester appealing."

"Not a bad choice considering our current alternatives."

"Where are you calling from?"

"Syros. I just had a wonderful chat with Sergey and Wacki."

"Where?"

"They paid me a surprise visit while I was having coffee at my friend Niko's place."

"What did they want?"

"To make me a very rich man."

"Just you?"

"I'm sure he'd be willing to expand the crowd. Son of a bitch really wants those files. Someone must have spotted us at the airport with the briefcase and Sergey figured out what was inside. He even threatened me."

"I didn't know he spoke Greek well enough to do that."

"Wacki translated for him. Did a pretty good job too. Only one screwup so far as I could tell, and from the way he looked and Sergey reacted, it might have meant something."

"What was it?"

"Sergey was saying how I should learn to play along, and I tried pulling his chain by saying he probably knew the 'perfect teacher.' When I said 'teacher' Wacki practically choked. He didn't translate the word, and I thought he didn't know it in English. I did, so I said it in English. That set Sergey off on Wacki about why I was talking about 'teacher.' I know enough English to tell Sergey was talking about 'teacher' as if teacher were a person."

"Who's 'teacher?'"

"I don't know, I was hoping you might."

"Not a clue."

"No problem, I have a friend at Europol I can run it by. I'll give him a call when we hang up. He might know something."

"We sure could use a break."

"And soon. I hate being off the job. First time in more than—"

"I know a hundred years."

"Sure feels like it at times. Take care. I've got to get back to my coffee commitments. I'm a busy man these days. *Yiasou*."

Andreas put down the phone. It was the house phone, so unlikely to be tapped as no one other than Tassos, Lila, and Maggie knew he was there. Or so he hoped.

Time to join Yianni for some fun in the sun, he thought. Andreas hadn't been a cop for anywhere near as long as Tassos, but he knew one thing for sure: Enjoy the downtime when you could, because the monsters lurking out there would be back soon enough.

◇◇◇

Sergey stopped on a dirt path that wound east away from the windmills along a ledge overlooking the water. He stood behind the other government-built hotel in town, a modernism gem designed by legendary Greek architect Aris Konstantinidis, and looked west at a small church sitting on a rise above the sea, just below and southeast of the windmills. Wacki had picked it as the place for Sergey's one-on-one meeting with the Albanian, assuring Sergey the church would be empty and only tourists came that way at this time of day.

Besides, the Albanian was not comfortable meeting with what he called "a Russian with big ideas" at a deserted spot. Sergey couldn't blame him. Life often ended abruptly in his line of work. No reason to take chances.

But now that the meeting was over and they'd reached an understanding, things should work smoothly from here on out. Each had something the other needed.

Everything was falling into place. Too bad for those cops. They'd had their chance.

◇◇◇

When not at home or in his office at police headquarters, Tassos always parked his car at Syros' city hall in spaces reserved for government officials. Suspended or not he wasn't about to change his routine. Besides, no one would dare stop him and he didn't give a damn about whatever bullshit the media might say about him, assuming any had the balls to come to Syros and confront him.

It was close to midnight, and Tassos' plans for coffee only and an early night had turned into *ouzo*, *tsipouro*, and whiskey with friends. He generally didn't drink much, but he was pissed off and Maggie wasn't around to keep him in line. He'd spoken to his Europol contact who promised to check if they had anything on a "teacher" character and get right back to him. That was hours ago. He'd better press him first thing in the morning.

Syros streets were relatively quiet at night. Not like Mykonos. He'd made his way down the alley from the taverna, and a block or so in the direction of his parked car, when he saw two men forcing a young girl into the doorway of a vacant, old storefront.

One man had his hand over the girl's mouth. She was kicking and shaking her head as if trying to scream, but no sound came out. They disappeared inside the doorway.

Tassos pulled his gun and moved carefully along the front of the building. The windows were covered over in old newspapers. By the time he reached the doorway the attackers and girl were gone.

He tried the door knob. It turned. He pressed his hand against the door. It moved. He pushed harder and listened. He heard what sounded like a scuffle, a slap, and the ripping of clothes.

No time to call for backup. The girl would be raped before they got here.

Tassos crossed himself and stepped inside. There was enough moonlight coming through a doorway on the right side of the rear wall for him to tell he was alone in the front room. He moved slowly toward sounds coming through that same doorway: the grunting of a man and the crying of a girl.

He paused at the doorway. They had to be inside and off to the left. He drew in and let out a deep breath, and swung into the room, gun barrel first. The girl was sitting on a chair smoking a cigarette and making crying sounds. On a chair next to her was a man grunting. There were two other men in the room, each with a shotgun aimed at Tassos' head.

The four began to laugh. Tassos did not. He dropped his gun.

The girl stood, walked toward him, kicked his gun away, smiled, and ran one finger up his arm and along his back as she walked behind him. Tassos waited for what was coming. Then he felt it. A sharp needle prick in his neck.

Chapter Twenty-two

I wondered how it would end. I knew it would. With all the mistakes I've made, my crazy chances, and lousy choices I'm surprised it hasn't come sooner. Maybe I've just been trying to hurry it along? Get out of here and on to the next place. If there is a next place, I want to see my wife, my son. It's been too long.

Lord, why didn't you give us even a single day together here on earth?

Tassos' mind wandered. *Lord, is it okay if I have sex with my wife in heaven?*

He laughed at the thought. At least he thought he was laughing. But he wasn't sure if he was awake or dreaming. He heard voices in a language he did not understand.

Perhaps I'm with my son and he's talking to me? I must learn to understand him. I feel the rocking of the cradle. As if we're in it together on the day he was born. But he was in heaven on that day and I wasn't with him. Only his mother was there.

At least he wasn't alone. Or she.

I feel the rocking, son. I feel the twisting. I hear your voice. I hear the engine. I…

Tassos caught his thought.

We are in a boat moving through rough waters. It is not you in the boat, son. But these people will have me with you soon, my child. I have no doubt about that.

He thought of Maggie. *I will miss you, my love.*

The rocking stopped.

◇◇◇

Sunlight was barely above the horizon when the phone rang. Andreas tried ignoring it. Then he heard Kouros' mobile ringing in the next room. Both ringing at the same time likely meant a conference call, and that meant only one caller.

He reached for the phone and fumbled for the answer button. "Maggie, what's up?"

"Tassos is missing!"

Andreas sat up on the edge of the bed. He'd never heard panic in Maggie's voice before. But he recognized the fear from what he'd once felt in his own voice when killers stalked Lila and he could do nothing to protect her.

"How do you know?" said Kouros on his phone.

"He promised he'd call me in Athens as soon as he got home last night from the taverna. He never called."

Andreas relaxed. "Maybe he just passed out and forgot to call?"

"That's what I thought, too, and why I didn't bother to call him last night. But this morning I tried his mobile and his home phone and there was no answer."

Kouros stuck his head in Andreas' room, covered his phone with his hand, and whispered, "Maybe he got lucky and didn't make it home?"

Andreas shrugged and said to Maggie. "I'm sure he'll turn up."

"I called Niko, Tassos' friend who owns the taverna, and he said the last thing Tassos said before he left was 'I'm heading home to call Maggie.'"

"Still," said Andreas, "he could have driven home and just forgot to call. Besides, if God forbid, there was an accident I'm sure we'd have heard by now."

"*There was no accident.* I called his assistant, Adonis, and he said 'not to worry' because *Tassos' car was in the City Hall parking lot all night.* One of the patrol guys had joked to him about Tassos tying on such a big one that he probably forgot where he'd parked his car."

Andreas felt it first in the pit of his stomach.

"What should I do? I'm sure something has happened to him," said Maggie.

"Don't worry. I'll make some calls as soon as we hang up and get back to you. By the way, what's the telephone number for Tassos' friend, Niko?"

Maggie told him. "Please, call me as soon as you hear anything."

"Promise. Bye."

Andreas looked at Kouros. "That doesn't sound like Tassos."

"If he's off with some woman no one is going to tell Maggie the truth."

"I know. That's why I'm calling his friend."

Andreas dialed the number and waited.

"Hello."

"Niko?"

"Yes."

"Hi, this is Andreas Kaldis, Tassos Stamatos' friend and I—."

"Have you found him?"

The knot in Andreas' stomach was now bigger, and tighter. "I was hoping you'd tell me not to worry."

"He left here a little drunk but it wasn't anything he couldn't handle. And I know he wasn't going anywhere but home."

"Could he have stayed somewhere else last night? Perhaps with a friend in town?"

"If you mean a woman, he could have but he didn't. I'm sure of that."

"Maybe if he was drunk someone gave him a ride home and he's still sleeping it off?"

"Are you suggesting that Tassos Stamatos would admit to anyone that he was too drunk to drive home? What Greek ever admits to that? Besides, as I said before, he wasn't that drunk."

Andreas fluttered his lips. "Okay, thanks. But let me know if you hear anything."

Andreas hung up.

"If he's not at home..." Andreas let the thought drift off.

He dialed another number. "Hi, this is Chief Inspector Andreas Kaldis. I'm trying to locate Tassos Stamatos and I understand—."

"Hi, Chief, it's Adonis, I work with Tassos."

"Oh, yes, how are you, Adonis?"

"Fine, thanks. I assume you're calling about his whereabouts?"

"Yes."

"After Maggie called I asked a buddy to drive by his house and wake him up."

Andreas let out a breath. "Great! So you found him?"

"Not yet. There was no one home. The neighbors hadn't seen him either. Maybe he stayed with someone in town?"

Andreas consciously kept his voice flat. "I think we have to take this to a different level, Adonis, and quickly. According to his friend, Niko, he was alone and headed straight home."

"What are you saying?" said Adonis.

"All I can tell you is that we're working together on an investigation involving some very desperate people who think he has something they want very badly. I'm afraid we must assume that Tassos has been kidnapped."

Pause.

"I knew he was clean. What do you want us to do?"

"Retrace the steps Tassos would have taken from the taverna to his car. Speak to everyone in every building along the way and check every security camera with a glimpse of his route to see if they caught anything."

"Will do."

Andreas paused. "I'm sure I don't have to tell you this, Adonis, but if the people who have him are who I think, we have a very small window in which to find our friend alive."

"You don't. Now if you'll excuse me I have to make arrangements for the citizens of Syros to undergo a period of woefully inadequate police protection. I'll call you back on this number as soon as we have anything, but by noon at the latest. Bye."

"Bye."

"Why don't we just bust Sergey's head until he turns over Tassos?" said Kouros.

"Nothing would please me more. But he'll deny everything, and pressure from us could push him to kill Tassos sooner. As long as he thinks you and I aren't on to his tie-in to the kidnapping he has no reason to kill Tassos before getting Christos' files."

"But Tassos doesn't know where Christos' files are. I hid them. He has nothing to tell them."

Andreas nodded. "I know."

Kouros rubbed his forehead. "Maybe we should tell Sergey we're willing to trade the files for Tassos?"

"I wish it were that easy. No way he's going to let Tassos live after this, no matter what we do."

Andreas stood up, walked over to the window, and pulled back the curtain. He watched the sunlight play along the sea. "Nor can he allow us to live." Andreas turned away from the window. "He knows we'll come after him for what he did to Tassos."

"He can't just go around killing cops," said Kouros.

"Dirty cops? At least that's how he'll try to play it. And if he can't make it stick, it won't be much consolation to us if we're dead."

"We have to do something."

"Yes, and the first thing is to get protection for your family and mine. Sergey is more than capable of going after them when he can't find us."

"And second?"

"Try to convince ourselves that we have a snowball's chance in hell of finding our friend in time if his Syros buddies turn up empty."

If there's a universal brotherhood among free-world cops, what binds them together is the unstated premise that civilians don't appreciate them. And in Greece, where cops are vilified as corrupt, lazy, and inept, and targeted with stones and molotov cocktails at public demonstrations, that brotherhood is very strong.

If a Syriot ever wondered precisely how many cops were on the island's police force, all that citizen had to do was count the number of uniforms on the streets around City Hall that morning. Every cop on the island, whether on-duty, off-duty, on holiday, or out sick, was there with a photograph of Tassos and a "you damn well better speak up if you know anything" attitude.

By ten that morning they'd found a waiter who the night before had been walking toward the harbor for a drink after work when he passed Tassos going the other way, toward City Hall. They'd said hello to each other, and according to the waiter, "He seemed fine."

When Adonis passed the news on to Andreas, Andreas told him to narrow the search to streets Tassos could have taken between where the waiter saw him and his car.

At ten thirty a sergeant found an abandoned store with an unlocked door. Inside the place was empty except for two chairs and a cigarette butt on the floor in a back room. A fresh butt. He called forensics and by noon a print matching Tassos' was lifted from the front door.

A security camera mounted on the roof of a bank just around the corner and across the street from the building caught a partial rear view of the top of a white van pulling up on the driver's side in front of the building, stopping for ninety seconds, and pulling away, all within twenty minutes of the time Tassos was said to have left the taverna.

Another security camera a block away caught a white van passing by at approximately the same time with the name of a butcher emblazoned on its side.

The butcher couldn't believe his good fortune when three cops showed up taking such an interest in his van. After all, he'd only notified the police of its theft that morning when he got into work and saw it was missing.

With that news, Andreas told them to make the van the target of their search. An hour and a half later a rookie cop in a patrol car found the empty van abandoned less than two miles from where they'd found Tassos' fingerprint. It was by a cove off the road to the seafront village of Azolimnos, south of the island's main harbor, just beyond the Syros Airport, and directly across the sea from Mykonos.

Andreas had Adonis on speakerphone as he delivered the news about locating the van. "I don't know what to say, Chief. Where they've taken him from here is anybody's guess."

"I know." Andreas looked at Kouros and shook his head. "Let me know if forensics turns up anything more from that building or the van. And keep checking those security videos. We might get lucky."

"Will do."

Andreas reached to turn off the phone. "By the way, Adonis. You did a great job. Tassos would be proud."

There was a distinct swallowing sound on the other end of the line. "Thanks, Chief, but if it's all the same to you I'd rather hear him tell me that himself."

Andreas smiled. "Well said. Bye."

He hung up and looked at Kouros. "I guess 'anybody's guess' means our guess."

"So, what's yours?"

"That they took Tassos someplace they know. Where they'd feel secure. My guess is that since Sergey doesn't know anything about the islands, he's relying on someone who does. I'd say Wacki, but it's hard to imagine him getting himself personally involved in anything as risky as kidnapping a cop."

Kouros nodded. "He's too much of a wimp for the physical stuff. But he'd know plenty of nasties capable of doing whatever Sergey wanted."

"For sure. They're clients in his clubs."

"Which means likely Athenian or local muscle," said Kouros.

"If Athenians snatched him and took him back to the mainland we'll never find him in time. If locals did it, they're probably from Mykonos, because Syros bad guys had no reason to get him off the island as fast as these guys did. They would know where to hide him there."

"Are you saying your guess is Mykonos?"

Andreas nodded. "It's our only possible shot at finding him alive. We've got three thousand islands in this country, all but a couple hundred deserted. Not to mention the number of boats out there. I'm just going for the long shot with the best odds. Kidnappers want a place where they feel safe and in control. And if they're from Mykonos, I'm picking here."

"Okay, so now what?"

"I'd like to do what our brothers on Syros did. Turn every cop on the island loose on finding him. But if I'm right about Tassos being here, as soon as Sergey hears about the search he'll likely panic and kill him."

Andreas scratched his head. "I think we've got to turn to civilians for help. After all, it's their island. And no one knows it better than they do."

"How can we do that and keep it quiet? Locals love to gossip. It's bound to get back to Wacki."

Andreas nodded. "Sometimes it seems almost everyone on this island is in Wacki's pocket, or someone like him, but there are a lot of good people out there who aren't. And some of them are indebted to Tassos. He's done good things for many of them, and if those folks aren't prepared to keep their mouths shut to save his life…heaven help this place."

"So, whom do we talk to?"

"Since it looks like they took him from Syros by boat, let's start with the coast guard."

Law enforcement on the seas and in the nation's ports was the responsibility of the Hellenic Coast Guard, also known as the port police, commanded by a harbormaster.

"I'll ask the harbormaster to find locals who might know something. He should know the ones we can trust not to gossip. After all, that's how the coast guard gets most of its information on what's happening in Mykonos waters. From folks like fisherman, ship captains, marine suppliers, boat agents, and union guys shuttling passengers between the cruise ships and the port. They're the ones who notice when something's not right."

"That's still a pretty big chance to take. Gossip is like breathing around here."

Andreas nodded. "I'll tell him to round up the ones he trusts the most, but not to tell them why, and to bring them here without letting them call anyone. That way we'll at least get a shot at convincing them not to talk. Besides, what other option do we have?"

"Prayer?"

"I haven't stopped since Maggie called."

"Amen."

Chapter Twenty-three

The coast guard SUV climbed a steep, paved mountain road along a rocky, gray-brown hillside. The road was originally dirt; and time, inattention, and the fiscal crisis seemed determined to return it to its roots. It also didn't help the residents' pleas for road repairs that the elegant homes that sprouted in the area during Greece's boom years were owned primarily by non-locals who did not vote on Mykonos. Local politicians with influence who'd favored the wholesale issuance of building permits to seasonal residents, and local businessmen who profited off a construction craze fueled by off-islanders' money, often had a very different attitude toward those same folks when asked to provide them with municipal services paid for out of public coffers.

"I remember when no one wanted to live out here," said a barrel-chested fiftyish man with salt-and-pepper hair and a full beard to match. He was in the back seat, on the passenger's side, looking down the mountain. "My grandfather used to say that even the goats had given up on this land. "Now look at it. Covered with people."

"The goats had more sense, Panayis. The people just had more money," said the man next to him of about the same age, but thick-waisted and clean-shaven.

Panayis laughed. "I wish my father had kept some of the land instead of selling it off. Maybe then I'd be as rich as you, Alex, and not have to spend my life working for a living."

"Fishing is a noble profession, my friend. I just prefer doing it as a hobby."

"Yeah, when you're not overcharging me for boat repairs."

A third middle-aged man in the backseat laughed along with Panayis. "Yeah, Alex, the last time you rebuilt an engine for one of my taxi boats you charged me almost as much as a new one would cost."

"That's only because you're my cousin, Manolis. If you weren't family I'd have charged you double."

Everyone in the SUV laughed.

A lean, spectacled man, older than the others and sitting up front, said to the driver. "I think it's time for an explanation. When you called and said you needed our help 'right away,' how could we refuse? After all, you command the coast guard on Mykonos. But we have a right to know what's going on."

The harbormaster said, "Absolutely, Vangelis. And I promise you'll get your answer in a few minutes."

Near the top of the hill the paved road twisted left up toward the air force's radar station and a dirt road cut off to the right. The SUV took the dirt road and bumped along for a couple more minutes before stopping on the right next to an arched doorway in a seven-foot high natural stone wall.

"I know this place," said Alex. "The owner's a customer."

Manolis smiled. "Then maybe you shouldn't go in. It could be a trap."

"*Malaka*," said Alex, equating him affectionately to a wanker.

The gate in the doorway swung open and Andreas stepped out. He opened the front and rear passenger's side doors and nodded toward the doorway. "Gentlemen, I'd appreciate it if you'd hurry. We have a lot to do in a very short time."

Vangelis set his eyes on Andreas. "Before I move from this seat, I want to know what has our former police chief dragging us out to the middle of nowhere?"

Andreas nodded. "It's simple. Without your help a man will die in a matter of hours. Now, if you please, let's hurry inside."

And they did.

◇◇◇

Once inside the house, Andreas offered them water, refused their request for *tsipouro*, and showed them to chairs arranged outside on the covered terrace. He and Kouros stood with their backs to the sea, facing the five men

"Let me get right to the point," said Andreas. "If any of you talk about what I'm about to tell you with anyone, the kidnap victim is as good as dead. And by 'anyone' I'm including your wives, girlfriends, and priests. Do any of you have a problem with keeping this strictly among ourselves?"

All gestured no, but Panayis said, "How long do we have to keep it secret?"

"I'll let you know, but if we don't find the victim by tomorrow morning, he'll probably be dead."

"Who is it?" said Alex.

"Tassos Stamatos."

For an instant the only sound was the wind.

"Who kidnapped him?"

"Where did it happen?"

"When?"

Andreas put up his hands. "I know you have a lot of questions, but most of them I can't answer."

Vangelis raised his hand and paused until the others were quiet. "I have only one question. What can we do to help our friend?"

The others nodded.

"Thank you," said Andreas. He told them everything he could about the kidnapping without disclosing who he thought was behind it.

Panayis was the first to speak up. "If they crossed over from Syros as late as you say and running fast, someone who fishes nights off of Rhenia might have seen something.

"Local sailors coming out of Syros headed for Mykonos know to aim for *aspros cavos*, the white-faced northwest cape of Rhenia. With the amount of moonlight last night that stone face would have been lit up like a beacon. And boats running fast in the dark get noticed. You're always worried the captain might be drunk, drugged, or up to no good. And if you don't recognize the boat or who's behind the wheel, you keep a damn close eye on it until it's past you. Let me make some calls." He pulled out his phone and dialed.

"Remember," said Andreas. "Nothing that might get back to whoever we're looking for."

Panayis nodded, and launched into an animated telephone conversation punctuated by *malaka* as the principal noun, verb and modifier. His face lit up in a Santa Claus-like smile as he hung up.

"We're in luck. Sometime after one in the morning an idiot in one of those inflatables went flying by him and three other boats, rocking the shit out of them."

"Any idea who it was?" said Manolis.

"No, but he wishes he did. All they could tell was that it looked like a Marvel."

"That's a Greek-made inflatable," said Alex. "There are quite a few of them around the island."

"Anything on the captain?" said Kouros.

"No one recognized him."

"How many people were in the boat?" said Andreas.

"Couldn't tell. It had one of those canopies that covers everything from the wheel forward."

"What?" said Alex.

"I said it had a bow canopy."

Alex rubbed his cheek. "There could be some dangerous people involved."

"We wouldn't be here if there weren't," said Andreas.

Alex drew in a deep breath and spoke as he let it out. "About a year ago the owner of a thirty-two foot Marvel had me fit it out with a custom canopy like the one you described. When I said it would ruin the primary function of the boat he told me, 'mind your own fucking business.'"

"Who was it?"

Alex said the name.

"Christ," said Vangelis. "He's the scummy bastard who brings in Eastern European prostitutes and calls them exotic dancers. I'm ashamed he's Mykonian."

"I guessed that was why he had me put on the canopy. So he could move the girls on and off the island unseen."

Panayis shook his head. "If he was driving that boat last night one of my guys would have recognized him. Everyone knows that asshole."

Vangelis said, "The talk among Albanians who work on my construction jobs is that he's the Mykonian front for the Albanian mob. Maybe one of his mob friends was using the boat?"

"Where's he keep it?" said the harbormaster.

"Depends," said Alex. "Right now in Ornos, away from the north wind."

Andreas looked at the harbormaster, "Do you think you could 'quietly' find the boat?" Andreas emphasized the word with finger quotes.

"We'll try. But we may have to use a helicopter."

"As long as it looks routine and doesn't raise suspicions."

The harbormaster nodded and made a call.

"Gentlemen," said Andreas. "If you were looking for a place on Mykonos to hide Tassos in order to do whatever you wanted to him, and get in and out unnoticed, where would you pick?"

The answers ran from the obvious—an off-the-beaten-track farmhouse, church, or old mine—to the not so obvious middle of the town. The latter suggestion took note that the boat would have arrived on Mykonos at the perfect hour for using the town's chaotic nightlife as cover, and with the right connections it would have been simple to smuggle him into town in a vehicle authorized to be there at those hours.

In other words, they had everywhere to look and nowhere.

Andreas was mulling over the possibility of going after the boat owner when the harbormaster said, "We got lucky. Around sunrise two of my guys in a patrol boat were on the eastern side of Mykonos, and decided to make a loop around the outer islands of Dragonisi and Stapodia. In a cove on the southwest of Stapodia, just below a church, they saw the boat."

"Are they certain?" said Andreas.

"We also know its owner's reputation. His boat is no stranger to us."

"Did they check it out?" said Andreas.

"No one seemed aboard and two men on the shore with spear guns and free-diving gear waved that everything was okay. Nothing looked suspicious."

"Lucky thing your guys didn't get curious," said Kouros. "I hate to think what might have happened had they unknowingly started pressing Tassos' kidnappers."

Andreas was excited. "It's the break we needed. What can any of you tell me about Stapodia?"

"There's not much to tell," said Vangelis. "It's an uninhabited, arid, brown rock in the Mediterranean surrounded by cliffs and accessible to the top only by a path that runs by that tiny church."

"It's about six miles southeast of Mykonos. About a mile long and four hundred yards at its widest part. I always thought it looked sort of like one of those German sausage dogs," said Alex.

"It's called a dachshund," said Vangelis.

"I used to go there with my father when I was a kid," said Manolis. "The north and east sides of the island are sheer rock cliffs. The south is too, but there the cliffs tend to angle in toward the center of the island and aren't as badly beaten by the winds as the north and east sides. The west is narrow and cliffy, too, but at least there's that path by the church heading up from the west to the top. Once you're at the top there's still not much level land. It's basically an island for hawks."

"Hawks?" said Kouros.

"Yes. In late summer, after the chicks hatched, my dad and I used to rescue the ones abandoned by their mothers because they couldn't fly. We'd bring them home and raise them until they were strong enough to fly. My father used to say it was the least we could do for all that nature did for us."

"There's a lighthouse at the top," said Alex. "No one lives there now that it's automated. But there's still a concrete cistern next to it for water."

"And that path is the only way up and down," said Vangelis.

"Sounds perfect for holding off an invading army," said Kouros.

"Unless you plan on coming in by helicopter," said the harbormaster.

"Too risky," said Andreas. "They'd hear us coming, might panic, and kill Tassos. Are you sure there's no other way up?"

"If there is, I only know one person who might know," said Manolis.

"Who's that?" said Andreas.

"Temi. He was the last lighthouse keeper. His family is from Ano Mera and they built that church on Stapodia."

"Where's he now?" said Andreas.

"Probably in a taverna around the square in Ana Mera drinking his homemade wine," said Alex.

Andreas looked at the harbormaster. "Can you bring him here?"

"I can try, but he definitely doesn't fit your non-gossip profile. When Temi drinks he can't stop talking."

"We don't have a choice. But, if we have to, we'll find some place to keep him incommunicado."

Alex smiled. "That won't be difficult as long as you let him bring along his wine."

Chapter Twenty-four

Temi had spent most of the afternoon at his old friend Frederiko's farm next to the reservoir in Marathi. His friend had supplied the homegrown vegetables and freshly caught fish, and Temi the homemade wine. By the time Temi and his small, dust-covered pickup truck reached his favorite hangout in Ano Mera, he'd fully attained the state of philosophic ecstasy so sought after by the ancients through wine.

His jolting ride in the harbormaster's SUV from Ano Mera's town square to the house at the top of the mountain had done nothing to diminish Temi's self-perceived clarity of thought on all things.

A small, thin man, with a craggy, walrus-mustached face and a black fisherman's cap perpetually perched upon whatever silver hair remained beneath it, Temi embodied the tourist's post card image of "old" Greece; and he relished that role.

Andreas offered Temi coffee. Temi refused and instead magically produced a small bottle of wine from a front pocket of his baggy pants.

"Later," said Andreas holding out his hand for the bottle. "But first I need your help with something very important."

Temi shrugged and handed Andreas the bottle. "Wine is also important. It captures the essence of sun, rain, earth, wind, all of God's unique natural gifts in one exquisite form for us to enjoy while bringing us closer to the Almighty."

This is going to be tough, thought Andreas. "Frankly, at the moment, I'm more concerned about keeping a really close friend away from the Almighty."

Temi twisted his head like a perched hawk trying to make out what had caught its eye.

"Do you know Tassos Stamatos?"

"Yes, of course I do. I knew him and his wife. Tragic what happened to her and their baby. When was it now?"

"Around forty years ago. His wife and son died in childbirth," said Andreas.

Temi nodded. "Yes, tragic."

"He needs our help and we're hoping you can answer some questions about Stapodia."

"Ah, Stapodia. My personal Delphi. How I miss my visions there."

"Is there another way to the top besides following the church path?"

Temi smiled. "Ah, I see you are also a philosopher," and waved his hands in the air. "All about us are the results of men who listen to the charlatans of change telling them that the way to the top is easy. Just allow money to lead you.

"Our beaches, our land, our culture, our children, our very souls are all we need offer in exchange. A simple transaction. Why not? Who cares about those yet to come? Or those who came before and left us as shepherds of this island paradise."

"I'm talking about a somewhat different path," said Andreas.

Temi nodded. "I know. But mine is for more than one man, it is for our island, our nation. We have lost our way."

"Please, Temi, is there another path to the top of Stapodia?"

"Follow Satan's path."

Patience, Andreas. "What are you talking about?"

"My dog. Satan was my companion there for many years. He knew a way. But he's gone and the path may be too. Who knows what could have happened to it in these frenzied times of build everywhere."

Vangelis said, "No one has built anything there since the church."

Temi grinned. "Not that you wouldn't have tried if you thought you could make money from it."

Andreas raised his hands. "Gentlemen, this is not the time to debate the pros and cons of development. We are trying to save a man's life."

"Communist," said Vangelis.

"*Malaka*," said Temi.

Andreas raised his voice. "*Cool it.* Please, just show us that other way up to the top."

The harbormaster unrolled a nautical chart on a stone table next to Temi.

Temi's head rocked back and forth, his eyes drifting on and off the map.

"Please," said Andreas pointing to the map. "Show us."

"I'm trying to remember. It's been a very long time."

Andreas held his breath and looked at Kouros. Kouros looked at his watch. Andreas didn't have to. He could tell it was getting late by the large orange ball about to drop into the sea off to the west.

"I think it was here." Temi aimed a shaky finger midway along the south side of the tiny drawing of the island.

"The path starts around here." He waved his finger in a circle around a small cove. "And runs like this up to here." He squiggled his finger from the cove to a spot directly above it and due south of the lighthouse. "I'm sure it comes out there because that's where I'd see Satan coming back from the sea. But I'm not so sure of the rest."

"Have you ever walked it?" said Kouros.

"Are you crazy? There's a simple path for man to follow. I had mine, Satan had his."

Stay with me on this, Temi, for just a little longer, Andreas prayed. "How long do you think it takes to climb to the top from the cove?"

"I could give you an idea if you were a dog. But, as a man, all I can suggest is that you take a look at it and judge for yourself."

"No time for that. We're climbing tonight," said Kouros.

"In the dark? Do you have a death wish? It's a cliff face."

"Is there any other way up?" said Andreas.

Temi gestured no.

Andreas shrugged. "Then what choice do we have?"

"What else do you want to know from me?"

"A lot. But give me a few minutes while I get our harbormaster to make some arrangements for us."

"What do you need?" said the harbormaster

"A squad of your best navy seals would do nicely."

He smiled. "Sorry, all out. You'll just have to settle for Yianni."

"Hi, Maggie."

"Andreas, what's happening? I haven't heard from you in hours!"

"Sorry, we've been making preparations to bring back Tassos."

"You know where he is?"

"We think he's in a lighthouse on a tiny island just off of Mykonos."

"Are you sure?"

"As sure as we can be."

"When will you know?"

"When Yianni and I break down the door."

"Just the two of you?"

"The coast guard is ready to play the cavalry if we need them. But this is the safest way to do it for Tassos."

"What about for you and Yianni?"

"There's something in my office I need right away. I want you to get it to me by helicopter and I don't care how you find one."

"You're not going to answer my question, are you?"

"Maggie. Please. Just do what I'm asking."

"Okay."

And she did.

Chapter Twenty-five

Small fishing boats were a normal sight around Stapodia in the pre-dawn hours. At least that's what Andreas and Kouros were hoping as the little *caique* squeezed in as close as it could to a tiny cove on the south central side of the island. They jumped into the boot-high water and scrambled across the sand into the shadows of the cliffs as Panayis steered his *caique* back out to sea. Up close the cliffs looked even more impossible to climb than in the photographs.

"I sure as hell hope that old man knew what he was talking about," said Kouros.

"Only one way to find out."

They were dressed head to toe in black camouflage, but the moonlight would give them away to anyone who bothered looking down the cliff face. Once climbing, the weapons in the packs strapped to the small of their backs would do them no better good than the 9mm Heckler & Koch USPs holstered to their thighs. They'd be dead in place targets for anyone above them.

It took twenty minutes to find the trail, a narrow ledge snaking back and forth across the cliff face and barely wide enough in some places for more than the soles of their shoes to slide along in parallel while their heels dangled out over the edge. Each man made sure to keep his weight on his rear foot until certain there was a firm place ahead to step.

Fifteen minutes into the climb Kouros whispered, "That dog must have been a fucking Chihuahua to make it up this path."

"Don't make me laugh," whispered Andreas creeping along behind Kouros, his face pressed against the cliff.

A cigarette lighter lit up off to the west, likely on the trail from the church to the lighthouse.

"What time is it?" whispered Kouros

"What difference does it make? We can't move any faster."

"I just wanted know how much longer to sunrise."

"You'll know it's here when those guys over there start shooting at us."

Twenty minutes of more finger-gripping, knuckle-scraping, rock climbing had them close to the top. The path widened and the two men moved more quickly until a section of ledge gave way under Kouros' front foot, nearly sending him and Andreas who'd grabbed him from behind crashing down to the beach. Both stood quietly for a moment staring down at the sea. Andreas patted Kouros on the shoulder and they resumed the climb, taking care where they stepped.

They reached the top less than fifteen minutes before the first rays of sunlight, but couldn't move on the lighthouse until they found the sentries. They knew there must be sentries. They crouched low to the ground so not to create a silhouette against the horizon, and scanned for whoever might be up there with them.

Kouros tapped Andreas on the shoulder and pointed one hundred yards to the west. A man with an AK-47 was standing by the top of the path, looking down. Andreas pointed to the cistern one hundred yards north of them. Another man with an AK-47 was behind it facing northwest. He looked to be guarding the front door to the lighthouse, just past the cistern and to the right. Another three minutes passed.

Andreas leaned in and whispered in Kouros' ear. "In seven minutes the sun comes up and we'll be lit up like a Christmas tree. It's now or never. You take the one by the path, I'll take care of the one by the lighthouse." He didn't have to say, "Do it quietly."A shot would mean the end of Tassos' life. Hard-asses who kidnapped a cop wouldn't dare leave him alive to identify them—and take revenge.

Andreas reached into his pack, felt around, and finding what he wanted, gripped it firmly in his right hand. He carefully made his way northeast, away from the cistern, before turning west. He stopped directly in line with the man's back.

Just keep looking the other way, he prayed.

Andreas slowly worked his way to about forty feet behind the man when the lighthouse door swung open. Andreas dropped to the ground and held his breath. Another man stood in the doorway, blocking most of the little light coming from inside. He said something to the man at the cistern, stepped outside, closed the door, and began pissing next to the doorway.

Goddamnit. Hurry up and finish.

The pissing man said something else, opened the lighthouse door, and disappeared inside just as the first rays of sunlight hit the top of the island.

Andreas pushed up from the ground and started toward the cistern. He could make out Kouros taking out the other sentry. The one at the cistern must have seen the same thing because he was swinging his gun around onto Kouros just as Andreas came up behind him.

Andreas thrust his right hand at the back of the man's head and just as quickly his hand jerked back at him. But there was no flash of light or sound. Except for the sound of the sentry and his gun crumpling to the ground.

Andreas waved for Kouros to hurry.

He looked at the gun in his hand. The little bugger had worked. It's what he had Maggie send him, a gift a few years back from a US military liaison assigned to the American embassy in Athens. He'd called it a QSPR, for Quiet Special Purpose Revolver, and said it was developed for use by tunnel rats in the Vietnam War, the brave ones who crawled into dark holes looking for the enemy with nothing but a flashlight, a pistol, and cast iron balls.

The American said it suppressed all the natural consequences of an explosion of gases rushing down a barrel to escape behind the bullet or shotgun pellets they were pushing. Silencers only muffled the effects. The QSPR stopped them cold. No muzzle flash, sound, or shockwaves. Only the faint click of the firing pin.

It was a modified six-round Smith & Wesson .44 caliber revolver with a barrel just over an inch long. The trick was in the gun's ammunition. It trapped the gases inside the cartridge so they never reached the barrel. Each cartridge was made of steel and housed fifteen metal shotgun pellets separated from the gunpowder by a piston-type device. When fired, the piston propelled the pellets out into the barrel and sealed off the end of the cartridge before the gases escaped. The weapon wasn't all that powerful, but at close range it was deadly.

But by the time Kouros reached him, Andreas had switched to the other gun in his pack, the noisier and far more lethal Heckler & Koch MP5K submachine gun. Kouros was carrying the same.

Temi had said the door on this side of the lighthouse was the only way in or out, just inside were stairs straight ahead leading up to the light, and off to the right at the bottom of the stairs was a room. That was it.

They listened by the door. Not a sound. Andreas pointed toward the room on the right.

Kouros nodded.

Andreas tapped him twice on the back and yanked open the door. Kouros was off like a sprinter to the crack of a starter's pistol. By the time Andreas swung in behind him, two men with shotguns sitting on chairs next to a body tied naked to a cross at their feet had bullets in their brains.

A man across from them with an AK-47, tried to fire but Andreas drew a circle around the man's center of mass and ran the string up through the top of his head.

A fourth man cowered in the corner by the feet of the body on the cross, a lit blowtorch in one hand. He dropped the torch and put up his hands. Kouros put a round in the man's knee.

"Whoops, it slipped," said Kouros.

The man screamed in pain. Kouros walked over, grabbed him by his throat, and dragged him to the doorway. "Any more friends around?"

The man kept screaming.

Kouros smacked him across the face with the back of his hand and pointed the machine gun at the man's other knee. "Shall we try for two?"

"No, no, just us and the four outside."

"Four?" said Andreas.

"The others must be down by the church. I'll be right back." Kouros opened the door, peeked outside, and crept out.

Andreas picked up the still burning blowtorch and motioned the hobbling man out into the other room. He told him to sit on the steps leading up to the light with his hands on the back of his head.

"Please don't hurt me with that."

"You mean this?" Andreas brought the flame close enough to the top of the man's head to singe his hair.

At the odor the man screamed.

Andreas turned off the torch, snapped a handcuff on one wrist, pulled the open cuff over the railing and cuffed the other wrist. "Not yet."

◇◇◇

Andreas kneeled down next to the body on the cross, bent his head close to the man's face, and said softly, "Tassos." He waited. He heard nothing. He tried again. He prayed.

It seemed like forever before he heard a struggling, "Andreas… Andreas…is that you?"

"Shhhhh, my friend. We're going home." He sliced the ropes binding Tassos' arms and legs to the cross, ripped the shirts off the two men Kouros had killed, and carefully covered his friend with them.

Tassos tried to speak. Andreas leaned down and said, "Rest easy, buddy, the helicopter will be here for you soon."

"It wasn't the pain…It was the helplessness. I knew they could kill me. I knew they would kill me. But I made them drag it out…I would be in control of my own death."

"You're going to be fine, don't worry." Andreas ran outside the lighthouse and pulled a military communicator from his backpack. "This is Kaldis, we have the kidnap victim and he's alive. Get that medevac chopper in here STAT. Officer down."

Andreas saw Kouros double-timing it toward him across the plateau.

"What happened?"

"Real brave guys. As soon as they heard all the fireworks they must have run the other way. They took off in the boat before I could get a shot at them or the boat."

"The coast guard will deal with them. They're out there waiting for them."

"How's Tassos? I called for the helicopter before I went after those last two fuckers."

"I just called it in again. Not good. I keep forgetting how old he is. Where the hell is that goddamned chopper?"

"They were at the airport waiting for the call. Every cop in the Cyclades, coast guard included, respects that old bastard. Trust me, they're coming as fast as they can."

As if on cue they heard the chopper coming in from the north. The pilot brought it in as close to the lighthouse as he could and before the rotors had stopped a doctor from Mykonos' private clinic was racing toward them.

"Where's Tassos?"

"Inside."

Kouros watched the doctor run to the door. "See, I told you a lot of people like that old bastard." Kouros coughed and sniffled.

"You did well, buddy. Tassos would be proud of you."

"He damn well better be, I used the crazy American Bowie knife he gave me for my birthday on that sentry."

Andreas put his arm over Kouros' shoulder and led him back into the lighthouse.

"I think we should pray," said Andreas.

"I already am."

The doctor called it critical that they get Tassos to Athens immediately. He had extensive burns on his body and was in shock.

Andreas and Kouros helped get Tassos into the helicopter, then helped the coast guard carry the dead down to the beach for transfer by boat to Syros. As the coast guard carried the last of the bodies out of the lighthouse the man cuffed to the railing kept screaming at a coast guard lieutenant, "What about me? You have to arrest me. I'm one of the kidnappers. I'm the one who tortured him. You must take me with you."

The lieutenant treated the screaming man as if he didn't exist, and just before leaving the lighthouse whispered something to Andreas.

Andreas stared at the handcuffed man. "So, you really did all those things you just said?"

"No, no, I just wanted them to get me out of here."

"Why? Don't you like it here? It seems rather cozy. How long have you been here? Wait, let me guess. About a day?"

"I just got here."

Kouros picked up the blowtorch. "You think you're pretty good with this I bet. A specialist, huh?"

"I'm not telling you anything. And you can't do anything to me but arrest me, you're cops."

Andreas laughed. "Not any more, Cinderella. Right now we're just friends of the fellow you were using this on." He took the torch from Kouros.

The man screamed, "*Help, help*!"

Andreas laughed. "You and your now very dead buddies picked the perfect spot. Yell as loud as you like. No one will hear you. You're all ours."

The man kept screaming.

Kouros took the torch away from Andreas and used it to knock the man out.

◇◇◇

The man awoke stark naked and tied to the cross. Andreas crouched by his head and Kouros stood by his feet.

"So nice of you to join us," said Andreas.

The man started to scream.

"Shhhh," said Andreas. "You'll have plenty of time to do that if you don't cooperate." He pointed at Kouros who promptly pulled an over-sized, double-blade knife out of a sheath on his side.

"If you look closely you'll see the blood of one of your late buddies still on it."

Andreas waited until the man's eyes had returned to somewhat normal size.

"So, I have a proposition for you. And it's a very simple one. I have four questions to ask you. For each one you answer to my satisfaction my friend will cut one cord binding you to the cross. For each one you do not, he first cuts off one testicle, then the other, then your penis and then either an eye or an ear depending on how he feels at the time. Then I ask the same questions over again and we keep cutting away until you answer them all…or you die…but that will take a while. So, shall we begin?"

Andreas never had to ask the second question.

Andreas and Kouros were standing outside the lighthouse looking west toward Mykonos. "You do know that if we let him live he'll do what he did to Tassos to someone else," said Kouros.

"Yeah, I thought about that. Thought about it real hard. Thought about leaving him in there tied to the cross with the door open so that the animals could get to him. Also thought about just tossing him off the cliff."

Andreas kicked at the dirt. "But do you know why I'm not going to do any of that?"

"Please don't give me a lecture on taking the moral highroad after what we've just seen."

Andreas gestured no. "Here's my thinking. If there is anything in this world that will motivate Tassos to get better, it will be knowing that the sick bastard who did all that to him was still breathing."

Kouros smiled. "Okay, I'll take that as an acceptable answer."

"Hey, don't lose heart, Yianni. We still have to figure out what we're going to do about the guy who's really behind what happened to Tassos."

"Yeah, mister blowtorch did get real chatty."

"I don't think he realized how much he was telling us when he said his only order was to find where a 'briefcase' was hidden."

Kouros drew in and let out a deep breath. "I feel it's my fault they did what they did to Tassos. If I hadn't hidden what they wanted he could have told them where it was. He really didn't know."

"Don't be so hard on yourself. You're probably the only reason he's still alive. If Tassos knew where it was he'd likely have told them and they'd have killed him as soon as they had it. No way they would let him live."

Kouros nodded. "Thanks."

"No need to say that. It's true."

"So what are we going to do about the Albanian mob? They're obviously working with Sergey."

"Quite a risk they took siding with a stranger against a cop as important as Tassos. This must have meant one hell of a big payday for them."

"It will get them run off the island," said Kouros.

"You really think so? For sure it will turn the heat up high enough to nail the others involved in snatching Tassos on Syros, but more than that, I doubt it. Albanians are a convenient scapegoat for a lot of problems on Mykonos. It's too easy to blame them for hotel-room thefts during tourist season, private home break-ins during the off-season, and car thefts year-round. If we get rid of all the Albanian bad guys, whom are the Mykonians going to have left to blame? Their druggie nephews? No one wants to hear that. They prefer the excuse, 'Albanians did it. Or the Pakistanis, or the *Tsigani*. Anybody but us.'"

"What really pisses me off is that with so many locals and cops knowing who's behind most of that shit, why haven't they been arrested? It doesn't take a brain surgeon to figure out how to catch them."

"No, just an honest cop doing his job."

"The truly bad guys on this island probably think they can get away with just about anything," said Kouros.

Andreas waved his finger. "Except kidnapping a cop."

"So, what are we going to do about mister blowtorch's Albanian mob boss? He said that's who ordered him to torture Tassos. Want to go shake his tree?" Kouros waved his knife.

"I doubt we'll get him to admit he ordered the torture of a cop. And once 'mister blowtorch' is safely in jail he'll clam up and deny everything he told us. We've got to get a direct angle on Sergey and the only way I see for doing that is by finding out who the hell is bankrolling him."

"He's certainly not going to tell us."

"Wish we could use your Bowie knife on him."

"Which reminds me," said Kouros. "We better get the prisoner down to the coast guard. They won't wait for us forever."

Andreas smiled. "Don't worry about it, they'll wait."

"How do you know that?"

"That lieutenant whispered something to me just before he left us alone with the prisoner."

"What was it?"

"'Take your time, Tassos is my godfather.'"

Chapter Twenty-six

Andreas hadn't been to sleep and it was approaching noon. He'd been summoned from the harbormaster's office to Mykonos police headquarters by the minister of public order and had spent the better part of fifteen minutes listening to Spiros rant on at eardrum splitting decibel levels. Luckily, it was delivered by telephone so most of the volume was directed at the police chief's office walls though a handset Andreas had put down on the chief's desk.

"How dare you organize such an operation without telling me? Without telling the local chief of police? And involving the coast guard without my authority? Just who do you think you are? Andreas, do you hear me? *Answer me*!"

Andreas picked the phone up from the desk. "Well, Minister, since you asked so nicely and the august chief of the Mykonos police force who played such a large part in your decision to suspend me is sitting here enraptured by our little conversation, I'll give you an answer. I did what I did to spare you both the embarrassment of having your names linked with mine."

Spiros screamed, "I'll see that you're prosecuted for murder!"

Andreas laughed. "Good luck with that. Why don't you suggest that to your colleagues in the party? My guess is you'll be out of government before you finish the conversation."

"*Are you insane*?"

"Obviously you're not keeping up with the latest news. Why don't you turn on one of those big screen TVs in your office? It's just about time for the news. Try Antenna."

Andreas waved at the police chief to turn on the television in the corner of his office.

Andreas watched as Greece's number one television anchor reported on Antenna Network news, "In a daring pre-dawn raid against a cliffside island fortress, Greek police overcame a heavily armed and numerically superior terrorist cell to rescue their kidnapped comrade, a hero cop who had uncovered the terrorists' plot to blackmail some of Greece's most prominent citizens.

"In a joint operation conducted by representatives of the police and coast guard, GADA's legendary chief of Special Crimes, Andreas Kaldis, and former navy seal, now detective, Yiannis Kouros, succeeded in freeing Cyclades Chief Homicide Investigator, Tassos Stamatos. Chief Stamatos remains in critical condition in an undisclosed Athens hospital under heavy police protection.

"I'm certain all of Greece joins us in praying for Chief Stamatos' speedy recovery, and gives thanks that in the midst of our country's crises we are still blessed with heroes on the order of Chief Kaldis and Detective Kouros who make us proud to be Greeks in the truest tradition of those who battled to the cry, 'We are Sparta!'

"The Minister of Public Order is to be congratulated for a job well done."

Andreas muted the television. "I'm sure you get the idea, Spiros. It's playing on all the channels and I understand the newspapers actually have some terrific photos of Yianni and me."

"I'll ruin you," said Spiros.

Andreas looked at his watch. "Can't imagine why you'd want to do that. But you'll have your chance in about ten minutes down in the pressroom. The film crews are waiting for you."

"Pressroom? I didn't call any press conference."

"But they're down there. I guess you could tell them to go home. Or you could present your ideas on prosecuting the three cops who've just given you the chance to look like a national hero.

"Maybe you should discuss this with your fellow ministers. See how they feel about your turning the first unifying good news this country's had in a long time into shit.

"Now, if you'll excuse me, I have to get back to Athens."

"Andreas…" Spiros voice fell off.

"Yes, Minister?"

"Goodbye."

Andreas left the police chief's office without saying goodbye. Kouros was downstairs in a group of cops watching television. They were slapping Kouros on the back and congratulating him.

"Let's go, Yianni. The plane leaves for Athens in twenty minutes."

"How the hell did the news channels get the story so quickly? And they're all using their big gun anchors to tell it."

Andreas said nothing, just waved for Kouros to follow him, and started walking the hundred yards or so to the airport.

When Kouros caught up, Andreas said, "You liked it, huh?"

"Loved it! What did the minister have to say? I could hear his screaming all the way downstairs but couldn't make out what he was saying."

"Forget about what he had to say. It's what he's about to say that matters."

"So tell me, already. How did you pull off all that television coverage?"

"Me? I had nothing to do with it." He put his arm around Kouros' shoulder. "It wasn't my fault Spiros decided to piss off my wife."

◇◇◇

Lila and Andreas sat on the bed in front of the television flipping back and forth between channels like kids jumping between cartoon shows.

"I can't believe this, I just can't." Lila was bouncing up and down on the bed. "I'm going to have to throw the absolutely biggest thank-you party ever. Every single one read it exactly as we wrote it."

"As *you* wrote it. That 'legendary' was a bit much."

"Not to me it wasn't. Besides with television if you say it's so, it is so, and I didn't want to give Spiros any wiggle room. I wanted him to know that if he didn't embrace you completely he was fucked."

"Whoa, such language." Andreas smiled.

"He's the one who decided to mess with my husband."

"Didn't you love it when Spiros said that the entire operation was carried out precisely in accordance with a contingency plan developed under his personal direction for just such a situation?"

"Spiros is a piece of work," said Lila, "but my absolutely favorite moment was when the Prime Minister jumped in on Spiros' act with a surprise appearance and kept praising you, Yianni, and Tassos by name. Spiros' cheeks were literally twitching from forcing a smile for so long."

Andreas wrapped his arms around Lila from behind. "You're terrific. Thank you for coming up with the idea and making it all happen."

"When you called and told me Tassos was safe, I wanted to make sure you were, too. We had to strike first, before Spiros had the chance to spin the news."

"Remind me never to cross you."

"Every day." Lila smiled.

"And to make a copy of all this for Tassos."

"How is he?"

"Maggie said it's still touch and go. No visitors allowed yet. Fear of infection."

"She must be hysterical," said Lila

"Inside, maybe. Outside she's a rock. She told me to give her a call when I have the chance. She said I should spend the afternoon with you and Tassaki and not think about work. Can't imagine what she thinks could possibly interest me home alone with you in our bedroom."

Lila clicked the remote and turned off the TV.

"Okay, it's time to prove why you're a legend."

There had to be places that were more depressing than hospitals, but Andreas couldn't think of any at the moment. He saw Maggie sitting on a hard-back chair in a dull green hallway outside the burn unit. A cop leaned on the wall across from her; another stood back by the elevators.

Maggie stood when she saw Andreas. She said nothing, just put her arms around him and squeezed. He hugged her.

"They're not sure he'll make it."

Andreas kissed her forehead. "That tough bastard will make it. Don't you worry. When we found him he promised me he'd make it. He said, 'Tell my Maggie not to worry.'"

She pulled back and looked at Andreas' eyes. "Did he really say that?"

"Absolutely. He didn't say much, but you were his first thoughts. It's what kept him going."

Why shouldn't I tell her that? I'm sure it's true.

Maggie smiled. "Even if he didn't, thank you for saying that he did."

Andreas kissed her again and dropped his arms.

"If you think there's a better hospital or other doctors that should see him, just ask."

Maggie gestured no. "This is the best place in Greece for burn victims. There is no where else to take him."

"Perhaps a hospital in another country has better facilities?"

"I understand they're doing all that can be done for now. Perhaps later. But not now."

"I know I don't have to say this, but if money ever becomes an issue—"

Maggie put her finger to his lips. "You're right you don't have to say it. I know."

"Lila sends her love. She'll be here as soon as you want to see her."

"You're a lucky man."

"You don't have to tell me."

"Good. Don't ever forget it."

Andreas smiled.

Maggie's face turned serious. "For the past thirty-six hours I've been living someone else's life. This couldn't possibly be happening to me…to us. Finding happiness together after all these years and then…" Maggie shook her head.

"Yesterday morning, after you called to say you'd found him, I rushed to church and thanked God for answering my prayers.

"As I sat there, I realized I must go on believing Tassos will recover, and live my life as if he will be home any day."

"Sounds like a healthy approach."

"Healthy or not it is the one I'm taking."

Andreas nodded.

"One of the first things I did when I got back to my apartment was check the messages on Tassos' answering machine in Syros. I didn't want anyone who might have called to worry, now that we knew he was safe."

Andreas nodded again.

Maggie opened her bag and handed him an envelope.

"This is a transcript of one of those calls. I think it's important. It came in after he was kidnapped. It may have to do with the people who did this to him."

"Who's the caller?"

"Whoever it was refused to identify himself or herself."

"Himself or herself? You couldn't tell from the voice?"

"The caller used a voice scrambler. I made a tape of the call if you want to listen to it, but I typed a transcript because I knew you'd want one…Chief." Maggie smiled. "Welcome back. I hear the suspension was lifted."

"And Spiros has promised all of us a raise."

"Good luck with ever seeing that any time soon. About the most you can hope for these days is that your hero pay won't be cut as much as we commoner public servants' pay."

"You're always my hero."

"Enough with the bullshit." Maggie waved the backs of her hands at him. "Now go read the transcript and find the bastards who did this to my guy."

Andreas smiled. "Seems I'm not the only 'lucky man' when it comes to finding the right lady."

"Damn straight, and don't forget to tell him exactly that."

"Can't wait."

◇◇◇

Andreas sat alone in his car in the hospital parking lot, air conditioner running. He opened the envelope and began reading the transcript.

"Hello, Chief Stamatos. I'm calling at the request of your good friend, Europol Inspector McFadzean. He said you're a man who can be trusted to respect confidences, and as I owe our mutual friend a very serious favor, I am repaying him with this call. But I cannot risk calling again, and so I must leave this as a message.

"As Inspector McFadzean appreciates and I trust you will as well, I cannot reveal who I am because I prefer living, and being identified as having provided this information would be inconsistent with that preference.

"I understand your question is, 'Who is Teacher?' Obviously, Inspector McFadzean did not know. Which is why you're receiving this call from me.

"My answer requires somewhat more of an introduction than you might think warranted, but it is necessary if you wish to understand the phenomenon that is Teacher. And I say 'phenomenon' because she is far more than just a mortal being. At least in the world to which she belongs. And rules.

"The world is no longer linear. There are no straight-line rules to follow, or confining borders to observe. Not in communication, not in business, not in political loyalties, and certainly not in crime. Those who seek to retain parochial influence within strictly drawn political borders fail to appreciate the implications of this new order. Today vast numbers live within various countries' legal borders but owe their allegiances elsewhere, to leaders outside borders and beyond a government's reach. Their loyalty is to a thought, an idea, one not offered in any embraceable form by the land in which they now live.

"It is the West's greatest nightmare. An insoluble situation many say. And one Teacher has exploited as ruthlessly as anyone on earth. She has convinced an army of the exploited that they have the power to change their lives. That any who desire simple protection from those who would do them physical harm should join her on the path to a better life.

"She preaches that words alone are not enough for those in mortal fear, and that praying for a better life is not the way. She proves her point by telling them what they already know: that the criminal beast can never be killed off in this world. Far too many want the sex and slaves and drugs that it offers. What *she* offers, on the other hand, is to tame the beast a bit. To teach those who traffic in evil that it is far wiser to pay the small share she asks for on behalf of her flock than face the assassination and torture she would bring upon them and their families.

"She lives in no one place. She has no family. She lives a private life away from prying eyes. It is said she has no vices because she's done them all and has attained a state far above what they promise.

"That is all the information I have to offer except for this bit of gossip.

"Virtually all in Eastern Europe who fear her are praying the rumor that she's terminally ill is true. They believe no one who assumes her role could be as ruthless as Teacher.

"Good bye, Chief Stamatos. I hope this is of help to you."

Andreas looked up from the transcript and stared out the window.

"Why is someone this powerful backing a low-life like Sergey? And why Mykonos?" Andreas knew he was talking to himself. He looked back at the transcript and shook his head.

"God help us."

Chapter Twenty-seven

Andreas sat behind his desk, watching Kouros read the transcript. He'd twice called out for Maggie, only to catch himself and get what he needed on his own. He didn't want to think about what life in the office would be like if she never came back. Or Tassos.

Kouros looked up.

"So, what do you think?" said Andreas.

"Sounds like an educated caller. Not a run-of-the-mill hood."

"Might not even be a hood. At least not of the traditional sort."

"You mean it could be someone who does business with Teacher?"

Andreas nodded. "A politician, military, journalist, maybe even a cop. But educated."

"How does the caller tie into Sergey?"

"I don't think there is a connection between the caller and Sergey. If the caller had something to do with Christos' murder or was tied in with Sergey or Teacher in whatever they have planned for Mykonos, why would it risk telling Tassos anything, no matterhow big a favor it owed Tassos' Europol inspector friend? The caller would have to know that Tassos was looking for the information to go after Sergey."

"I'd still like to know who the caller was."

"Me too, but since the caller doesn't seem to have anything to do with our problems, and we don't have the manpower to allow us the luxury of satisfying our natural curiosity, let's just accept the caller's message for the gift that it was and go on from there."

"And where precisely would 'there' be?" said Kouros.

"If we assume that Sergey's financial backer and likely boss is Teacher, and it sure looks that she is, why is she involved in this hotel deal with Sergey? It seems such small potatoes for Teacher and her crowd. I don't see a payday coming out of it anywhere close to what she must make everyday extorting drug dealers and sex traffickers. She must have something else in mind for the hotel. Something that made them so desperate for Christos' files that they kidnapped and tortured a cop."

"I see.... We're back to where we started. Nowhere."

Andreas tapped a pencil on his desk. "Wacki?"

"Not yet, but give me time."

"Glad your sense of humor's back." He flipped the pencil at Kouros, who caught it in mid-air.

"If Teacher is as infamous with Eastern European bad guys as the caller said, I can't imagine that Wacki doesn't at least know about her."

Kouros twirled the pencil between his fingers. "And from the way big-ego Wacki is playing seeing-eye dog for Sergey, my bet is he's doing it because Teacher told him to."

Andreas nodded. "Nothing else makes sense. I think it's time we head back to Mykonos."

"Are we still hiding out or am I free to till the soil?"

"I won't ask what that means. But, yes, we're done hiding out. After all, we're national heroes."

"Good, that should help with the tilling."

Andreas smiled. "And I know the perfect hotel for national heroes."

Sergey had spent thirty-six hours sunning, dining, drinking, dancing, and demonstrating to all of Mykonos his presence there. It was difficult to miss him and his entourage of three Asian, African, and Irish beauties. The women were almost as tall as he, and when clothed—as opposed to virtually naked on the most prominent beach on the island—they dressed in white linen accented by earrings, necklaces, and bracelets of solid gold.

They danced together in the style and form of proper ballet as Sergey undulated and swayed among them, dressed in skintight blue and white, his silver hair flowing freely about his face.

No one could take their eyes off him.

But, now, with the first news of Tassos' rescue, Sergey had disappeared. No one, not even Wacki, had seen him for a day. He'd left firm instructions not to be disturbed by anyone, a not-unusual request to the hotel front desk from one who partied as hard as Sergey.

But Sergey had not slept. He kept running over in his mind how Andreas and Kouros could possibly have found Tassos.

There must have been a betrayal, he thought. There was always a betrayal. It was to be expected. That was why betrayal must be punished harshly and swiftly.

Wacki was the likely one. But he'd not known anything of the plan. He only knew of Sergey's meeting with the Albanian. Perhaps now, with all the news, he'd guessed that was the purpose of the meeting. But he had no way of knowing before.

Sergey stared at the wall.

Unless the police came to Wacki after Stamatos disappeared and pressured him into talking about Sergey's meeting with the Albanian. That would have given them the lead they needed to find the cop. He should look into that.

Perhaps the men the Albanian used were simply inept and made a mistake that betrayed their location. No matter, it was still betrayal. Failure was betrayal, and it had to be punished.

Teacher would want that.

He nodded.

Thankfully, I did not fail. My plan was right. It was those charged with carrying it out who had failed.

Indeed, his plan had eliminated a false lead. Stamatos did not talk because he did not have the files. But now Sergey was certain who did: Stamatos' two cop colleagues, Kaldis and Kouros.

Yes, we are closer to our goal because of my plan.

But he would not seek praise from Teacher by informing her of his success just yet. He would wait until he had the files. It should not be difficult. Kaldis and the other cop saw what happened to their friend. They would not want to risk similar fates for themselves. Or their families.

But Sergey knew he must hurry. He couldn't afford to have Teacher become impatient for results.

Teacher had not heard from Sergey in two days. No matter, she wanted him to show initiative, learn to function on his own. Besides, she'd heard from Wacki and knew what was happening, even if Wacki hadn't quite figured it out correctly.

Wacki first called to say Sergey was partying with hookers 24/7, as wildly as a profligate tourist liberated from the prohibitions of his homeland.

That worried her.

Wacki's most recent call was about the kidnapping and rescue of the cop, and of a one-on-one meeting Wacki had arranged for Sergey with the Albanian whose people had been killed and captured in the rescue.

She was no longer worried. Sergey's wildly visible behavior was his obvious alibi for the kidnapping. Everyone knew where he was every moment of that time. Yes, there were details Sergey had neglected to mention to her, but that was understandable and not as if he had lied to her. After all, children did strive to please their Teacher.

In her world one learned to deal with surprises, adversity, and police. This mess was of Sergey's own making. It would serve as a test of his capacity to overcome far more brutal challenges yet to come if they were to succeed on Mykonos. And if they failed, she had no risk or exposure beyond an amount of money less than what she generated in a day on just the interest on her bank accounts.

But failure was not an option. There was far too much more at stake than her investment.

Teacher hadn't told Sergey what first captured her interest in his proposal, and doubted even now that he realized the full potential of what he'd stumbled upon. Since antiquity, East and West met in Greece to engineer fortunes later made together in other lands. American presidents meeting Saudi princes on Greek-owned yachts and British and Russian leaders sharing unobserved pilgrimages to isolated Greek locales were but modern celebrated examples of a long tradition of highly profitable international intrigues. That relaxed style of doing business remained as integral to the fabric of Greek life today as it was to the ancients.

It did not matter to Teacher's plans whether Greece stayed in the EU or not, because Mykonos would prosper on or off the euro and the country would remain unstable long enough for her to establish and consolidate her presence on the island. Nor did it matter if the hate-mongering, anti-immigrant element in parliament rose to greater power. She knew that sort well; they attacked the weak and defenseless, not the organized and ruthless. Besides, if necessary, it would be no problem to purchase their cooperation.

In her plans for Mykonos, Teacher saw the opportunity for expanding her influence far beyond the Eastern block. The murdered club owner, Christos Vasilakis, had the right idea: Once you had the rich and powerful living out their fantasies under your roof you owned them forever, as long as your demands were manageable. Mykonos was the perfect venue for creating such a magical draw, because major players from around the world already flocked there each summer looking to party, many open to irresistible temptations of the sort Teacher knew would soon have them using their influence to help her reach out across the world.

Things would be different in those new lands. There she'd leave behind her old practices and preach a different message, one of love, understanding, and forgiveness. Many others had done the same: Left behind their dark dealings with the devil that had amassed them fortunes and moved on to build golden bridges to heaven through good works. Mykonos was Teacher's chance at redemption, at reuniting with her slain children in heaven.

And all that she hoped for would come to pass if Sergey simply did as he'd promised.

He dare not disappoint me.

The room clerk wasn't sure he'd understood the request. "We want a room up against that Russian bastard's ass."

"I'm sorry, sir, I don't understand."

"I said, 'We want a room up against that Russian bastard's ass.'"

Andreas raised his hand. "What my colleague means is that we would like a room adjoining Mr. Tishchenko's.'"

"Sorry, sir, but there is none available."

"Does that mean they're all occupied or just 'not available?'" said Andreas.

The clerk forced a smile. "It means just what I said. Now if you'll excuse me there are guests behind you waiting to check in."

"No reason to show attitude, fella," said Andreas.

"I'm not. I'm answering your question. Now, please," and he waved for the couple behind Andreas to step forward.

Andreas looked at the couple. They were in their sixties and appeared American. Andreas spoke in English. "We're going to be a while here. Perhaps several hours. Why don't you come back later?"

The clerk raised his voice. "How dare you speak to guests of our hotel like that. If you don't leave immediately I shall call the police."

Andreas smiled. "You're new on the island, aren't you?" He pulled out his badge.

The clerk glared at Andreas. "Those rooms are reserved for special guests of the owner. I cannot do anything without his permission."

"Then get it. We're not budging until we have the room."

The clerk placed a call and explained the situation to the person on the other end of the line. You could hear screaming through the phone. The clerk handed the phone to Andreas. "He wants to speak to you."

Andreas took the phone. "Hello there."

"Who the fuck do you think you are coming into my hotel and trying to strong-arm a room out of my clerk? I'll have your fucking badge."

"I love it when you talk dirty, Lefteris. I'm looking forward to many more such moments over the next several days as I watch you match invoices against every good and service purchased by every guest of your hotel and restaurants over the past year. Who knows where we'll go from there?"

A decided pause came from the other end of the line. "Who is this?"

"You don't recognize me? I'm hurt. It's Andreas."

"Kaldis?"

"In the flesh."

"Why didn't you tell me it was you in the first place? Of course you can have the room. As my guest."

"No need for that."

"Why of course, you're a national hero."

"So, you heard?"

"How could I not? Terrible thing. How's Tassos?"

"Better," he lied.

"I'll pray for him."

"Thanks. So, what have you heard about who did the kidnapping?"

"Only what's on the news."

"Lefteris, *mou*. Don't con me. It doesn't become you."

"I'm not."

"I'm sure. But why don't you come over for a coffee anyway?"

"If you insist."

"I do."

"Fine. I'll come by after you're set up in your room."

"Sounds good. Here, I'll give you back to your clerk."

Andreas handed the phone to the clerk. Screaming began immediately and ended abruptly. The clerk handed Andreas a key. "Sorry, sir, may I help you with your bags?"

"That won't be necessary." Andreas turned to the couple behind him. "Sorry about that."

The man said, "No problem. We haven't had this much excitement since leaving Pittsburgh. Just wish we understood what was happening."

"Me too."

Andreas and Kouros sat at a table by the hotel pool, watching tourists stream into town along the harborfront road.

"Where do they all come from?" said Kouros.

"Take your pick. I count two enormous, three huge, and two large cruise boats anchored between here and the new port."

"There must be more buses than motorbikes on the road into town from the new port."

Andreas nodded. "And all headed this way loaded with tourists expecting Mykonos to live up to its reputation as the place to visit for wildly sensual experiences."

Kouros shook his head. "It's hard to imagine where they expect to find one in the few hours they're in port. Most won't even make it to a beach. It's all about wandering through the town in herds."

"Too bad they don't spend money here. They're told on the boats that 'Mykonos is expensive,' and so they shy away from purchasing anything but the most touristic trinkets. And with all their onboard food and drink for free, it's the rare cruise boat tourist who buys more than a coffee in town."

"Sounds like a huge potential market to exploit," said Kouros.

"Yeah, but if someone figures out how to do it, a dozen others will knock off the concept immediately, killing the idea for everyone. One frozen yogurt shop today, a half dozen more tomorrow."

"I guess the trick is to come up with something that will attract tourist money but can't be imitated."

"Good luck with that. Hard to imagine any real money-making idea involving tourists that hasn't been thought of before by someone on this island."

"I wonder if that's what Sergey has in mind?" said Kouros.

"Like I said, 'hard to imagine,' but who knows?"

"I wonder if he's upstairs. It didn't sound like anyone was in his room."

Andreas shrugged. "We were just as careful not to talk in our room. No reason to risk him being able to hear us."

"Do you think he knows we're in the next room?"

"After all the trouble we went through making that scene with the clerk? I damn well hope so. My guess is the clerk called him while we were on our way up to the room."

"Do you think the clerk told him about your conversation with Lefteris?"

"Not sure, but that's why we're waiting for Lefteris here, where everyone can see us. Including him." Andreas nodded in the direction of Sergey's room without looking up. "I want the cocky bastard to know we're coming for him."

"Speaking of bastards, look who's heading toward the hotel."

Andreas turned his head. *"Wacki!"*

Wacki jumped and swung in the direction of the voice. He forced a smile and went back to walking toward the hotel.

"Come here!" shouted Andreas.

"I can't."

"You damn well better or else I'll come over there and drag your sorry ass back here."

Guests at several tables began squirming in their chairs.

Wacki stopped, turned, and walked over to Andreas' table. "Why are you hassling me?"

Andreas pointed at a chair across from him. "Sit."

Wacki did. He glanced over his shoulder up toward Sergey's room.

"Don't worry, if he's not up there watching I'm sure someone will tell him about our little meeting."

"I don't know what you're talking about."

Andreas smiled and patted Wacki on the shoulder. "This little meeting. And if he is watching, I want him to know we're the best of friends."

Wacki didn't move.

"Speaking of the best of friends, I know you heard about what happened to Tassos."

Wacki nodded. "Yes. I'm sorry."

"I just bet you are," growled Kouros.

"And I assume you heard who did it?" said Andreas.

Wacki didn't move.

"Funny thing. Guess what they were after."

Wacki shrugged.

Andreas patted Wacki's cheek with his right hand. "The very same thing your boss wanted from him. Small world isn't it?"

Andreas patted Wacki's knee. "And it gets even smaller. Everyone we nailed on Stapodia was from Mykonos. Hard-asses. The kind only someone with deep connections into the dark side of this island would know."

Andreas leaned forward. "I wonder who that someone could be?"

Wacki looked away.

Andreas waited until they were eye to eye. "How long have you been working for Teacher?"

Wacki's eyes widened for an instant. "I don't know what you're talking about."

Andreas leaned back. "What you know or don't know doesn't matter a rat's ass to me as long as *I* know. I hear Teacher's not a forgiving employer. How are the health and pension benefits?"

Wacki's left eye began to twitch.

"No matter. With how badly you and your buddies fucked things up, my guess is you won't be in need of either much longer."

"I don't know what you're talking about."

Andreas smiled. "Of course you don't. But as I said before, what you know or don't know doesn't matter. All that matters is that Teacher knows you're a fuck-up."

Wacki scratched his cheek and looked away.

"Now run along."

Andreas stood and waved to a man walking toward him across the lawn. "Lefteris, my friend. Good to see you. Please, join us. We have much to talk about."

Andreas stared at Wacki. "Like I said, 'run along.'"

Andreas watched Wacki walk away. As he reached the lobby door Wacki looked back over his shoulder at Andreas. Andreas immediately smiled, waved, and blew him a kiss.

Wacki hurried inside, looking straight ahead.

Wacki knocked on the door.

"Come in."

Sergey stood at the window holding back the curtain and looking out.

"Hi, boss."

"What was that all about?"

"You mean Kaldis?"

Sergey didn't respond or move from the window.

"He wanted me to know he thinks you and I were involved in the Stamatos kidnapping. He said the kidnappers were after the same thing you wanted and that everyone involved came from Mykonos."

"What did you say?"

"I didn't know what he was talking about."

"Anything else?"

Wacki forced himself to keep looking at the back of Sergey's head. "No."

"Are you sure?"

Wacki knew that question would come. He'd gone over his answer a dozen times on his walk up to the room. Teacher had made it abundantly clear that absolutely no one but Sergey and he were to know of her connection to the project. If Wacki told Sergey of Kaldis' suspicions there was no doubt Sergey would tell Teacher in a way that would end badly for Wacki. If anyone would be the bearer of bad news to Teacher it would be Wacki. But not now, he needed time to think.

"Yes, I'm sure. But I did hear him say to Lefteris that they had a lot of things to talk about."

"What sorts of things?"

"He didn't say. He told me to leave."

Sergey dropped the curtain. "He's bluffing. He knows nothing. He's just trying to frighten us into making a mistake by getting in our faces."

Sergey turned and walked toward Wacki. He rested his forearms on Wacki's shoulders and stared into his eyes. "But we won't make any mistakes, will we?"

Wacki held Sergey's stare. "No, boss. We won't."

Sergey held the stare then patted Wacki on his shoulders.

"Good. As long as we do not panic we have nothing to fear."

"What about his conversation with Lefteris?"

Sergey shrugged. "What of it? Lefteris is like you. He knows nothing of my plans. He has nothing to tell him."

Chapter Twenty-eight

"What was that all about?" said Lefteris sitting down and waving for a waiter.

"We were just discussing mutual acquaintances," said Andreas.

"If they're 'mutual' with Wacki, my guess is they're guys you put away." He waved again at the waiter. "Or ought to."

"We'll see what we can do about that," said Andreas. "But for now I just want to talk about the hotel."

"What about it?"

The waiter came running. Andreas waited until Lefteris ordered for everyone and the waiter had left.

"Why do you think Sergey is buying it?"

"Because he wants to be in the hotel business. Why else?"

"That's my question."

"But what other reason could there be? He can't sell the property. All he's permitted to do is what the lease allows."

"Does it make sense to you that a foreigner like Sergey is willing to pay so much just to operate a hotel?"

"I'm not interested in making sense out of what's going through someone's mind who wants to give me a lot of money."

"Indulge my curiosity. We both know that no matter what you're actually making running this place as a hotel, on and off the books, the price he's paying can't be justified."

"I pay every cent of my taxes."

"Yes, I'm sure. Then if I were you I'd be straining my brain for justification to the tax authorities as to why a stranger to the hotel business is buying a lease on a hotel whose total profit over the past five years is less than a single year's bank interest on the purchase price."

"You seem to know a lot about the deal."

"I'm a national hero, remember. People tell me things. Besides, that memorandum of understanding you signed with Sergey and submitted to the ministry of tourism disclosed the purchase price and the bank accounts of your friend Sergey that will make you a very rich man."

"So what do you want me to do, guess?"

"Go for it."

Lefteris shrugged. "Fine, I'm always up for party games. How about turning it into a house of prostitution? The lease doesn't permit it, but at times it seems that way anyway. Then again, on this island the paying clientele would be limited." He smiled.

"Maybe a high-end house?" said Kouros.

"You guys are serious about this, aren't you? Okay, from my experience here's my bottom line opinion on a high-end prostitution operation. Classy hookers working this kind of high-roller destination would end up turning it into a wedding chapel for old farts and young tarts."

Andreas laughed. "Catchy phrase."

"Mottos for businesses. It's my gift. My favorite was, 'Don't fret, get wet, lay a bet.'"

"What level of whorehouse was that supposed to be?" said Kouros.

"No, wise-ass, it was my motto for turning this place into a seaside casino."

"A casino?" said Andreas.

"Yeah, I had the idea twenty years ago, when the ministry of finance was still giving out casino licenses. I even negotiated a modification to the lease with the ministry of tourism that would allow the place to operate as a casino if I ever got the license."

"What happened?"

"The ministry of finance stopped issuing licenses. All you can do these days is buy an existing one, but you can't move it to a different location. Once you have the license it's regulated by the ministry of tourism, but my friends there can't help me with getting one for Mykonos. That's all in the hands of the ministry of finance and brutal politics."

"What sort of politics?"

"Many kinds, but the most obvious is that the nine casinos already out there don't want more competition. And certainly not of the sort Mykonos could bring to the table. Can you imagine what a casino would do for Mykonos? It would turn the place into the Las Vegas of the Mediterranean."

"And that's a good thing?" said Kouros.

Andreas rubbed his forehead. "Don't you think the island has gone about as far off in the 'nightlife direction' as the Mykonians can take?"

"Maybe, but it has only profited the handful of locals who control it. Look, I love this place as much as any Mykonian. I grew up here and raised my family here. But I'm a realist. There is no going back to the old days. None. All we can do is try to protect the future, make things fairer so that no longer will one man get rich and another go to jail for doing exactly the same thing just because one has connections and the other does not.

"If we'd commit as a community to turning our island into a worldwide entertainment destination, a Las Vegas on the sea, it would become a year-round tourist attraction, and not just a place for partying kids in the summer."

Lefteris turned his hands palms up and shrugged. "But none of that is ever going to happen. Even an ex-prime minister couldn't get a license for a casino on Mykonos. The big boys here have all the juice and the big boys elsewhere don't want Mykonos to have a casino. And you don't have to look very hard to see how nasty some of them are willing to play."

"You mean like casino employees jumping out of windows in what are called 'suicides'?" said Kouros.

"You got it. Those boys play for keeps. So, unless you're prepared to play by their rules, stay away."

"Sounds like good advice," said Kouros.

"It's the same advice as I gave Christos."

Andreas leaned in. "Christos Vasilakis?"

Lefteris nodded. "He came to me about a year ago. He remembered that I'd negotiated a lease modification to operate the hotel as a casino and wanted to know if I'd be willing to go partners with him if he could get a license from the ministry of finance."

"What happened?"

"Nothing. I said no. I'm not a fool. Christos and I were friends since he came to the island. The only way he'd be able to pull that off would be by squeezing some very serious balls. I wanted no part of that sort of aggravation at this point in my life. Besides, I took it more as a big show for his *putana* girlfriend."

Andreas cleared his throat. "She was *with* Christos when he talked to you about getting a license to turn the hotel into a casino?"

Lefteris nodded. "Tits and all."

Don't fret, get wet, lay a bet.

Andreas and Kouros walked along the harborfront. It was filled with tourists speaking every language but Greek. Still, the two men spoke quietly, just in case Greek might be a second language for some.

"Son of a bitch. He's planning to go into the casino business," said Kouros.

Andreas nodded. "It all fits. Ties everything together. Christos planned on using his files to extort a license for a casino on Mykonos. The girlfriend passed the idea on to Sergey, he went to Teacher for financing, and here we are. Two bodies later and Sergey's on the verge of bringing Russian gangsterism to Mykonos."

"As tough as Greek bad boys like to think they are, the Russians will chew them up. Wholly different rules. No one, not a child, mother, you name it, is off limits."

"And once here, they'll want a piece of everything they can get their hands on," said Andreas. "Those big clubs with bullet-proof rooms for protecting all that cash they generate each night will need tanks to hold off the Russians."

"Las Vegas may not be a bad comparison for the way Mykonos could end up. I hear it's surrounded by desert filled with never-to-be-discovered bodies. Mykonos has the Aegean."

"Let's hope it doesn't go that way."

"What's to stop it? If all it takes is money to do whatever you want, those with the most get to call the shots," said Kouros.

Andreas put his arm around Kouros' shoulder. "If you're right, there's nothing you or I can do to affect the end of that story; it's all up to the Mykonians. But there is something you and I can do about one miserable motherfucker named Sergey."

"What do you have in mind?"

"Not quite sure yet, it's percolating, but whatever it is will require us back in Athens. Time to head home."

"Before lunch?"

Andreas smiled. "Who's buying?"

"Spiros."

"Good, I know the perfect place."

Sergey watched the two cops leave the hotel gardens and walk along the road toward town. He'd sent Wacki away ten minutes before.

He clenched the curtain in his fist as he stared out the window. All that rat-faced fool ever wanted to do was gossip. He couldn't be trusted. He knew Wacki was aching to see him fail. It was the nature of his kind. Sergey couldn't risk involving Wacki or any of his people again in anything serious. They were useless. He must return to using those he could rely upon to do as they were told.

Sergey unclenched his fist, stepped back from the curtain, and looked at the phone.

He wondered if he should ask Teacher to find the two men he'd told to disappear? The fates knew he was wrong before. Yes, that's why they didn't allow him to find and eliminate them. The fates looked after him. They always did.

◇◇◇

Teacher hung up the phone. Sergey seemed so cheerful. Was he mad or just trying to please her? He said, "All is going well," "Right on schedule," "Nothing to worry about," "The license will be ours soon."

Such confidence.

But then came the real reason for his call. He wanted her to find the killers of Christos, to bring them to Athens. She thought he would want them eliminated. But he said, "No." Surely he knew the risk in their returning to Greece.

It spoke of desperation. That was not good. Desperation led to misjudgments.

A misjudgment at this moment could be fatal. No gambling meant no international money crowd. The sex, the drugs, the party atmosphere would not be enough to draw them away from other places offering the same. They needed the magic of a casino to bring it all together.

She clenched her fist. Without that casino license her plans were ruined. She would be trapped in this life for the rest of her days.

She looked at the photograph of the young girl on her desk and relaxed her hand.

Am I desperate? Have I misjudged?

◇◇◇

Halfway to Ano Mera, just beyond the island's garbage dump and overlooking the wind and kite surfers' Shangri-la of Ftelia Bay, sat what many Mykonians viewed as the most blatant example of how far their island had gone in the wrong direction: A strip club with signage leaving nothing to the imagination about what was available inside for a price.

"I still don't understand how that place stays open," said Kouros.

"Of course you do."

"Okay, but how do they get away with putting up signs like that on an island with fourteen hundred churches?"

"Maybe that's why there are so many churches. There's a lot of sinning to atone for going on in places like that."

Kouros laughed. "Where are we headed?"

"My favorite place. Fokos Beach."

"Great. I haven't been there in years. Could use a trip back to old Mykonos after all this dark side shit we've been putting up with."

"Aha, the true danger of a cop's life. We see the worst and wonder if there is any better."

A few minutes later they entered Ano Mera and took the second left, just before a tiny square. They followed a paved road that narrowed down to barely a lane and a half as it wove between borders of old low and new high stone walls. Beyond the walls, beige-brown fields and pastures ran off in all directions toward hills of still different shades of brown, peppered everywhere with tiny white churches, old homes, and new construction.

After about a mile the road turned to dirt, widened to two lanes, and ran north along a valley floor beside a mile-long rainwater reservoir. The valley's brown-gray hillsides were veined with old stone walls and filled with wild rosemary, savory, thyme, and goats. The only signs of man were power lines along the road and a modern windmill perched on a hilltop off to the east, generating power to operate the reservoir.

Anywhere but on an Aegean island one would marvel at the deep blue of the man-made lake, but on Mykonos it literally paled in comparison to the sea.

"The natural beauty of this island is extraordinary."

Andreas nodded.

The road made a wide arc to the right, and just before turning sharply left Andreas slowed by a man and boy fishing in the water.

"Nice of you not to coat them with dust from the road."

"I didn't want you to miss this."

As Andreas made the swing to the left the far end of the reservoir came into view.

"What the hell?"

Andreas didn't have to ask what had caught Kouros' attention. "That's about what I thought you'd say when I heard you hadn't been out here for a while."

Hovering above the end of the reservoir, as if devouring the hillsides beneath them, loomed a mass of white villas.

"How could somebody so screw up such a beautiful place? Damn them," said Kouros.

"I think they already are damned. Last I heard not a single one's been sold, and the asking price has been reduced by two-thirds."

"Serves them right."

The end of the reservoir stood seventy-five feet above sea level. Beyond it the road dropped steeply down toward a wide, sandy cove and a taverna of natural stone set fifty yards back from the sea at the widest part of the beach. The cove was edged distally in black- and rust-color stone and framed by virgin brown hillsides, azure blue waters, and brilliant Aegean skies.

It was a picture postcard vision that magazines and moviemakers often used to present the paradise known as Mykonos to the world. *Sans* villas. And where locals and longtime fans of Mykonos escaped to remember how very beautiful their island could be.

They parked beside the broad stone steps leading up to the taverna's outside terrace. They'd barely made it up the steps when the owner recognized Andreas and dragged both of them over to his table. He had his grill man cooking octopus, calamari, and fish, his wife turning out zucchini pie, *moussaka*, and more types of salads than Andreas could imagine, and his daughter pouring wine until Andreas had to threaten to arrest the entire family if they didn't stop.

In other words it was a terrific time.

The drive back to the airport was a cautious one. Kouros drove, though neither would have passed a breathalyzer test. Nor would either have scored a record for such a test on an island where virtually no one feared being stopped for erratic driving of any sort.

As they neared the airport Andreas began drumming his fingers on the dashboard.

Kouros looked over from the driver's seat. "Do I detect inspiration?"

Andreas nodded. "I think I have an idea on how to get things rolling."

"Are we talking about something like the 'rolling' boulder opening scene of *Indiana Jones and Raiders of the Lost Ark*?"

"As I recall, the boulder was chasing the hero."

"I guess I should go for a different movie."

"Good idea."

"*The War of the Worlds*?"

Andreas shook his head and waved a hand toward the road ahead. "Drive."

Kouros smiled. "Liked that film, Ryan Gosling, too."

Chapter Twenty-nine

"Morning."

"Chief Kaldis! What are you doing here?"

"Sorry to startle you. I've come to see the minister."

"Is he expecting you?"

"No, it's a surprise. Just tell him I'm here, please."

Andreas stood by the secretary's desk as she dialed her boss, whispered into the phone, stuttered in reply to some comment, and looked up. "He's very busy."

"Please tell him that I must see him on a matter of great importance."

She went back to whispering, nodded to the phone, and hung up. "I'm sorry, Chief, but he can't possibly see you today."

"No problem, just tell him I stopped by to let him know I plan on running for his seat in parliament in the next election and I'm on my way over to ask the Prime Minister for his blessing."

The woman's jaw dropped. "You want me to tell him that?"

Andreas smiled and nodded.

She called and whispered again.

The door to Spiros' office burst open. "Andreas, get in here."

Andreas mouthed, "Thank you," to the secretary as he passed by.

Spiros shut the door, pointed Andreas to a chair in front of his desk, and went to sit behind his desk.

"You're joking of course. You can't be serious about all that. You're not a politician, you couldn't possibly put up with all the bootlicking I have to do day after day."

"Who knows? At least you have influence, the ability to get things done."

"But it's a horrible life, and —"

Andreas held up his hands. "Stop. I just wanted you to know what I could do if I ever wanted. But, as long as I feel I have your unconditional support in my job—"

"You know that you do. Always have, always will."

Andreas smiled. "Let's just say there is a reasonable basis for disagreement on that score and leave it at that."

"Fine, that's a mature way to look at things."

"With one proviso?"

"Proviso?"

"Yes, I want you to set up a one-on-one meeting with me and the minister of finance right away."

"Why?"

"You don't want to know."

The old rage returned to Spiros' face. But he spoke softly. "I really must know."

"Sorry, I can't tell you. For your own good."

"Then I can't arrange the meeting."

"No problem, I'll ask the Prime Minister to do it when I see him later."

"You're wasting your time trying to blackmail me with a threat to run for parliament. The Prime Minister would never agree to allow you to run for my seat."

"Blackmail? That's a rather harsh term to apply to someone who simply wants to participate in the democratic process. Is your tape recorder running, again? I have an idea. Instead of meeting with the minister of finance this morning, why don't you and I go see the Prime Minister and let him decide if he'd rather have this hero cop run for your seat as a member of his party or as a member of the loyal opposition." Andreas smiled.

Spiros bit furiously at his lip. "I'll only agree if you let me attend the meeting at finance with you."

"You might regret it if you do. I'm telling you that up front."

"Don't threaten me!"

"I'm not threatening, I'm warning you. But if you want to come, fine. Just arrange it for today. And tell him it's urgent."

Spiros bit at his lip a few more times before calling his secretary. "Call Panos at finance and tell him I must see him ASAP on an urgent matter."

He hung up and glared at Andreas. "Satisfied?"

"Very."

◇◇◇

"Panos, thank you for seeing us on such short notice."

"When the minister of public order says it's 'urgent,' I take it seriously. Please sit down." He pointed to two chairs in front of his desk."

Andreas walked to the edge of the desk and extended his hand. "Andreas Kaldis, Minister."

"Oh, you two haven't met? Sorry about that, I should have introduced you."

"I know of Chief Inspector Kaldis by reputation, and for having the loveliest wife in Athens, next to mine of course." He smiled and shook Andreas' hand.

Andreas nodded. "Thank you."

"So, Spiros, what can I do for you?"

"It's a delicate matter that I thought would best be explained by Andreas. That's why I brought him with me."

Andreas tried to suppress a smile by squeezing hard at the bridge of his nose with his thumb and forefinger. "Feel free to take the lead if you'd like, Minister."

Spiros, cleared his throat. "No, as I said, I think it best that you take it from here."

Andreas thought he saw a slight grin on Panos' face.

"I'm sure you're familiar with the recent kidnapping and rescue of a fellow police officer."

"Who in Greece isn't? Congratulations."

"Thank you." Andreas leaned forward. "In connection with the investigation that led to the rescue I learned of a plot to blackmail members of the government. The simplest way to put this, Minister, is I'm here to tell you that you are a target."

Spiros bolted forward in his chair. "What?"

Panos' grin was gone. "What are you saying? How dare you suggest that I would do anything to compromise my duty to my country?"

"I'm sure that's not what Andreas was saying. Were you Andreas?"

"Minister, you are in charge of the office that creates new casino licenses. The kidnappers tortured that police officer in an attempt to get him to reveal the location of a cache of audios, videos, and photographs secretly recorded over decades by Christos Vasilakis. It is not just the behavior of members of government and prominent citizens that they were after, but incriminating materials related to their families." Andreas put his hands out palms up.

"And who's to say what one might be willing to do to spare themselves or their loved ones from ruination?"

"I have nothing to fear," said Panos.

"I understand how you feel." Andreas shook his head. "But there are some things in there—"

"What sorts of things?" said Spiros.

"Spiros, shut up." Panos ran his fingers through his hair.

Andreas said, "I'm the only one who knows what's in those materials. The kidnapped inspector and my assistant have never seen them. And there's no reason for anyone else to ever know."

Panos snickered. "And what is it you want in return, Chief Inspector?"

"Nothing but a little cooperation that will allow us to quietly put an end to this matter once and for all."

"Yes, yes, just as I suggested," said Spiros.

Panos shook his head and glared at Spiros. "Please, Chief Inspector, continue."

"Very soon someone will attempt to access your ministry's records. I'm not sure what the pretext will be, whether it will be an official or unofficial request, but it will come. And when it does, this is what I want them to find."

Andreas' explanation took five minutes, during which Panos quietly took copious notes and Spiros said not a word.

At the end Panos stood up, extended his hand to Andreas, and said, "We have a deal."

◇◇◇

"Wacki, could I talk to you for a minute?" It was the Mykonos police chief calling out to him from a table at the Kadena harborfront taverna close by City Hall.

"I'm in sort of a hurry, Mihalis, what is it?"

"Sit, please, it won't take long."

Wacki looked at his watch and sat.

"Glad I bumped into you. I have to ask you some questions about your friend, Sergey."

"Me? Why are you asking me? Ask him."

Mihalis gestured no. "I can't do it that way. I'm doing a background check on him and have to ask his known associates about him."

"What sort of background check?"

"Just routine."

"Chief, I'd like to help but how can I if I don't know what it's about?"

Mihalis leaned in. "All I'm authorized to tell you is that it's a direct request from the office of the minister of finance. Sergey's applied for some sort of license and the ministry is required to get a police background check on him before giving its okay. There's a lot of heat on me to get this report back to them ASAP, so my guess is unless I come up with a reason to say no, he has his license."

Wacki shook his head. "No reason I can think of to deny him a license. He's a model citizen as far as I can tell."

Mihalis smiled. "I thought you'd say that. Thanks."

Wacki stood up and hurried away, wondering as he did, what license?

◇◇◇

Wacki knocked on Sergey's hotel room door. "Hey, boss, it's me. Open up."

No answer.

Wacki went downstairs and asked the desk clerk, "Are you sure he's in his room? There was no answer when I knocked. Or yelled."

The clerk shrugged. "I haven't seen him go out. Maybe he went out the backdoor and is down at the harbor for sunset."

Wacki grunted and left the hotel.

Time to call Teacher.

◇◇◇

Sergey stared at the door from inside his hotel room. He'd ignored Wacki because he could not stand him. He was always in his way. Never helping, just trying to make himself look important. Today the two men Teacher found for him would be in Athens. Now things would get done. And quickly.

◇◇◇

"I hope you'll be comfortable in the guest bedroom," said Lila.

"Yes, thank you very much," said Kouros.

"Good, and as soon as my husband gets off the phone I'll leave the two of you alone to talk. Don't forget, if you need anything, just ask Marietta."

"Thank you."

Andreas closed his mobile and hugged Lila. "Thanks, my love."

"No problem. Yianni is like family. Besides I feel safer having two cops in the house." She turned and left them alone in the library.

Kouros looked at Andreas. "Chief, that guest room is bigger than my whole apartment."

Andreas laughed. "Tell me about it. It's what comes from being an honest cop."

"Does Lila happen to have a sister? Even an ugly cousin."

Andreas shot him an open palm. "But Lila's right about you staying here. Until we take down that bastard, things could get very nasty. No telling which of us he'll come after next, but he will."

"Me, me, me. I want him to pick me."

"Don't be a macho wise-ass. These guys aren't brave. Just ruthless. Could be a bomb or grenade launcher. Dirty and distant is their trademark. Unless you're an old man or a girl."

"Thank God Tassos is off the critical list."

Andreas crossed himself. "Maggie said they might let her in to see him tomorrow. She'll tell him only what she thinks will make him feel better."

"Five dead and three in jail should start him along the great yellow brick road to happiness."

Andreas shook his head. "You sound like his clone."

"How long do you think I'll have to stay here?"

"Why? Do you have a cat to feed at home?"

This time the palm came from Kouros.

Andreas smiled. "That was the finance ministry on the phone. They received a fax from Mykonos police that their chief had spoken with Wacki about Sergey applying for a license and there was 'nothing negative to report.'"

"Did Wacki take the bait?"

"Won't know until it happens. All we can do is hope Wacki runs true to form."

"And straight back to Teacher."

Andreas nodded. "If he goes to Sergey, we're fucked."

"It's a gamble."

"This whole thing's a gamble. Starting with my suggesting to the minister of finance there was something on him or his family in Christos' files when as far as we could tell there wasn't."

"He could have hung us out to dry."

"Nope, just me. I said I was the only one who knew what was in the files, then I watched as his mind ran to whatever painful moment in his past or his family's past conceivably might be out there. Never ceases to amaze me how much more threatening imagined risks are than the known."

"Whatever, it worked. So now what do we do?"

"Wait."

"Want to watch a soccer match?" said Kouros.

Andreas turned on the television. "Whom are you rooting for?"

"The winner."

◇◇◇

"Hello, Teacher, it's Wacki."

"Yes, I know."

"I'm sorry to call so late, but I was trying to reach Sergey and couldn't find him so I thought I'd pass this information on to you. It might be important and I didn't want to sit on it overnight."

"Just tell me what it is, please."

"This afternoon the Mykonos police chief questioned me about Sergey."

"What did you tell him?"

"That he was a 'model citizen.'"

"Why are you bothering me with this?"

Wacki began to stammer, but caught himself. "It wasn't what he wanted to know that mattered it was *why* he wanted to know."

"And 'why' was that?"

"Sergey applied for a license from the ministry of finance and the police were doing a mandatory background check at the request of the ministry."

"Did the police say what sort of license?"

"No."

"Did the police say it was for a license in Sergey's name?"

"I, I can't swear to that but the chief did say that with all the pressure coming down on him from the ministry to hurry along the background check it looked as though *he* would get *his* license."

"Thank you."

"You're very welcome. I hope—"

"Wacki, for the time being I want you to keep this conversation and your conversation with the police chief just between us."

"You mean don't tell Sergey?"

"Do I have to repeat myself?"

"No, Teacher, no. Absolutely. I understand completely. Tell no one."

"Very good. Good night."

"Good night."

Teacher hung up the phone and stared at the ceiling. Her eyes moved to the backs of her hands, and the black and blue marks along her arms.

She hadn't been surprised when she'd received the news about her health. No one wanted to think such things were possible, at least not about yourself and not out of a past you'd put so far out of mind. But she'd been a prostitute, and this was to be expected. She'd battled her illness for years, but with no one to share her burdens she was growing weary of the war.

Then Sergey entered her life with what seemed the answer to her prayers.

Her eyes shifted to the photograph of the young girl. She dropped her head.

I must make inquiries.

Chapter Thirty

It was early morning when the email arrived from Teacher's colleague in Athens. It read simply: ATTACHED ARE ALL FILES ON THE APPLICATION YOU REQUESTED.

The contact was thorough. The attachments included a copy of an application for a casino license on Mykonos. It was stamped as submitted to Greece's ministry of finance the day after the hotel owner had agreed to sell his interest in the hotel lease. Listed as the applicant was "Sergey Tishchenko."

That was not as they had planned. It would be foolish to hold a license in a single individual's name because the license would lapse should anything happen to that person.

Why would he do this? He surely knew better than to steal from her. Perhaps he thought of it as insurance against her killing him should she become disenchanted with him, as the license would end with him?

She smiled. She admired that sense of self-preservation. Her smile faded. As long as he did not plan to steal from her.

She read on. The application was filled with the words of lawyers.

He couldn't have done this on his own. He had help. But from whom? Wacki? Not a chance. But there had to be others involved in preparing this application, persons she did not know. She did not like that.

Teacher cleared her throat and finished reading the application. It contained financial representations and divulged sources of funds necessary to complete the project and bond the performance obligations of the casino. She knew the accounts, they were hers that she'd put in Sergey's name for purposes of the application.

She looked for questions about the hotel lease, but there were none. The application focused on the applicant's financial abilities and background, not on specific details of the facility to be operated within the approved venue. That would come later, after the ministry approved the license. She read on and lingered for a moment over the signature of Sergey Tishchenko.

The next document made her pause. It was a one-line memorandum from the minister of finance to the section chief responsible for casino licenses. Above the signature of the minister was typed, DO WHATEVER NECESSARY TO APPROVE THIS APPLICATION ASAP. The directive was dated the day after the cop was kidnapped.

That document could only mean one thing. But Sergey had never told her he had Christos' files. He'd kept that from her. There was no way this minister would have given such firm instructions in writing other than in mortal fear of what was in those files. It would also explain how the kidnapped cop was found and rescued so quickly. The cops who had Christos' files must have turned them over to Sergey in exchange for their friend's release, and then killed his captors as a message to any others who might consider kidnapping cops. That's what she would have done in their position.

Why had Sergey not told her? Was he waiting to surprise her with the license?

Subconsciously, she drew a deep breath, but stopped at a wince of pain. What could he possibly be thinking?

She looked at the last document. She read it twice. It was formal approval by the minister of finance of the issuance of a license to Sergey Tishchenko authorizing him to operate a casino on the island of Mykonos, dated yesterday.

He'd not told her the license was approved. Maybe he didn't know? No, he would have known immediately. That minister would have told him.

Teacher stroked her forehead. This was all far too strange to be true. Perhaps he believed she would die and that once she did all that was in his name he'd be able to keep for himself? How could he be so foolish? So shortsighted?

She was prepared to treat him like a son, groom him to succeed her, and he betrayed her? No, that could not be.

She shut her eyes and rocked back and forth in her chair. She would not judge him on this alone. There was another step to take. Another inquiry to be made.

It took until late afternoon before Teacher's Athens contact got back to her with the additional information. But she now knew what had happened. It was a clever ruse, but had failed. She also knew whom to punish.

◇◇◇

The lights illuminating the Acropolis had just gone on, and Lila was sitting on a sofa sipping a glass of wine and looking across to the Parthenon when Andreas walked into the apartment.

"Perfect timing," said Lila. "Come sit with me." She patted the seat.

Andreas walked up behind her, bent down, and kissed her on the cheek. "I'll get a glass of wine and join you."

Lila picked up a little silver bell from the table in front of her and rang it.

"Yes, ma'am," said Marietta, looking in from the next room.

"A glass of wine for Chief Kaldis, please."

Marietta nodded and left.

"I know. You would have preferred to do it yourself."

Andreas shrugged as he walked around the sofa and sat next to Lila. "I've given up that battle."

"Where's Yianni?"

"He said he had to meet a cop friend." Andreas smiled. "I told him not to stay out too late."

"I just heard from Maggie. The doctor said Tassos could have visitors tomorrow but only for a brief time, and only in the morning."

"Terrific. Yianni and I will be there first thing tomorrow."

"Any word on what's happening with Sergey?"

Andreas gestured no. "All we can do is hope Wacki took the bait, Teacher followed up, and she believes what we planted. If she thinks she's being conned, no telling what that maniac might do."

"You seem concerned."

"Trust me, I am."

◇◇◇

The next morning, a somewhat hungover Kouros and mercilessly chatty Andreas made their way to the hospital. They parked in the lot reserved for doctors and entered the hospital through the main entrance. Andreas told Kouros to "follow the color purple" for the elevators to the burn unit.

"I wonder who came up with this idea of putting colored lines in floors for directions. Pity the poor colorblind," said Andreas.

"Could you please stop talking for just a while, Chief. I'm trying to clear my head for Tassos."

As they reached the purple elevator bank Andreas said, "That mercy pitch won't work. Although if you told me why you got in so late last night, perhaps I could be convinced to shut up for a while."

"Fuck you."

"Such language, and to your boss, no less."

A tall man also waiting for the elevator and carrying a box of flowers looked away. Andreas couldn't blame him. Their back and forth banter probably qualified them for outpatient status in the psycho ward.

The elevator doors opened and the three men stepped in. Andreas pushed the button for five and with his finger still poised above the panel asked the man with the flowers, "Which floor?"

The man didn't respond but instead reached over and pressed "6."

Suit yourself, thought Andreas.

They got off the elevator, nodded to the guard, and walked down the hall toward Maggie sitting in a chair at the end of the hall. As soon as she saw them she jumped up and hugged them.

"He's so excited that you're coming."

"Where's the other guard?" said Andreas.

"Spiros thought one was enough."

"Bastard," said Andreas.

"Just take it easy in there, please. The doctors don't want him getting worked up."

Andreas nodded.

"And whatever you do, don't make him laugh. Thankfully, they didn't burn his face, but he'll be in pain if he starts to laugh."

"I'll let Yianni do all the talking. That should keep things from getting funny."

"Like I said, guys, don't make him laugh."

"Can we go in now?" said Kouros.

"First, we need to go into that dressing room to cover our street clothes and hair and put on a mask." She pointed at a door to the left of a pair of large, swinging doors marked BURN UNIT. "It's to prevent infection."

They dressed as Maggie said, walked into the burn unit, and stopped outside a room on the right at the far end of the hallway.

"This is his room." She led them inside. The lighting was dim and the only sound a distinct background hum punctuated by an occasional ping. Tassos lay on his back hooked up to intravenous lines, monitors, a tube down his nose, and more tubes coming from beneath a cover over his body.

"You look like shit," smiled Andreas.

Maggie shot him a look.

"Sorry, I was told not to make you laugh."

Tassos struggled to say, "Never have before, so, don't worry about starting now."

Kouros said. "Glad you're feeling better."

"When I heard what you did to those bastards I felt better real fast. Thanks."

"No need to," said Kouros. "You'd have done the same for us."

Tassos was quiet for a moment. "The doctors told me that if you hadn't gotten to me when you did I might not have made it."

Andreas and Kouros looked at their feet.

"But I don't believe him. I think he was just trying to make you two fuckups look good."

Andreas and Kouros burst out laughing.

"Stop that this instant. All of you."

"Easy, my love, I'm feeling no pain." Tassos' voice sounded stronger, less struggling.

"They gave me some really good meds. Besides, the doctor told me I was lucky getting my burns the way that I did. If I'd been electrocuted or caught in a fire, I'd be in much worse shape. Hard as that may be to believe."

"You really do look great," said Andreas.

"Now I *am* worried. So, quick, before the nurse throws you out of here, tell me what's happening. Maggie's already told me about Teacher and the mysterious caller. My guess is the caller was my contact at Europol covering himself by acting as if he were a third party. He's been involved in some, shall we say, unorthodox arrangements over the years, but if he were involved in what's going on with Sergey he never would have left that message."

Andreas quickly briefed him on what they knew and what they'd done.

"Boy, now you're the ones playing with fire. Let's just hope Teacher doesn't figure everything out."

"You're beginning to sound like Lila."

The door swung open, and a figure in the doorway waved at them.

"It's time to go," said Maggie.

"Damn these rules," said Tassos.

"Don't worry, we'll be back as soon as the doctors say that we can," said Kouros.

"And next time I'll bring Lila."

"Give her my love."

They all blew kisses to Tassos and left.

As they walked up the hall Andreas said, "He looks better than I thought."

"You really perked him up."

Andreas nodded. They walked through the swinging doors, headed toward the dressing room, when a man hurried out of the dressing room. He didn't bother holding the door open for them.

Malaka, thought Andreas. As he reached for the door handle one word raced through his mind: flowers.

He swung around looking for the man. "Yianni that's the guy from the elevator with the flowers. Get Maggie back to Tassos' room and don't let anyone near that dressing room. Keep everyone away. It could be a bomb."

Andreas ran down the hall to the elevators and asked the cop, "Did a tall guy just get on the elevator?"

The cop gestured no.

"Get down inside that burn unit, last room on the right, and ask Detective Kouros for instructions. And hurry."

The cop ran down the hall.

Andreas thought, if he didn't take the elevator…the stairs! Andreas ran back down the hall and stopped twenty feet before the burn unit at a door on the left marked STAIRS.

He opened the door. No one was inside and he heard no one on the stairs. Up or down, which way did he go? Andreas bolted down ten steps and stopped.

If it's a bomb, how would he know when to set it off unless he knew we were inside the dressing room? For that he'd need a visual on us.

Andreas raced back up the steps and slowly pushed open the door. He peeked across the hallway. The man needed a visual on the room…a visual on the room. There it was. A linen closet across the hall.

Andreas carefully slipped out into the corridor making sure the door made no sound as it closed. He crossed quickly to the far wall and hugged it as he moved toward the linen closet with his gun in his left hand.

Please, God, don't let him have a deadman switch on that detonator. He looked at the hinged, far side of the door. It angled in a bit, enough to mean the door was open slightly on the side closest to Andreas.

Andreas crossed himself with his right hand, edged up flush with the doorjamb, and kicked at the bottom of the door two feet up from the floor with enough force to send a soccer ball sixty yards.

He heard the grunt before he saw the man stumbling backward toward the rear of the closet, a cellphone in his hand. Andreas stuck his gun between the man's eyes and with his free hand motioned for the phone. The man winced and handed Andreas the phone.

Andreas had cuffed him by the time Kouros found them in the closet.

"The bomb squad is on the way."

"Who's with Tassos?"

"The cop from the elevator. I told him to shoot anyone he doesn't recognize trying to get into Tassos' room."

"Do you know this guy?" Andreas grabbed the man by his hair and lifted up his head.

"Yeah…from the video. He's the tall one of the two who murdered Christos. Where's your buddy, asshole?"

"You're wasting your time. He doesn't speak Greek. That's why he didn't give me his floor number on the elevator when I asked for it."

"Lucky break for us that you remembered."

"Tell me about it." Andreas crossed himself. "Get someone over here who speaks Polish. I want to know where his buddy is. And how he knew we'd be here this morning."

"He won't talk," said Kouros.

"Just make sure the interpreter doesn't have a queasy stomach."

Andreas patted the man's cheeks. "A man who was about to blow up a hospital filled with sick and injured people will talk. Believe me, he'll talk."

◇◇◇

Sergey looked at his watch. He should have heard by now. Tassos Stamatos' girlfriend always was at the hospital by now. All the man had to do was get close enough to her to leave the flowers, blow her away, and get out in the confusion.

Then her cop friends would know he meant business.
He'd better not have fucked things up.
Sergey looked at his watch again.
At worst, there was the back-up plan.

Chapter Thirty-one

The interpreter was a slight, dark-haired, blue-eyed, policewoman in her early twenties. Kouros told Andreas she could be trusted. "She wants to be one of us."

The woman smiled. "The name is Petrova. An honor to meet you, Chief."

Andreas nodded. "It's important that the subject understands things will get very nasty very quickly if he doesn't cooperate."

"Don't worry, I've studied acting and love all the *Dirty Harry* movies."

Andreas looked at Kouros, leaned in toward his ear, and whispered, "Is she by any chance your 'cop friend' from last night?"

Kouros smiled at Petrova and Andreas had his answer.

"She's totally fluent in Polish, Chief."

Andreas smiled. "Good, let's go inside."

Inside was an operating room. Two cops were standing on either side of an operating table. Between them and strapped to the table, naked but for a surgical gown, was the attempted bomber.

Andreas told the two cops to leave and not let anyone in. "No matter what you hear coming from inside." He waited until they left, and nodded to Petrova.

"Well, my friend, you have finally reached the end of the road. Welcome to Greek justice," said Andreas.

Petrova translated.

The man laughed, spit at her, and said in Polish, "You are a woman talking for a man. Why should I listen to you?"

Petrova translated his words and as she finished reached down under the man's gown, grabbed his testicles, and squeezed until he screamed. She kept squeezing as she said. "Either answer or I'll pull your useless balls right off you."

Still squeezing, Petrova repeated her comment in Greek for Andreas and Kouros, punctuating it with a hard yank on the man's testicles before letting go.

Andreas looked at Kouros. "My compliments. A fine choice."

Kouros smiled.

"So, shall we continue, numb nuts?" Andreas smiled.

Kouros shook his head and Petrova laughed as she translated.

The man said nothing.

"Good, now that you understand how very serious we are, I have a few questions for you."

"I want a lawyer."

"Request denied."

"I'm not talking."

"Permit me to explain the ground rules. You came into a hospital planning to kill innocent people. You're also caught on video as one of the killers of a well-loved man on Mykonos, and if you happen to be the lucky one the victim's dog got a piece of, your DNA is all over a murder scene. Any way you look at it, you're in prison for the rest of your life."

"So why should I talk?"

"You want to make a deal?"

"It depends," said the man.

"On what?"

"On what you're offering."

Andreas shook his head. "Now that you've established that you're willing to talk and the only question is price, let me explain the deal I'm willing to make."

Andreas walked over to the table and patted the man on his shoulder. "Like I said, you're off to prison for the rest of your life. The question is whether you'll be able to walk, or see, or piss with your own dick during your remaining years."

Andreas stepped to where the man could see Andreas' eyes. He spoke slowly, allowing Petrova to translate as he did. "You tried to kill someone I consider family. So I don't care what it takes to get you to tell me what I need to know to protect her and the rest of my family. If you live or if you die is not of my concern. Only yours." Andreas held up his right hand and Kouros slapped a scalpel flat against his palm.

"So, shall we begin by removing your nose?"

Andreas swung the scalpel down and across the man's face narrowly missing the tip of his nose.

The man jerked back violently trying to pull free of the restraints. "You're crazy."

Andreas nodded. "Very."

"We didn't know you would be here. We were only going after the woman."

"Who's 'we'?"

The man stared at the scalpel. Andreas twirled it between his fingers.

"I shall not ask you again."

"My friend."

"The other one with you on Mykonos?"

"Yes."

"Where is he now?"

"I don't know."

Andreas brought the scalpel toward the man's right eye.

"Honest, I don't know! Teacher found us and sent us to Athens. We've been staying at some place in Athens. I have no idea where it is."

"How did you know where to find the woman?"

"Sergey made arrangements with old friends of his now living in Athens. There are a lot of people from the old country here. They located her, showed me the layout of the hospital, and gave me what I needed to do the job. Afterwards, I was to take the metro to Omonia Square and someone would meet me there. It's much easier to do these things here than back home. Everyone is trusting and no one is expected to follow rules. I failed only because I did not expect you to be with her."

"Sergey told you to kill the woman?"

"Yes."

"Why?"

"I don't know."

"And what if you failed?"

"My friend has his own instructions."

"What are they?"

"I don't know. Sergey gave us our orders separately. He said in case one was caught he could not inform on the other."

Andreas put down the scalpel. "I see he knows the quality of his men."

◇◇◇

Andreas and Kouros stood outside the operating room watching the prisoner led down the hall in handcuffs and shackles. He was cursing at Petrova, who followed along, translating his insults for the benefit of the other Greek cops.

"He should enjoy his trip to Korydallos," said Kouros.

"Bet he'll slip and fall a few times along the way."

"He's just lucky Petrova's not wearing stiletto heels."

"Let's not go there," said Andreas.

"She's a very nice person."

"I'm sure. And speaking of nice people, let's check on Maggie."

They took the stairs to Tassos' floor. Maggie was sitting in the hall outside the entrance to the burn unit.

"Why are you sitting out here?" said Andreas.

"If I were with Tassos he'd know something was wrong. I didn't want to worry him."

Andreas nodded. "He'd be right to worry. They were after you."

"Me? Why me?"

"Wish I knew."

"If Teacher is on to our plan, I'd think she'd be looking to take all of us out," said Kouros.

"It makes no sense why she'd only be going after Maggie. I'm the logical one to target," said Andreas.

"Maybe they're following someone else's orders?" said Maggie.

"That could only be Sergey," said Andreas.

"Which means Teacher may not be on to us," said Kouros.

"Yet," said Andreas.

"So what do we do?" said Maggie.

Andreas smiled. "Pray for the best and prepare for the worst."

It was late afternoon and Wacki was banging away furiously at Sergey's hotel room door. No answer. He'd been to the front desk twice and was assured by the clerk that Sergey was in his room because the clerk had personally connected calls going out of that room to Athens through the switchboard.

"Boss, please, open up. It's very important."

Still no answer.

He leaned against the door, cupped his hands around his mouth, and tried to whisper through the edge of the door.

"Teacher is on Mykonos. She wants to see us right away."

Wacki heard the bolt turn and the door opened.

"What are you talking about?" Sergey looked as if he hadn't shaved in days. He was wearing sweatpants and a tee-shirt stained with spots of coffee down the front.

"Teacher is here. On a yacht docked in the old port. She called and wants to see us right away."

"Us?"

"Yes, us."

"I need to shower."

"No time."

Sergey walked into the bathroom and turned on the shower. Wacki stared at his watch.

Thirty-five minutes later Wacki and a showered, clean-shaven, immaculately dressed Sergey presented themselves aboard the two-hundred-twenty-foot motor launch *Medea*.

As soon as they walked into the main salon, Sergey spread his arms and smiled at the woman in sunglasses sitting in an overstuffed chair off to his right. "Teacher, what a wonderful, unexpected surprise. I hope it is the first of many such visits."

Teacher smiled and put out her hand. "Always nice to see you, Sergey."

Sergey immediately came forward and kissed her hand.

"Please, sit," she said.

Sergey sat in one of two straight back chairs in front of her. Wacki stood.

"Both of you, please."

Sergey glanced at Wacki. Wacki did not take his eyes off of Teacher as he sat in the second chair.

"Thank you, both, for coming."

"Our pleasure," smiled Sergey.

"I'm on Mykonos because I want a face-to-face update on the status of our project."

Sergey glanced at Wacki. "In front of him? He doesn't know anything about it."

"I can't believe he would betray us." She looked at Wacki. "Would you?"

Wacki gestured no twice. "Absolutely not. No way."

"Good," said Teacher."

She looked at Sergey and smiled. "So, please continue."

"Certainly, Teacher." He crossed one leg over the other. "We are on target to have the casino license within a matter of weeks."

"Weeks you say?"

"Yes, there have been some delays. Nothing unexpected, but delays nonetheless."

"How are things going with the ministry of finance?"

"Our representative is ready to make the introduction to the minister the moment we have the necessary materials."

"You've had no contact with him yet?"

"It would be premature to fire a gun without ammunition."

"Good point."

"Have you spoken to anyone about our plans?"

"Of course not."

"I mean a lawyer, someone to help you with all the applications and paperwork necessary to gain the license."

Sergey looked surprised. "I'm sorry, I did not know that was my responsibility. I thought you would want to use people of your own choosing."

"Yes, of course. How silly of me. It must be all this medication. It's making me forget."

"How are you feeling?" said Sergey. "That was the first thing I wanted to ask when I saw you, but thought it inappropriate in his presence." He dipped his head in Wacki's direction without looking at him.

"No, not at all. I am feeling much better than many wish. I hear their prayers for my death and it inspires me to go on."

"May they rot in hell," said Sergey.

"Too good for them," she smiled. "And what about the ministry of tourism? How is the approval process coming along for the assignment of the hotel lease?

"No problem whatsoever. We're all set. Lefteris says it's only a matter of our signing the final papers."

"And when will that occur?"

"I thought it best to coordinate the timing of the assignment of the lease with the issuance of the license from finance. After all, why be stuck operating a hotel without a casino license?"

"I thought you said there was 'no problem' with the license, that it would be only 'a matter of weeks.'"

"Yes, but I saw no reason not to be cautious."

Teacher nodded. "Caution is a good thing. There are people out there trying to take advantage of us." Teacher looked at Wacki. "Trying to turn one of us against the other."

Sergey said, "Him?"

Teacher shrugged.

"I know he talks behind my back. Probably to you. But I thought it just typical, petty, Greek jealousy bullshit."

Wacki sat perfectly still.

"He has told me many things."

Sergey struggled not to glare at Wacki.

"But nothing unexpected."

"Tell me his lies. I'll refute them all."

Teacher shook her head. "No need for that, I have only one question for you."

"Ask."

"It is a simple question."

Sergey blinked. "Please, just ask it."

Teacher moved her face close to his. "Remember when you told me, 'Lefteris' eyes popped wide open when I gave him our offer'?"

"Yes."

"Did you ever tell Wacki how much you were paying Lefteris for the hotel?"

Sergey paused. "Why are you asking that?"

"Please, just answer the question."

"As best as I can remember, no."

"You mean there's a chance you told him?"

"No, I'm certain I didn't."

"How can you be so sure?"

"Because the price I offered Lefteris was the price he accepted. We never had any conversation about price. I simply handed him a piece of paper with my offer on it and he accepted it."

"Did Lefteris tell anyone?"

"Not that I know of. In fact, he told me he didn't want anyone to know the price."

"What about the ministry of tourism?"

"Well, yes, he had to inform them."

"And what price did he tell them?"

"The one we agreed upon. The one you told me to offer."

Teacher leaned back. "Good."

Teacher stood up. "Sergey, please help me to the upper deck. I've arranged a wonderful celebratory dinner for the three of us, sailing around this beautiful island in the moonlight."

"Sounds delightful," said Sergey taking Teacher's arm.

She nodded to a man dressed all in white standing at attention at the rear of the salon. He spoke into a communicator, the engines roared to life, the lines were undone, the anchor came up, and the boat was away.

Chapter Thirty-two

Maggie dropped into bed exhausted. I'm getting too old for this craziness, she thought. Her next thought was of tomorrow, and she was asleep in minutes.

The window at the rear of Maggie's first floor apartment in the working class Pangrati section of Athens wasn't completely closed. A screen kept the neighborhood cats out, but not the breezes that made Athens' summer nights bearable.

The man was very quiet, very professional. He took his time removing the screen and carefully lifted the window without a sound. He slid inside like a predator who'd done this a thousand times before.

The apartment was dark. He listened for a sound. Nothing. He knew the woman was here. He'd seen her come in an hour and a half ago. The lights had been out for over an hour. She had to be asleep. He moved on his toes, making not a sound.

The bedroom must be straight ahead. The door was closed. He listened. He heard nothing. He pressed softly against the door. It moved without a sound. The room was filled with moonlight. There was a body in the bed, red hair on the pillow.

He took the stiletto from his pants pocket, silently flicked it open, quickly stepped across the room, and drove the blade into the woman's neck. Three times, quickly. Each time expecting something that did not happen.

A light went on as a closet door opened by the foot of the bed and a man in a dress said, "Surprise!"

The killer lunged at the vision, slashing away at it with his knife.

Or at least he tried to.

When the attacker woke up several hours later, he had two broken knee caps, a compound fracture of his right wrist, four broken ribs, a broken nose, broken jaw, fractured cheekbone, and double hernia.

When Maggie Sikestes woke up the next morning in her boss' guest bedroom, detective Yianni Kouros promptly apologized for the bloodstains on the dress he'd borrowed from her. He also thanked her for providing him with the opportunity for some of the most fun he'd had in years, plus credit for arresting the last of Christos Vasilakis' killers.

◇◇◇

The *Medea* sailed south, away from the harsh rush of wide open seas funneling through Mykonos' narrow straits with neighboring Tinos.

The farther out to sea they sailed, the more ethereal Mykonos' southern coastline became. A pearl and diamond necklace of light strung along the shore.

"Such beauty, a true paradise," said Teacher taking off her sunglasses and looking off toward shore from the upper deck dining room.

She looked at Wacki. "You must feel blessed to be a part of all this."

"Yes, ma'am. Absolutely."

Those were about the only words Wacki had spoken in the two and one-half hours he and Sergey had been on board. He looked like a frightened mouse waiting for the cat to pounce.

"Did you enjoy the dinner?" She asked.

Wacki nodded. "Yes, terrific."

"What about the wines. They were special, weren't they? Very rare."

"Yes, yes," he nodded. "Never had better." Wacki's face now looked as if the cat were toying with him.

"And you, Sergey?"

He sat to Teacher's right, directly across from Wacki. He reached over and patted her hand. "I cannot ever remember a finer meal, or better company." He looked straight into Teacher's eyes as he spoke.

"Wonderful, I'm pleased." She did not move her hand but with the other waved to the man all in white.

"Yes, ma'am."

"Please, pour the wine."

"More?" said Sergey.

"It is very special, a 1975 Chateau d' Yquem. You will enjoy it I assure you. For the occasion I picked the best I could find closest to your birth year. It is a few years older than you, but the newer vintages proved sadly disappointing."

"How thoughtful." He smiled and tossed his head to flip his hair away from his face.

Teacher said, "I always planned to come back to Greece. I have not been here in decades, except for our brief meeting ten days ago."

She shook her head. "Only ten days. It seems much longer. So much has happened in such a short time."

The man produced a bottle and showed it to Teacher. She nodded.

He placed a glass in front of her, poured out a bit, and waited.

She sipped it. "Magnificent. I'm sure you'll enjoy it."

The man placed a glass in front of Wacki and poured. He did the same for Sergey, and filled Teacher's glass.

Teacher raised her glass. "To Mykonos and our soon to be Mykonos Magick."

Sergey and Wacki repeated the toast and drank.

"I must say, Sergey, when you came to me with your idea I never thought you would be able to pull it off. It seemed so farfetched, so risky. It made no sense that you, a foreigner, could succeed where so many others had failed."

Sergey nodded. "Thank you for having faith in me."

"But times were different, I told myself. Foreigners with skill and proper backing could gain a foothold that a generation ago seemed impossible. And, as you pointed out, where there is little moral reluctance, the ruthless are unstoppable."

Sergey nodded.

She looked at Wacki. "Would you like more wine?"

He gestured no.

"Please, I insist. I cannot re-cork a bottle of such quality."

"Sure, whatever you say."

She nodded to the man in white and he refilled all three glasses. They toasted again, and drank.

"I'm not sure I'll be back this way."

"Why?" said Sergey, suppressing a yawn.

"Too many bad memories. Too many disappointments."

Sergey yawned widely, but did not respond.

"But you, Wacki. You did not disappoint me. You ran true to form."

Wacki tried to smile but the right side of his face was twitching.

"I judged you correctly. I knew you were jealous of my great fondness for Sergey, that you would do what you could to undermine him in my eyes."

Teacher shook her head. "But never did I think you would go so far as to lie or attempt to deceive me."

Wacki literally shook. "I never did. I never would."

Teacher stared at him. "That's what I thought. And that's why I spoke to you earlier today and asked you my one simple question."

Sergey said, "You spoke to him before we came on the boat?"

She kept her eyes on Wacki. "Yes."

Sergey tried to flip his hair, but couldn't complete the motion.

"And your answer to that question is the only reason you're still alive."

Wacki looked unsure whether to laugh or cry.

"What was the question?" said Sergey.

"'Did Sergey ever tell you how much he was paying Lefteris for the hotel?'"

"The little lying shit. What did he say?" Sergey mumbled more than spoke the words.

Teacher turned to Sergey. "Precisely what you said. 'No, he handed Lefteris a note with the price and I never saw it.'"

She kept her eyes on Sergey as she said, "Isn't that right, Wacki?"

"Yes, ma'am."

Sergey blinked his eyes. "I don't understand. What is the problem?"

"The problem is that the amount you offered Lefteris is not the amount you told me. Not the amount we agreed you would pay."

"What? How can you be saying that? It's not true. What has that little bastard been doing behind my back?" Sergey struggled to get to his feet, but the man in white pressed him back down into his chair.

"Sergey, I had such hopes for you. Such aspirations. How could you have betrayed me? Robbed me? How could you have thought you would get away with it?"

"Rob *you*? Never!"

"That's what I would have thought. And why, when you failed to tell me that you already had the casino license, I still did not believe it was to take advantage of me."

"License. What license?"

Teacher shook her head. "It does not matter any more. I found my answer elsewhere."

Sergey's head began to droop.

"Honest, I never—"

"*Stop*! Enough of your lies. I've seen the memorandum of understanding submitted to the ministry of tourism signed by you and Lefteris. And whether he is your accomplice in this fraud upon me or not, I have seen the price."

"I don't…know…what…"

Teacher rose to her feet, "You paid him only two-thirds of what we agreed. You stole from me."

She walked behind him, took something from the man in white, and whispered in Sergey's ear. "I thought of you as a son.

You were my salvation, my chance to escape from Hell. How could you have betrayed me?"

"I did—" His words were lost in a gurgle of blood as Teacher slid the razor-sharp blade across his throat, then drove it repeatedly into his heart.

Covered in blood, she stood panting and staring at the body bleeding out onto the dinner table. She looked across at Wacki, dropped the knife, and went back to her seat at the head of the table.

She reached for her wine glass. She stared at the bloody fingerprints on her glass, and drank. She put down the glass and stared at Wacki.

"I shall take his body with me so that I may bury him at sea."

She took another sip. "It is a tragedy when one you trust does not prove worthy."

She stared at Wacki. "That would never prove to be you, would it?"

Wacki's voice cracked. "No. Never. Absolutely never."

Teacher nodded. "Good. I will be around far longer than many think. In time someone will take over for me and I hope whoever that is will be able to trust you as well."

"Yes, absolutely."

"For whoever follows me will likely be even more ruthless than I. That seems to be the way these days. Show how you can be tougher than your predecessor."

She paused to take another sip. "I want you to go back to Mykonos and wait. We will forget about this hotel deal. Sergey will simply disappear, the hotelier Lefteris will be disappointed, and rumors will spread but die away.

"Still, a seed has been planted, and the possibility looms in the minds of those who matter that there is great profit to be made for those willing to sell their birthright. We just must be ready for the opportunities. They will come in many forms as Greeks struggle to find a new direction. You shall be my eyes and ears on Mykonos."

She picked the wine glass and said, "To our future together in paradise."

Wacki picked up his glass but did not drink, only stared at the body of Sergey.

Teacher smiled. "Don't worry, the poison was in his glass, not the wine. *Chin-chin.*"

A week had passed and, according to the Mykonos police, Sergey had vanished from the island.

Andreas took it as good news, but remained careful where he parked his car. The best news by far was that Tassos was back to his cantankerous self. At first he'd pondered about calling it quits, taking his pension, and settling down with Maggie.

Maggie's response to Tassos' suggestion was instantaneous. "If you intend on hanging around with me 24/7, I'm taking a second job."

Kouros was packed and all set to leave Andreas' and Lila's apartment when his hosts opened the bottle of champagne he'd given them as a thank you gift and began toasting his farewell.

"To no more assholes, just good friends," said Andreas raising his glass.

"Interesting toast, darling."

"You're right. I should have said, 'To my fantastic wife and her childhood friend, the minister of tourism."

"Which reminds me, do you think it's okay to tell her to put the real memorandum of understanding back in the ministry's files?"

"Not yet. Besides, it's only going to mean something to someone who gets into her files who shouldn't be there. The minister knows where the real one is if she needs it."

"The minister is such a straight shooter…How did you ever convince her to substitute the real memorandum for our phony one?" said Kouros.

"I told her my husband was convinced our lives were in danger if the 'wrong people' saw the real one."

"Speaking of people'in danger,' our boss is about to get his balls cut off courtesy of the minister of finance," said Kouros.

"How do you know that?" said Andreas.

"Before coming here, I stopped by the office to give Christos' files back to Maggie for safekeeping. She told me she just got off the phone with her girlfriend, the finance minister's secretary, who said that in connection with the ministry's ongoing tax fraud investigations her boss was about to release a list of Greek government officials with undisclosed Swiss bank accounts. And Spiros' name is on it."

"That should get him a real warm reception in the press," said Lila.

Andreas shook his head. "I warned him not to come to that meeting with me. I knew that somehow he'd find a way to piss off the finance minister," said Andreas.

"It's his gift," said Kouros.

"Sounds like you two may soon be working for a new minister."

"I'll believe it when I see it," said Andreas.

"Any more word on Teacher?" said Kouros.

"Nope, and I like it that way. I prefer staying off her radar screen."

"Funny, isn't it, how we ended up teaching Teacher a lesson." said Kouros.

"I think the better word is ironic," said Andreas.

"Interesting. Did you two know that the word 'irony' comes from a stock comic character in Ancient Greek theater?"

Kouros and Andreas looked at each other with blank stares.

"You guys would be perfect for the role. Eiron brought down his opponents by making himself seem less than he actually was."

Kouros shook his head. "You have us confused with that American TV detective, Columbo."

"Yeah," said Andreas. "Here in Greece, cops are more like Sisyphus. Always pushing the same damn boulder up the same damn hill. Sometimes I feel like just letting go, jumping to the side, and watching to see what the hell happens."

"I think you need a vacation," said Lila.

"Why don't you guys come with me?" said Kouros."It'll be a blast."

"Where to?" said Lila.

"To Mykonos, of course," said Kouros. "Where else?"

Andreas nodded. Mykonos in August. Where else indeed.

To receive a free catalog of Poisoned Pen Press titles, please contact us in one of the following ways:

Phone: 1-800-421-3976
Facsimile: 1-480-949-1707
Email: info@poisonedpenpress.com
Website: www.poisonedpenpress.com

Poisoned Pen Press
6962 E. First Ave. Ste 103
Scottsdale, AZ 85251